A Merry Little Christmas

CONTINGENCY

A Merry Little Christmas Contingency

Cover: Melody Jeffries Design

Editor: Sue Copsey

ISBN: 978-0-6456910-6-1 (paperback)

ISBN: 978-0-6456910-7-8 (ebook)

For Clare
This book was fuelled by you

A Merry Little Christmas Contingency

A MOONSHINE ROMANCE NOVEL

BROOKLYN DEAN

Series Note

A Merry Little Christmas Contingency is a novel in the interconnected Moonshine Romance series. Each novel can be read as a standalone, and in terms of the overarching series timeline, many events cross over between the books, weaving each story together.

Please note that this book is set at Christmas, with the main narrative events occurring <u>prior</u> to those in *Meet Me in Moonshine, The Write Way for Love,* and *The Insufferable Adam James.*

Content Warnings

Dear Reader,

While this book is intended to be a sexy little romantic comedy, it does include content you should probably be aware of.

Please be advised that the story *A Merry Little Christmas Contingency* contains:

explicit language and crude humour (AKA Australian English), ableist language, a main character with a physical disability, anxiety representation, some mummy issues, sexism and gender stereotyping, sexual content, and tinsel in strange places.

Author's Note

This story is a homage to a December 'Down Under' and inspired by the complete lack of snow in a Southern Hemisphere Christmas.

While I'd *love* a white Christmas, here in Australia our festive season is hot, sticky, sweaty, and (in my opinion) pretty sexy, with all the scantily clad people hanging out at the beach and all.

So, to that effect, and with an Aussie Xmas flair, this book is best paired with:

- 'shrimp on the barbie' (jokes! They're *prawns*)

- a sugar biscuit (not *cookie!*)

- and a refreshingly cold cocktail (let's go a Shandy or a Sunrise. Not Egg Nog because warm milk in summer is *not* a great idea).

For additional adult reading fun, add this to your Christmas List this year: *Find a fun new use for tinsel.*

There is also a curated Spotify playlist to accompany this book.
Scan the QR code to start listening.

Lastly, thank you for being here. You look lovely today, even if
you don't feel it. And, if you've made it this far, your sense of
humour is pretty darn great too!

Merry Christmas, my friend.

I hope you enjoy Billy and Bre's story.

With love,
Brooklyn

Prologue

Breanna Henderson's Life Plan.

Signed and dated New Years Eve, Age 13.

Steps to Living a Happy Life:
   1- Adopt a dog.
   2- Travel the world.
   3- Never. Have. Kids.
   4- Always come home for Christmas.

1

Tradition

Billy

THE PERSISTENT PANTING AND GRUNTING that wafted through his open window was, to say the least, distracting. Eyebrows drawn low, Billy's blue eyes wandered often to the swaying curtains. He waited.

The book had grown heavy in his fingers long ago, but he needed something to cling onto, other than the pure hope that she'd climb into his window tonight, as she did every 1st December, and take up residence in his bedroom until the end of Christmas. Billy had been about to give up on the idea, worrying she wouldn't show up, fearing their tradition was no longer ... until the telltale rustling of the bushes below preceded the shuddering of the ladder against the house, and the muttered curses of the woman as she climbed higher.

The hardcover he'd been reading fell heavily to the mattress. Gripping the windowsill, Billy peered beyond the billowing curtains. The warm summer breeze hit him before the sight of her did.

"Need a hand?" Billy called out into the night. He thought that was rather funny, considering he had only the one to offer.

The shadow-woman struggling up the old red ladder huffed. "Piss ... off!"

Gripping the ladder rung tightly, she finally looked up, her face dotted with colour from the tiny fairy lights framing the massive downstairs windows. "I can do this, William *Bloody* Carmichael."

"I am sure you can, Breanna *Bruce* Henderson." She could do anything and everything she set her mind to.

He tried to force the usual gruffness in his voice to mellow into something smoother, to no avail. The sight of her red hair bobbing closer and closer left his throat too tight to speak further. She was here. Finally. This was happening.

Dragging his hand down his beard, Billy smothered a smile, watching as she continued grunting with effort, hauling herself up to his second-storey window. Heavens above, the noises she was making! His cock twitched at the thoughts the sounds invoked. Those were his grunts to tease out of her, his to swallow. At least, at Christmas they were. Billy bit down on his bottom lip. Christmas ... and any other time she offered, more accurately. He wouldn't get bogged down in details. He was simply grateful she had returned home for Christmas and was climbing in his window. It was a lingering tradition from their teenage days, when sneaking in and out of their parents' houses was a common pastime, and it was only the beginning of their annual festivities.

Clearing his throat, Billy forced his words out. "I honestly did not expect to see you tonight."

A resigned sigh blew from below. "I know. But I can't just ignore *years* of our rituals, Billy. What would our younger selves say if I stopped showing up? I can't break our Friends-With-Festive-Benefits plans now!" She gave another groan as she hauled herself closer to the window, a slash of her red clothing blinking into focus as a downstairs light switched on. Breanna waved into the window and a warm greeting – his mother's voice – drifted through the glass, before the light flicked off.

"Good night Mrs C!" Bre called into the darkened room below before continuing the climb.

Billy's family adored having her as part of their annual festivities, even if they didn't quite understand the relationship between their youngest son and the neighbour girl they'd claimed as their own long ago.

What *were* Billy Carmichael and Breanna 'Bruce' Henderson? Best friends? Occasional lovers? They had stopped trying to label it years ago, simply accepting that they were two sides to the same zipper – each rather useless without the other half. Together? They were unstoppable. Intricately woven and unbreakably strong.

At least, that was how he felt. And while Billy had always imagined he'd be married with a few kids by the time he was in his thirties, on nights like this, when everything felt right in the world, he remembered that all he'd ever wanted was right here – his family farm, the high-spirited noises of the Carmichael clan downstairs, and the quieter world that existed upstairs, only for them. This was his favourite place, where 'home' truly existed.

When Breanna's arousing little noises floated around him, the rest of the world ceased to exist. This was as good as life could ever get for Billy. This tiny slice of Heaven that was so different from the way they interacted almost every other day, working in sync behind the bar at his tavern, The Pope, or gorging themselves on pizza and watching old movies.

That's how they'd been, until recently.

Billy knew exactly when everything changed, if he were being honest, but he wouldn't be the first to acknowledge it. Bre was never backwards in coming forward, so he figured he'd wait for her to approach the elephant in the room, but ...

The distance between them had been growing over the last few months, and he'd increasingly found himself looking forward to the additional time they spent together here at his family farm, simultaneously worrying things would continue to be different, while hoping their traditions stayed the same.

Bre continued her climb, the second storey feeling like a skyscraper as he waited for her to arrive.

"Bruce," Billy started again, using her childhood nickname,

"don't you think ..."

"I give very few fucks," she huffed, "about what people think." Resting her forehead against the ladder, she added, "Just go ... lay down. I'll be there ... in a ... minute."

Breanna resumed her climb, grunting like an animal in heat. She'd never had this much difficulty scaling the building before, but then again, it was a particularly muggy December evening, and she was in a padded velvet Santa Suit. Plus, he knew she'd been working extremely long days at her garage, restoring her beloved 1943 Ford Utility, before pulling double shifts with him managing The Pope. Now, she'd come home for Christmas, to work the farm with him and organise his raucous family and their events, like she did every year. It was no wonder Bre sounded fatigued. They'd both been so busy lately, but that's what made coming home all the more exciting. The pace of Christmas was slower, somehow, and they made the time to connect.

A warm breeze blew through his family's Christmas tree farm, thickly scented with pine, baked cinnamon, and the tang of eucalypt. Billy loved a summer Christmas, with its hot meals shared in cold air-conditioned spaces, and the way the pool congratulated you on a hard day's work with a cool, consuming hug.

He especially loved all the clutter of tinsel and decorations, too big and gaudy to be anything but beautiful; the small family heirlooms, and newer carved-wood decorations. His father made those by hand and his mother made everything famous with her booming social media accounts. She'd started by documenting their Australian family Christmases several years ago, and the internet had gone crazy for Holly and Nick Carmichael, their Christmas Tree Farm Down Under, the charmingly festive rural aesthetic ... and all the images of their four strapping lads in their traditional plaid, chopping down trees with their shirts off.

Nobody did Christmas like the Carmichaels, and the local Moonshine residents – and millions of online followers – went nuts for it. Personally, for Billy, Breanna's presence was the most integral part of the festivities.

Ducking his head back into the bedroom, Billy tried to wipe the smirk from his face. Tried and failed. God, this was his favourite night of the entire year. The best Christmas tradition he could've imagined – Breanna Henderson in a Santa costume ... then absolutely nothing at all.

It was all part of The Plan – a list created when they were teenagers. They hadn't deviated from it at all, because – as Bre said – it was tradition. Breanna Henderson was nothing without a plan, always scribbling lists and providing tick-boxes. It made her a great manager for his business, and it was an asset here on the farm, too. Always busy, December became downright unmanageable without a seasoned planner at the helm. Everyone here had a job, and even though his parents were the business owners, Bre was irrefutably The Boss.

That's what made ignoring her demand to wait for her on the bed additionally enticing. Was it a festive fetish? Wanting his sexy Santa to scold him for disobeying orders? Maybe. Though he knew Breanna loved it when he took charge. She relinquished so little of her control, but for Billy, she'd let go entirely.

Cock throbbing with the images that flashed through his mind, Billy paused by the window, ready to pull her into his childhood bedroom, press her close, and kiss her like his life depended on it. What he wouldn't give for two complete arms, to be able to scoop her up and carry her across every threshold, their lips locked – but only at Christmas.

He rarely lamented his disability, but there were times Billy wished his right arm extended its full length, and that he had another set of fingers to run through her hair, over her skin, to trace the outline of her lips.

He'd been dreaming of it all day, resulting in numerous spilled beers and quite a few broken glasses behind the bar. Some days, having ten fingers would have made all the difference. Billy reached absently for his right forearm now, hand falling through thin air where warm flesh and muscle still existed in his mind's eye. It had been amputated at five years of age, but he still marvelled that it was missing. The forearm still itched and ached. And often, late at night, his right hand reached across the sheets for Breanna Henderson.

"Finally!" Her perpetually stained mechanic's fingers gripped the window frame and she hauled herself onto the ledge, panting. "Whose idea was this, anyway?"

Billy cocked an eyebrow and grunted in response; no use wasting words on a rhetorical question. The second her feet landed on the floor, he fisted the collar of her white, fur-lined Santa suit, Billy dragged Bre's face closer. Smiling, he slanted his lips over hers. Bre's mouth, warm and sweet, indulged in the kiss, but her body language ... she seemed too tense.

"Hey." She smiled up at him, eyes bright before turning her back to him. Unwilling to let go, not just yet, Billy slung his arm around her slight shoulders. Slowly, she melted back into him, and he smiled into her hair.

"Welcome home, Bruce."

She chuckled. "Some things will never change. That nickname, and this room!" She stepped from his grasp and made a show of surveying his bedroom, as she did every year. He watched her compile a slow, meticulous mental catalogue to see if anything had changed. It hadn't. The room was a shrine to their younger selves: The vinyl player and neatly stacked records, the overstuffed bookshelves, The Angels, Van Halen, and AC/DC posters still tacked to the walls alongside Pammie in the red bikini, and the random googley-eyed things she insisted on gifting him every holiday. They stared out, unblinking, and unchanged.

Bre often joked that Billy had a 'steel trap' memory, yet how the google-eye tradition had started, he couldn't remember. His room was littered with rocks, books, pinecones and a million other objects, all sporting bulging eyes. Even the posters had been google-eyed one year, completely changing Pamela Anderson's vibe from sexy to silly. He loved it.

"This place!" Her eyes, crinkled in the corners, darted to his appreciatively.

"It's ours," Billy said, the deep tone of his voice echoing around the room, dulling the screech of the cicadas outside. Mouth dry, his throat felt gravelly and unused as he squeezed the words out past the knot at the base of his neck – the knot that only seemed to grow whenever Breanna was near.

Bre had seen it all before, of course, but the room, her close examination as she picked up things and put them back down; Billy saw it for what it was – a delay. And a moment for them to assess their dynamic. Had things changed so much? The way her familiar body moved was ... different. Or was it just the costume?

Settling onto the bed, Billy pushed his back into the headboard, his long, tattooed legs stretching towards her as he placed the book low over his hips.

"Wait, Billy, I thought the deal was YOU in your birthday suit and ME in this ridiculous Santa suit! But you cheated!"

Billy only blinked.

"Billy! I came here in the spirit of tradition ..." She motioned to herself, how she'd gone all out this year and padded the costume. She was rounded, festive, and absolutely magnificent, hair piled into a messy bun atop her head. He'd seen that familiar bun sliding under cars as she fixed engines, and flopping front then back like a rag doll as she found the right rhythm to chop massive blocks of wood. He'd seen that same red hair slide low on her neck, curling under the lip of her Elmo helmet as she tried, over and over again, to master a skateboard in their youth.

She'd done it – all that, and more. That messy bun – the knot of hair he loved to loosen – was a sign of hard work. Cheeks flushed and a light sheen of sweat dotting her forehead, it seemed that tonight, climbing the ladder fit that criteria.

He wanted to be the one who painted those cheeks red, then trace each freckle as the colour slowly faded once more. He couldn't help but make some primal, throaty noise of appreciation. He had no words to adequately convey it, how his body responded to hers. He'd try, although his tongue tied whenever she was around, his voice sounding gruffer than usual, his tone deeper – and it was already rough and deep.

Beautiful. God, she was beautiful. He would have told her, if he hadn't felt like he should tiptoe on eggshells. No, he'd keep the observation to himself until he was sure everything was back to normal between them. *Normal* ... What exactly was normality nowadays? He still remembered that day, six months ago. The sight of Bre's hair spilled across the bar, her big eyes looking back over her shoulder as his fingers dug into the soft white flesh of her bare hip, the way she'd moaned his name over and over and ...

"Billy!"

She had the uncanny ability to see right through him and read his thoughts, but he refused to be embarrassed. He used to think it was because they had been such close friends for so long, but he had never been able to see through her in the same way. He hadn't had to. She'd always been the better communicator, whether verbal or otherwise, and her somewhat brutal honesty was one of his favourite traits. Breanna Henderson never held back. Not about anything, or in any way. She had tasks and to-do's, tick lists and back-up plans galore, and she ensured their completion. If she wanted it, she got it by sheer strength of will, *making* everything happen.

Except now. Now, with her Santa suit still firmly *on* and the physical distance between them growing, she was most definitely holding back. Tugging at her outfit, Bre was clearly hot and bothered. Christmas in Australia was usually a sweltering affair – and not just because of the weather. Why didn't Bre just strip off? In Christmases past, the outfit would barely make it through the window before becoming a festive puddle on the floor.

Unsure what to do, he scratched at his thigh.

"Billy, the only thing covering you is tattoos. *Usually*." She threw a small smirk his way, before picking up a chipped ceramic cookie monster mug with wonky, wiggling eyeballs. "But tonight you have boxers, and a book! I see you went for the big volume?" A large, special edition volume of *The Grinch* hid his groin from sight. "Wise choice."

Her brazen eyes roamed as she chuckled, the sound music to his ears. The tension in his body melted. This was all going to be fine. He knew it. Despite this weird, stilted start, soon, everything would be back to normal.

"You're reading *The Grinch* in ... what is that?"

"French."

Her eyebrows lifted. "Why?"

Clearing his throat, Billy shifted under the heat of her gaze. Whatever game she was playing, he'd join in. Bre knew what she wanted, and when – if – that was him, he'd take whatever time she offered.

"Knowing the English version exceedingly well," Billy said, "the French is not too difficult." He adjusted *Le Grinch*, watching her swallow. "Bruce, can we–"

"I brought you a present," she interjected, changing the subject yet again.

Retrieving the rather large Santa sack he'd somehow failed to notice, Bre removed a sprig of mistletoe and flowering gums, their red bursts exploding from gumnut caps. Bound with a too-large red bow, the posy sported two odd-sized googly eyes, glued at awkward angles. The bundle came hurtling at his bare chest.

"You like?"

A burst of laughter rolled through the room like thunder, and Bre grinned at his response.

"This is perfect, Bruce. Thank you."

"I don't want my present," she said. "Not yet, anyway. This year *I'm* finding the pickle, and I'm going to open my present in front of everyone and make a huge deal, like Liam and Connor do."

"If anyone can find a needle in a haystack – or a pickle in a pine tree – it's you," Billy said earnestly, as he did every year. It was an odd tradition, but one as old as themselves.

"So ... you gunna string it up?" Bre's eyes flicked briefly to the roof, and the twirling ceiling fan, before returning to *Le Grinch*. "You know mistletoe started this."

"Actually, Adam James did." Bre's words mirrored Billy's thought exactly.

Exchanging wide smiles, he added, aloud, "And I have never been more grateful for childish dares in my life."

"But I don't want to talk about Adam. Not now. URGH!" Breanna's bun wobbled as she shook her head. "None of this is going to plan, Billy. You and your Mr Happy jocks, *Le Grinch*, me ... The Plan is ..." she sighed out the last word, "fucked."

The Plan. Her Santa suit. His birthday suit. Friends with festive benefits. 'Fucked' was a crass but accurate adjective for their sexy Christmas tradition. 'Fucked' was The Plan, the box they loved to tick. Christmas was *their* time to cross that line between friends and behind-the-bar colleagues into unrestrained sex-on-every-possible-surface territory. Nothing compared to this. It was worth it. *She* was worth the wait. But ...

"Bre ..." He tried to put words to his feelings, forcing them out to address her hesitation. "We don't have to carry on the traditions anymore ... if you choose not to, I–" He couldn't help but move to her, to rub his thumb across the freckles high on her cheek. Freckles he'd mapped out like constellations, connecting the dots time and time again. She was goddamn glowing, lit from inside like a Christmas trinket, and gleaming. Yes, it was probably also a sheen of sweat – it was summer, and she was in a velvet suit after all – but that didn't matter. Breanna Henderson could be covered in kangaroo shit, and she'd still be the most amazing woman in any room.

Breanna read the truth of it in his expression. Her chin dipped, bun flopping onto his face.

"Bre? Are you … crying?" Breanna Henderson was *not* a crier. Not once had he witnessed it. Not at five when she came to visit him at the hospital, after his arm had been amputated. Not at eight when she crashed her bike so badly on the old dirt road that he'd had to pluck rocks and gruesome chunks of flesh from the wound. Not at fifteen when she jumped from the rafters of the barn, missing the haystack landing point entirely, breaking her leg in three places. Not even at funerals had Breanna Henderson wept. Her best friend, Jillian, had lost her mother recently, and while Billy had seen distress and sorrow plain as day on Breanna's face, not one single tear had escaped her hazel eyes.

But now …

"You can't want this, want *me*," she sobbed, pushing his hand from her face before wiping her face free of sweat and tears. She needed to get the costume off, and cool down. Billy's eyes dropped to his favourite freckle – the one resting on her top lip. The spot he loved to kiss, every Christmas – *only* at Christmas. Well, *almost* only …

"You can't want me like *this*," she said, plucking the fur-trimmed costume from her body where it stuck in wet patches. Hot and flushed, Bre was spectacular. And he'd tell her so.

"You are–"

"All gross and disgusting," she sniffled. "And I've been trying to call Jill, and I know she's a boomerang and she'll always come back, but I feel like she's ignoring me. I don't blame her, really, because I keep ruining all my friendships and–"

"Untrue," he interjected.

She took a shaky breath, pressing her lips together when Billy continued, thumb wiping an errant droplet as it rolled past her nose. "Jillian is a bit ... broken ... right now. Give her time." Her sigh rolled against his palm. "She might be your best friend, Bruce, but you are mine. And you can't ruin us." He rushed to add, "Even if you changed your mind and changed the plan. There is no pressure from me, Breanna. You could not ruin anything we have, because we are friends first, always."

Friends with benefits had been her idea, but he'd never denied the chemistry that sizzled between them. Whatever she offered, he would take it with both hands – metaphorically speaking.

He brushed a stray lock of rosy hair behind her ear. "And you are not gross and disgusting. Far from it. Though ..." Scratching his bearded chin, Billy considered her costume. "Speaking of our costumes ... You know our deal was supposed to be the sexy Mrs Clause kind of Santa outfit. Yet you insist on teasing me with this concealing abomination every year."

"Oh, you want the *uncovered* version, do you?"

Bre's fingers dug into the fluffy white seam of the costume, ripping the Velcro apart in one swift movement. The sound split the room in two, sending his stomach plummeting to his feet.

Billy froze. He always froze. That familiar tightening around his ribcage constricted to near suffocating. Silence enveloped the room as he watched Breanna's clothing hit the floor and she sighed blissfully at the fresh air against her skin. Bare and beautiful, she stood with hands splayed on her hips, determined and defiant, daring him to look. This was the woman he knew. Brave and fierce and–

"Well? Anything to say now? Still want to tell me the plan is ... doable?"

He'd been rendered speechless, and she knew it. But this time ... it was different. *She* was different. He was kicking himself for not noticing earlier.

A foot shorter than he was, she stepped back, pulling away so he could see her ... All of her. She was fearless, shameless, and honest – traits he'd always admired. He needed to be the same, but he couldn't lift his gaze to meet hers, eyes locked on her body.

He watched Bre's chest rise and fall, the sound of her quick breaths hitting his ears in short waves. Billy soaked in every freckle scattered across her body, noting the slow roll of goosebumps prickle across her skin as she waited for him to respond. Swallowing hard, he stared.

"You sure you want all of this, Billy?" Her hands roamed over her breasts, which looked heavier than he'd ever seen them, her nipples – darker – down her ribs to her hips, which curved and flared like never before, before circling her stomach, where a tight bubble of skin bulged.

"Bre." His tongue managed to find words. "You're ..." His

voice caught, chest was unbearably tight. "You're pregnant?"

2

Nothing Kills Romance
Like an Air Mattress

Bre

DECEMBER HAD ALWAYS BEEN her favourite month – until she was pregnant. Now, her ankles swelled before she even slid them from the bed, and scalding hot lines of pain, like heated needles, stabbed the soles of her feet as she carefully stepped over Billy's hulking frame on the floor. She felt heavier and slower than ever before, though the woman in the mirror often didn't look as horrid as she felt.

The woman in the mirror had a tight little baby bump, but when Bre looked down ... that swollen gut seemed infinitely larger. And right now, that belly was pushing its entire weight onto her bladder.

Stumbling to the bathroom, she looked longingly at Billy's silhouette. Nothing killed the romance like an air mattress being blown up ... after a surprise pregnancy announcement to your best-friend-with-benefits ... in his parents' house. She'd imagined December first, over and over in her mind. She had planned and prepared for how and when she'd tell Billy about the baby, but nothing could have prepared her for last night.

They hadn't fought, exactly, but she knew Billy wanted answers – and deserved explanations – but she'd refused to discuss it further. The bottom line wasn't the pregnancy, per se, but the fact that she didn't see why anything had to change between them. She was just six months pregnant now, that was all. Sex was completely doable, she'd even read up on it in that *What to Expect* book, just to be sure. No, the only thing that could have changed between them was a level of expectation – she expected that he would fall on his metaphorical sword and sacrifice his future to save her from this strange, unplanned present.

Billy Carmichael was the most upstanding man she'd ever known, and she knew that once she told him about the baby, he'd get down on his knee and make promises he'd actually keep. He'd try to secure a future for her that didn't involve being that horrible small town social outcast – a single, unwed mother. A slut. A hussy.

All their lives, and especially at the tavern, when the locals became loose-lipped, they'd heard those horrid terms slung around town. Women had sex just as much as men, unfairly labelled for their behaviour, especially if it resulted in a baby. Her towering best friend, she knew, would be so full of pity that he'd sacrifice himself by marrying her to save Bre from that judgement. And that was not what she wanted.

She'd had months to figure this out now, and amidst the uncertainties, there was one thing she knew for sure – Bre refused to trap Billy, especially because of his own damn chivalry. She refused to let him act on that innate quality all Carmichaels seemed born with – to protect her, simply because she'd been born with a vagina.

As children, she'd cleared it up, this notion that she was something less because she was a girl. She'd stood on her own two feet and been such a tomboy they'd named her Bruce, her straight up and down figure and oil-covered overalls confirming that she was 'one of the boys'. Unfortunately, nothing screamed 'vulnerable femininity' like her new beachball belly and swollen mammaries.

Bre didn't want to be seen differently, and she certainly didn't need well-meaning sympathy. She – and her baby – were never going to be someone's chore. She didn't want the pity or the questions or the too-good intentions of her best friend. That was exactly why she hadn't wanted anyone to know about the unexpected, yet not unwelcome, pregnancy.

She didn't *need* help. Or a man. She would admit, however, that when they'd tiptoed around the question of whether their traditional festivities were still on the table, Bre had certainly *wanted* Billy.

Her body ached for him, desire coursing through her like she had taken some kind of aphrodisiac. She'd never been hornier in her life than when she was pregnant and naked before him, eyeing *Le Grinch* and those ridiculous Mr Happy jocks that covered less of him than his tattoos. She'd forced herself to stay still, rooted to the spot, and watch as his dark eyebrows clashed together, thinking a million questions he didn't ask.

Usually, she had zero reservations. Christmas wasn't for being shy or hesitant, it was their once-a-year no-holds-barred clothes-completely-optional festive fuckfest. But how could she stick to their plans now? Without even meaning to, Billy would treat her differently, and she couldn't bear it.

Over the years, he'd seen her naked plenty of times, and she'd been hopeful that nothing would change, but last night … it hadn't been the same. Despite the pounding in her chest, and the equally strong beat much lower down, exhaustion had dragged Breanna to Billy's bed, alone.

He'd sat for a long time, staring at the gifted mistletoe she'd hot-glued eyes onto, before setting up camp on the floor. For a quiet man, Billy's thoughts had been extraordinarily loud.

For a loud little person, she had been awfully quiet, mentally working down the lists in her mind:

- Come home for Christmas.

- Resume the 'benefits' part of friendship with Billy (see addendum in planner – Bre's Sexy Bucket List).

- Explain everything.

She hated a list she couldn't complete, and at this rate, her carefully curated Sexy Bucket List was going to end up screwed into a tiny ball and thrown in the bin – much like her love life in general. That last point? For the first time in her life, Bre's tongue was tied, and explanations, while needed, would change everything between them ... forever.

As usual, Billy was patient with her, waiting quietly for her to elaborate. But very few details came, stilted and forced, and the awkwardness between them became a pressing weight that pinned her down. Her lips clamped shut while her mind whirled, writing then re-writing the list of 'right words' to say in this awkward as hell situation.

Eventually they'd fallen asleep, separated by all the things that weren't being said and the cavernous valley of spine-prickling tension between their respective mattresses.

Now, as she watched his broad frame rise and fall, the increasing light of dawn offered new hope for a new day. Shadows still clung to every surface, despite the morning call of the currawongs beyond the curtains, but with time the darkness would. Time healed all wounds, too. How much time might Billy need? She absently searched for a clock, unsurprised to find it didn't exist.

Clocks weren't required in Billy's world. He'd never known a time that wasn't 'beer o'clock' at The Pope, or 'up at sunrise' and 'bed at sundown' here on the farm. The timelessness of it, the natural ebbs and flows of their world – it felt *right*. Like there was no beginning or end – just up and down, natural, and rhythmic, a relentless pounding that would never end; that she *never* wanted to end. Aaaaand there she went, getting all horny again. Pushing hair from her face, she sighed. Maybe all her plans, and their traditions, would have to go out the window this year.

Coming back here each December, helping his family with the business and the festivities, it felt like home. She'd never doubted she'd end up here again this December, but she'd desperately hoped nothing would change between her and Billy, despite their somewhat strained last few months. Bre knew she'd been distant. Billy deserved a better friend.

Where once they'd clear the bar then head upstairs for a private drink and an old film, she'd decline, saying she had an early morning the next day. Their midday coffee dates at Friday's Café had fallen by the wayside – not that she was supposed to drink Friday Evan's jet-fuel strength caffeine while pregnant. She'd told him she was too busy, which she was, but in reality, Bre could never be too busy for Billy Carmichael. The idea of saving up her time with him, of hoarding it until now, had been a mistake. Now, it was too late.

Every small moment of retreat had drawn a line in the sand, and last night that line had cracked into a chasm. Clearly, nothing was the same, and it was her fault.

Carefully, Bre tiptoed across his room, opening then closing the door to the ensuite she'd helped build all those years ago, when Billy's parents, Nick and Holly, decreed their four teenaged boys were too unmanageable to share the one family bathroom. To stop the morning fights, Nick ordered each son to address their issues in a productive manner. With Bre's new lodgings completed by then, the boys turned their attention towards home renovations, under the watchful eye of their father. Literally building the changes they desired in the world had been a revelation to Breanna. Her own mother would have never let her pick up a hammer, let alone the air-compressed nail gun the Carmichaels shoved in her hands.

"They were some hard years," she told the white tiles, noting how clean the bathroom was, and how nice it would be to vomit into this sparkling toilet bowl, rather than the ones at The Pope. Billy's tavern was impeccably clean (for a pub) but pregnancy-induced vomiting in a public restroom was not Bre's idea of fun.

She'd always had an aversion to public toilets, the precise reason Billy ran a tight ship with frequent cleaning schedules. Still, every time she gripped a toilet seat, heaving, she was never sure if it was the baby or the idea of someone else's arse germs that made her feel so ill.

The slightly minty bathroom air filled her lungs as she relieved her pressurized bladder. Looking down, she whispered "good morning" to the beachball that had taken up residence in her stomach. Six months of growth and change, of hiding under loose clothing, and shitty posture, and now she'd finally revealed herself. Revealed the truth – the foetus the ultrasound technician had unceremoniously joked about looking like a turd.

A sudden wave of sickness rolled through her. "I need breakfast, little one, or I'll barf till midday." It was yet another new, not-so-fun addition to her daily rituals. Luckily, the Carmichaels' kitchen cupboards were used to raiders. "I think we should have vegemite toast, little shit."

After flushing the toilet, it took her three attempts to stand up. She imagined the baby, sloshing around beneath her skin, an olive in a martini glass, sliding side to side as she gathered her legs under her.

"Finding the centre of balance when you're a whale on land is rather difficult," she mumbled to her reflection, a thinner, less green version of the person she felt right now. Flicking off the light, she allowed her eyes to adjust before opening the door and surveying Billy in the slowly growing light. He hadn't moved. The mountain of a man lay on his side, his back an expansive art-covered canvas, atop a rapidly deflating ... no, *deflated* ... air mattress. Well, that explained the hissing she'd heard all night.

Bre had dreamed it was a tortured snake, slowly wheezing its last breath from somewhere outside, but the mattress beneath Billy's bulk was probably equally as anguished. Her heart gave a low, heavy throb. Billy Carmichael was a good guy. The best, in fact. She'd known it since they were kids.

Unlike everyone else in her life, Billy never imposed. He never tried to make her apologise for who she was. He'd just ... been there. Often quietly reading and always a solid presence. He'd been a pseudo-brother, and she was one of 'the boys' until, one night, years ago, when Bre's to-do list required a date.

"It's just a wedding! Please, Billy, I can't go alone. Not again. Everyone is getting married so early, but I haven't had a boyfriend since tenth grade when Alex McKenzie slipped his fingers up my skirt and ... it's not important. You know the story, anyway. He told everyone at school. Point is, the eligible men of Moonshine are either all dating, married, pining a lost love, or so far up themselves I'd have to hold a mirror all night to catch their attention! But you, my best friend in the whole world, *you* are like me. Single by choice and happy to ignore the pressure to live on a big block of land with five dogs and a dozen kids! Those were our parents' dreams, but we have independence, and our own business aspirations. We're our own people. We can help each other out!"

Poor William Carmichael never stood a chance.

"I see that eyebrow raise, Billy. Okay, how about I sweeten the deal?" she'd said, all those years ago. "I'll give you anything you want. *Anything*. Hell, at this point I'd exchange sexual favours for this wedding – oh, you'll come? REALLY? THANK YOU!"

He'd assumed she'd been joking, of course. Been shocked when she drove him home, followed him to his apartment above his beloved tavern, placed a soft, melodic record on his vinyl player and oh so slowly removed her clothes.

She still remembered the surprise in his eyes, the tremble of his big, square-fingered hand against the soft underside of her barely-there breast, and how his brilliant blue eyes had darkened with desire. His hand had slid into her hair, tugging her head back, forcing Bre to look up at him. Words rumbled through his chest, reverberating through the hands she'd planted there: "Are you certain, Bruce?"

"Never been surer." Honesty, plain and simple. "If you'll have me ..."

Billy had kissed her then – their first kiss, aside from the barely-there peck that Spin the Bottle forced on them as idiot teens. This kiss had been hot and hard, lighting a fire within her she hadn't known existed, and she'd swallowed all hesitation.

Bre swore fireworks had burst within her body that night. They'd spent many nights curled into each other on the couch, or side-by-side in a bed, but they'd never spent a night together, before then, naked, and willing to explore.

Come morning, that fire in his eyes was tempered. Bre, unusually awkward, had joked about "friends with benefits" and "maybe again at the next wedding, if you're lucky" and "how about a festive fuck every Christmas?" She'd hated how callous the words sounded, even as they spewed from her mouth. But Billy had nodded, sealing the deal with a swift, hot kiss.

Casual sex with Billy had never been awkward. In fact, the familiarity of her best friend's huge, solid body wound around hers had provided more comfort, enjoyment and orgasms than the few official boyfriends she'd had over the years. Fucking Billy was fun in a way regular relationships weren't, probably because he approached her body like she approached broken vehicles – something challenging and fun, a new hobby that needed to be learned and tested, examined part by part.

More weddings, anniversaries, and events requiring dates flooded their calendars. Christmases and a few official boyfriends came and went. Then, she'd found out she was pregnant, and things didn't seem so fun and carefree anymore.

Her plans with Billy were built around a lack of responsibilities, with no second guessing. With a baby growing in her belly, all she did these days was feel guilty and doubt everything.

Why did she have to do this? Insist on upholding these Christmas traditions when – he had been right last night – everything had changed. *She* was changing. She couldn't deny him for trying to back out, but she needed him more than ever. Not just for sex but also for comfort and reassurance, the continuation of their lifelong friendship. Things had always been so easy between them, and she wanted – no, *needed* – that to continue.

A sob rose within her, a sad little bubble that slid from her gut to her throat, plucking at her tear ducts.

Blinking at the google-eyed Def Leppard poster, Bre tried to slow her heartbeat and her breathing. This hormonal thing was a trip. She never cried. *Never*. But now? She was a wrecked car leaking engine oil, threatening more damage with every drop and every memory that refused to stay locked away. She needed food in her system, or she was going to vomit on the giant man lying on the floor.

"God, pregnancy is a bitch," she quietly told some old, too

small clothes in the tallboy drawer Billy kept for her. Dressing quickly, she sighed at herself in the mirror. Even in the near-light of dawn, she could see that the red t-shirt, stretched too tight over her stomach, made her look like a Christmas bauble. Huffing a very bad word that Billy would have described as 'bawdy', she peeled the shirt off and threw it to the floor.

Her appearance was rarely a consideration for Bre, but there was definitely a time and a place for new clothes – and that was about two months ago. Called a tomboy and a beanpole all her life, she had no idea what to do with herself now that she had curves.

Not just curves, but breasts. Hips. Thighs. Places she'd never noticed before now swelled and filled her clothes in all sorts of strange ways. It was like she'd finally hit puberty ... just twenty years too late. Now, because of those damned curves, her pants refused to zip up, the buttons on her overalls remained open at her hips, and her t-shirts had shrunk into halter-tops. Opening the drawer beside hers, she quietly rifled through the familiar fabrics of Billy's clothes.

William Carmichael had always been big, broad-shouldered, and towering. His shirts hung to her knees, comfortable and airy – exactly what she needed right now. Even with a belly, his old Mighty Ducks jersey was sure to fit her.

Twisting her hair into a bun, she wound the old hair tie from her wrist round it in three quick loops and grabbed her favourite hat from the hook on the door. *SHIT SHOW SUPERVISOR* it proudly proclaimed in white embroidered letters. Years ago, the Carmichaels had gifted her the cap that told everyone on the farm who the real boss was. She adored it. Sweat-stained and sun-faded, the old hat was easily her favourite possession, aside from her car, Edsel.

Tiptoeing to the stairs, she descended from Billy's bedroom and straight into the huge Carmichael family kitchen.

To describe it as the 'heart of the home' wouldn't have done the cavernous space justice. It was warm and earthy, full of light and eclectic bright colours. The sweet air perpetually smelled of freshly baked biscuits. Herbs from the garden dangled in posies between iron pots and pans from vaulted, exposed wooden beams, and arched windows drew the Christmas tree farm and bushland beyond into the room itself.

It had long reminded Bre of a good witch's kitchen, or at the very least some kind of earthen fairy, because there was almost certainly a magic that Holly Carmichael kneaded, basted and baked here.

Where was Holly? Billy's mother couldn't be too far. Amidst her festive content creation, Holly found joy in ensuring everyone who set foot on Carmichael lands was welcomed and fed.

The kitchen opened into an equally impressive dining room, both serving a huge volume of traffic throughout the day. Bre had rarely seen the long wooden table or benchtop without a selection of food and drink, made available to the family, farm hands, and seasonal workers who made the pilgrimage each year to the Carmichael Christmas Tree Farm.

Stomach grumbling, Bre spied a plate of oat biscuits. Stuffing one into her mouth, Bre's eyes rolled skyward, praising whichever god was responsible for Holly's cooking prowess. "There's an orgasm in my mouth ... about time, too." Mouth watering, she munched.

From its hiding place, tucked into the band of her underwear, her phone vibrated.

"Oh, shit." Her palms were sweating. "Jesus freaking Christ in a manger." Biscuit crumbs fell on the screen as she read the name splashed across the screen: Revv Ryder.

Hey Breanna baby! ETA= 2hours.

Can't wait!

Are you as excited as I am?

AND I'm bringing a surprise!

You have a surprise, she thought ruefully, one hand on her belly as the other brought another biscuit into her mouth.

"Shit, shit, shit!"

3

Too Many Men

Bre

"SHIT, SHIT, SHIT!"

"None of that language, please, young lady!"

"FUCK!" The phone flew from Bre's hand. Normally, she was unflappable, cucumber cool and generally made of sterner stuff. Now, though, after a horrid night of tossing and turning, half happy to be here, half wondering what the hell to do to fix things now she *was* here, and fully horny, Bre watched her phone arc in slow motion, before it crashed to the floor. The glass screen, like last night's hope of naked fun times, was smashed to smithereens.

"Well, that was … unlike you." Holly eyed Bre suspiciously, as cookie crumbs fell from her open mouth to the floor in a slow, embarrassing trickle. "Have the dropsies today, Breanna?"

"HOLLY!" She dived for her phone, as if hiding it would make her feel better about the potential pain she was about to inflict upon this woman and her family. "What are you–" All this extra blood in her system was making her light-headed. Gripping the back of a chair, she tried again. "You scared the shi ... uh, heck ... out of me!"

Holly chuckled, pushing her dark hair off her face with the back of one flour-dusted hand.

"You know there's nothing I love more than lurking in my own kitchen to scare the unsuspecting neighbour girl who may as well be my very own daughter." She laughed again, resuming her work. "Actually, as usual, I'm just preparing to feed the army. Nothing sinister. Well, except for all the arsenic, but no one's complained about the taste of it yet."

Bre's smirk refused to hide. "And they say the special ingredient is *love*."

"Fools." Holly beamed. Dusting her hands, Holly Carmichael, tall and refined, took Bre in with a familiar sweep of her eyes, head to toes, then up again, assessing. How this slender woman birthed four of the biggest human males Bre had ever seen, she'd never know. All of her sons had inherited her height and thick brown hair, but only Billy had inherited that swiftly raised arch in his brow that spoke volumes.

"I'm fine."

Holly's gaze flicked back down to Bre's abdomen, a smile tugging at her lips. "Looks like you're doing *very* well. Though

I wasn't *expecting* you down so early."

Bre's stomach rolled, a long queasy feeling spreading through her. "I ... need food."

Holly nodded sagely, trying to suck the smile back between her lips. "Anything you want to talk–"

"Nope."

"Well." The smile grew, despite Holly's efforts. "When you decide to start replying in multisyllabic words ... or even if you just want to grunt small words at me, darling," she added as an afterthought, smiling softly, "I'll be here to listen. You've never had trouble voicing yourself before, so I doubt you'll start playing coy now."

That arched brow was back, challenging Bre, who bit her tongue, refusing to take the bait. No way was she confirming or denying, but the truth was plain to Holly, a seasoned mother-of-four, that she, Breanna 'Bruce' Henderson, was well and truly 'Up the Duff'. There was a bun in her oven. A pea in her pod. She was with child. Knocked up. Preggers, and she was eating for two. The list of euphemisms had been growing in her mind since she'd made the discovery, months ago.

"And let me guess –" she motioned to Billy's Mighty Ducks jersey, "– you haven't gone shopping for clothing that will fit that bump. Trust me, you'll need Spandex. Stretch and comfort now trump your usual swimming-in-too-big denim and cotton t-shirt obsession. And while we're speaking of uncomfortable necessities ... Does your mother know?"

Bre only snorted, reaching for another biscuit.

Her mother was one item on her 'Things to Deal With' list that never seemed to get struck off. Bre guessed Elanor Henderson felt much the same way about her daughter.

"My mother has nothing to do with this. Or me ... generally." *Not unless she wants something*, she wanted to add.

Six months ago, Bre had been seeing someone – a few someones, if she counted a string of bad blind dates set up by her mother as 'dating'. By Bre's age, her mother insisted, she should be well and truly married. Elanor Henderson wanted her daughter settled and pumping out grandkids, burdened like all the other thirty-something-year-olds, with a mortgage and a husband.

There must be something inherently wrong with her, Elanor had argued. Why else was Breanna still single and dressing like a dirty barn brat instead of wearing pretty dresses like her friends? Having few close female friends, Bre guessed her mother was drawing a comparison between herself and Jillian Maitland, who was the definition of feminine grace. In stark contrast to Bre's baggy t-shirts, jeans, boots, or dirty work overalls, Jillian's wardrobe, bursting with bright colours and pretty florals, would have made a fifties housewife proud.

Jillian was still single too, Bre often wanted to argue, but she was also grieving the loss of her mother. That was a valid excuse for singularity, or so Elanor would argue right back.

Sometimes, Bre wished that same excuse could be hers – a dead mother, one could only wish! – but every time her mind travelled down that morbid rabbit hole, guilt swept in like a ghost, tugging at Breanna's edges until she almost – *almost* – felt grateful to still have her interfering, argumentative mother in her life. Elanor Henderson was well and truly alive, and unafraid to make herself known.

"Seven dates," Elanor had warned, "should be more than enough to find a man to settle down with, especially in such a small town as Moonshine, where the single men are on the hunt for a wife to complete them."

"Complete them?"

It had taken Bre a long time to process this, mouth opening and closing as arguments filtered in and out of her mind. Her brother Seth had been much quicker to react, snorting his dinner into his nose.

The next few minutes had been spent whacking his back, thankfully taking attention away from Bre and the predicament Elanor had forced upon her. She'd been a fool to think Seth's opinion on the matter would count, and while he'd tried, ultimately, Elanor would not be ignored. Seven dates.

Bre had buried her face in her hands and slumped over the table, sighing, "Fuck me."

"Such foul language for a young lady!" Then, "Hopefully, one of them will! *After* marriage, of course!" Elanor had sniffed, turning to mutter about her indelicate daughter's potty mouth, the soap required to wash out the filth, and how corrupting those Carmichaels lads were on her sweet Seth and Breanna. "Not enough soap in the world ..."

Graciously organising the dates around Breanna's work

schedule – long days at her garage, Rust Busters, and her nights at The Pope, Elanor sent the would-be suitors to the local tavern for after-shift meetings. None of the men had thought it odd to meet a single woman at the local pub, very late at night – yet another reason why Bre questioned her mother's taste.

At least Elanor hadn't insisted on acting as her chaperone on the dates she'd pre-arranged. Apparently, that had been Billy's job, as "the only quiet Carmichael. You know… the one with all the muscles who puts his brains to use with running his own business, even though it's a –" Elanor's nose had scrunched, "– tavern."

Billy was the one person Elanor deemed worthy of protecting her adult daughter, and he'd been unceremoniously appointed to the job. Thankfully, Billy had taken on his task of assessing Breanna's potential suitors in his own, silently diplomatic manner. By the time Breanna finished her shifts, most of those seven would-be-husbands had been judged unworthy, so unsteady they could barely stand. Her boss and friend plied each one with alcohol until they forgot why they were waiting at the pub in the first place.

One had missed their meet time, too busy hunched over the toilet bowl. The second had finished the evening ramming his tongue down another woman's throat in the darkened corner by the jukebox. The third had ceremoniously thrust out his hand, burped out the word "charmed", then vomited something bright green all over Breanna's Doc Martens.

"Midori," Billy had murmured, kicking the mop bucket with

a grimace. "Sorry."

Despite being covered in toxic green, she couldn't blame Billy. He'd always looked out for her. Later, they'd laughed until their ribs ached, pondering what wedded bliss to a man who gorges Midori cocktails while waiting to meet his potential wife might be like. It probably threw up a few red flags, if she was honest. The other dates hadn't been great, either.

There were simply too many men in her life during that strange time. Only one potential suitor had a shred of romantic potential, and they'd had a great night together – not that she'd ever admit that to Elanor.

"Mum and Dad probably know I'm here," Bre told Holly, resigned, as her foggy brain re-entered the present. "Somehow they see everything, even if I'm only here for a few minutes."

Holly nodded, flipping long lines of golden pancakes on the eight-burner stovetop.

"This will certainly be a fun Christmas," Holly said, chuckling.

Loosing a breath, Bre's eyes slid to the huge arching window. Beyond the thick trees, and the burnt remnants of a wooden fence, her parents' house hid in the bushland.

"No, it won't."

That eyebrow arch had Bre scrambling for more words. What she wouldn't give for a coffee right now. Clearing her throat, she added, "We ... still don't talk very much."

Holly clicked her tongue, dancing around the kitchen, the pots, pans and plates her partners. The motion so reminded

Bre of Billy. His movements were a rougher, more masculine version of Holly's gentler moves, but his ability to whirl around a workspace was almost hypnotic and had long ago earned him the nickname of Holly's 'little fournado,' despite no longer being anywhere near 'little'.

"Tis the Season, you know ..." Holly said, pouring juice from a large pitcher into a coffee mug that demanded *KEEP CALM AND DRINK COFFEE*. Sliding it towards Bre with a wide smile, she added, "for little miracles."

Bre snorted.

This wasn't the Christmas of the movies. There was no slow, soft snow to lay down and make angels in, no hot cocoa by the fire, no iced-over steps to slip on and fall into Mr Right. But there was, and always had been, magic in an Australian Christmas.

Bre didn't consider herself a terribly romantic person, but even she had to admit there was something special in the way the trees baked in the sun and filled the air with a sweet thick scent, and how deliciously cold ice-cream slid down a parched throat. She loved hot, sweaty days in the fields of Christmas trees followed by cooler, just as sweaty nights in Billy's bed. She loved watching condensation climb like frost up the window of Billy's bedroom while the temperature reached boiling point outside ... and within the sanctuary of his four walls, too.

December was sweat and sun and sex. December was licking down Billy's heavily tattooed chest, fingertips exploring his skin in search of new ink. There was always something new to discover. December was Billy's body, huge in comparison to hers, flexing and shifting as he dragged trees on and off the trailer for customers, one handed. Billy after a long day of work, an immobile mountain sunbaking by the pool, body glistening with the rapidly vaporising water. Billy towering over her, on his knees, behind her, pulling her flush against him, nibbling on her earlobe, dragging her long hair down over her nipples, tickling overheated, bare skin ... Billy, Billy, Billy.

"Breanna, dear?"

A flutter low in her belly brought her back to reality once more, a flood of heat swamping already flushed cheeks. *Damned hormones.* Bre cleared her throat, blinking away the visions that danced behind her eyelids.

"December is just a month," she told Holly, wishing she believed it. Bre wasn't a liar. Better to fill a room with silence than deception. Or so she'd always thought, until last night, when Billy's thoughts had been so loud, they might as well have had the difficult conversation, anyway.

A voice spluttered behind her. "Just a month? Just. A. Month! What poppycock! Holly, this wee lass should leave our residence immediately! She's quite lost her marbles if she thinks she can say rubbish like that here, of all places!"

Grinning widely, Bre turned to face Nick Carmichael. Barrel-chested and wide as his sons, grey sprouted from his temples and ran in lines down his neat beard, making him look like a fierce Highland warrior – and a total silver fox, if ever there was one.

Bre rushed into his open arms, almost spilling her juice. "Mr C!"

"Aye, lass, tis me. The one and only." He appraised her in that same up-down once-over as his wife, his tone softening. "But you're not one and only, are ye now? May I?" After an initial hesitation, Bre gave a tiny nod and Nick's large, weathered hand gently curved across her stomach. "Hullo, wee one." If warmth had a sound, Nick's voice was it. Drawing back, he offered a watery smile.

"Dad, stop being weird."

"Yeah, Dad, stop being weird."

The twins, Liam and Connor, bounded into the kitchen. Only ten months older than Billy, and in their early thirties, they were easily identifiable as Carmichaels, their physical makeup so similar they could have been cloned in a lab. Every Carmichael had been blessed with striking genetics – light blue eyes, dark hair, tall stature, and broad frames.

Smelling of the earth and completely covered in pine needles, like twin echidnas, the brothers took their seats at the table, grins playing at their wide mouths.

"Bruce! Glad to see you're still hanging around like a bad smell," Liam said, his fork spearing the pile of pancakes Holly placed on the table.

"Ready for Christmas, Bruce?" Connor chimed in, hoarding the maple syrup, mischief plain on his face.

"Of course she is! Bruce without a plan or a list is an existential crisis waiting to happen!"

Liam wasn't wrong.

"About this Christmas," she began. "I'll need to go over a few of the finer details of those lists I sent you, and Seth–"

The twins chuckled. "Heard from Seth lately?"

Holly and Nick exchanged tired glances but Bre only grinned.

"What have you done to him this time?" she asked, knowing full well their implacably cheeky mood would be the result of some shenanigan involving her brother.

"Nothing."

"Seth's fine."

Plucking a pine needle from her son's hair, Holly tutted, and the twins' grins grew even wider.

"Mister Seth Henderson should be gracing us with his presence *sometime* today ..." Connor chuckled.

"*If* he can untie himself from the tree," Liam added.

"Boys! What did you do?" Holly's hands went to her slight hips. "You might not be children anymore, but your father and I are still able to punish you, especially while you're under our roof!"

Liam and Connor exchanged glances before turning to their father for moral support. Nick didn't tear his attention from the sports column.

Liam started. "Mum, calm down. He's just–"

"Tied to a tree ..." Connor interjected.

"Butt naked ..."

"*Buck naked*," a deep voice corrected, preceding heavy feet down the stairs. "*Buck* naked is the older etymological form. *Butt* naked," Billy continued, "is a lazy derivative that entered the popular vernacular in the seventies."

She couldn't help but stare as he descended the final steps and entered the massive kitchen. Bre's breath caught. It always did, even though she'd seen it a million times before – the expanse of his tattooed chest, and the long plane of Billy's stomach. Still, she forced herself to breathe in and out. Repeat. Look away. To remember the strange paradox that while Billy was so casual with this language lesson, she'd ruined their friendship with her inability to speak.

And, she reminded herself begrudgingly, she'd ruined everything with her ignorance of simple math. She'd ignored the simplest equation human beings had ever known – that *intercourse* minus *contraception* equals *impregnation*. Tugging a singlet shirt over his head, Billy nodded a greeting, clearly having exhausted his allocation of words today.

"Well said." Holly's eyes lit up, beamed at her youngest son, who filled the doorway with his broad, muscular body.

"Word nerds, the both of you," Nick chimed in, pulling his wife down for a kiss, full of adoration.

Shaking her head, Bre tried to lighten the mood, to portray a sense of normality. "Who talks like that?"

"People," Billy said, delicately folding his large body into what looked like a laughably small chair by comparison, "who read."

Three more words, directed at her. Good. That was a start.

Usually, Billy was the quiet, pensive one and she was the talker, but now she found herself wanting him to fill the awkward silences between them.

Open, honest and often called 'too blunt', Bre was the walking definition of 'Too Much Information' … usually. But now? She waddled too much to be a walking definition of anything but a penguin! And more than anything she couldn't – didn't *want* – to talk about anything, let alone it. *It*, of course, being the baby. The paternity.

"Good morning, William!" Holly beamed.

"Son," Nick beamed, knowing only his wife got away with using Billy's full name.

"Brother!" Liam and Connor cried in unison, mocking their mother's tone. Their jollity died, however, as Billy shot them a look filled with warning. Their pancakes suddenly became extraordinarily interesting. "Boss," they amended as Billy shot them a look, rubbing eyes dry and red from a lack of decent sleep.

Words weren't necessary for Billy, and they certainly weren't his preferred mode of communication. The twins knew this better than anyone. Liam and Connor often worked as security for their brother at Moonshine's favourite watering hole, The Pope, and were attuned to Billy's non-verbal communications across the loud, crowded tavern.

Bre had personally witnessed him stop a bar fight with one pointed finger and an equally pointed look from those cool blue eyes. One brief glance or a nod of his head and the brothers knew which patron Billy wanted removed from the premises.

To look at him, you might be forgiven for assuming Billy Carmichael was some kind of rugged mountain man from a fairytale. He could be a towering menace in shadow, especially when in one of his rare bad moods. But Billy was the wallflower in most social situations, too big to disappear despite his wish to do so. He was the quiet, observant, book-lover who preferred the silence of libraries and museums.

Serene, he would label it. *Awkward and stifling*, she'd argue right back, forced to tilt her chin up, up, up to his heavily bearded face and the bright, light blue eyes that smiled down upon her. She aimed most of her retorts straight ahead, hitting his chest that was easily three hands wider than most men's.

All of him was big in ways that made her mind boggle. He didn't have the pretty-boy gym muscles of their good friend Adam James. Adam was, admittedly, lovely to look at, but he was too smooth and evenly tanned, spending so much time shirtless outdoors. Billy's body was more akin to the gods of old – dark hair curled over even darker inked skin, his physique hardened and honed like a lumberjack's – the result of years of hard, consistent, physical work. Nothing stopped him – especially not his disability.

Billy's mere presence filled the air with a quiet authority that was undeniable. He rendered words unnecessary, which was ironic, because he insisted Bre verbalise everything.

And his hair! The man's facial hair was his most expressive feature. Billy's eyebrows spoke volumes, and his beard and moustache were able to swallow his entire mouth or part like the Red Sea when he smiled, revealing brilliant white teeth. Billy's physical strength and ability to kick someone's arse into next year were mere footnotes.

The woman who'd gifted that hair was speaking, smiling around the table, aiming a wink at Bre. Swallowing a quick gulp of juice, Bre fought the rise and fall of her emotions, which were ebbing and flowing with her nausea. What was Holly saying? Did she need to respond?

No, Billy was responding, his voice rougher than usual, like gravel slowly grating on rocks. "Everything is fine."

"*Fine.*" One of the twins air quoted with big fingers and a grin.

"We all know that's code for *not* fine. Bruce's snoring keep you up?" the other said, before lunging at the pile of crispy bacon their mother had just deposited on the table.

"I do *not* snore."

"Uh, yeah, Bruce, you do." Liam earned the punch.

"Hey!"

Nick scowled. "No fightin' at the table!"

"I thought our babies had grown into thirty-year-old men," Holly lamented with a sigh. "I was wrong."

"Some things never change," Bre's mouth said before her brain had time to think.

Billy stiffened at the word: change. Something flashed across her best friend's face – a thought half formed – but it was gone before Breanna could blink. Clearly, he wasn't commenting.

Everything had changed. And it was all her fault.

Equally wordless, Nick split his newspaper, sliding one half across to Billy, who spread it across the table, immediately immersed. Bre tried not to view it as a dismissal. He always read the paper, she reminded herself. Billy was in no way *extra* concentrated on the tiny print of the sports section this morning. And he definitely didn't glue his eyes to the page just to avoid engaging with her across the long wooden table. An Olympic champion of a reader, Billy was also a notoriously closed book – except with her ... usually. Perhaps if she gave him some time and space, he'd come around. She hoped so.

Plonking down a big bowl of fresh strawberries, Holly gripped Billy's shoulder.

"Doesn't Breanna look lovely this morning? *Glowing*, some might say," she said to no one in particular, but numerous pairs of light-blue eyes lifted briefly, flashing varying degrees of acknowledgement at Bre before resuming their breakfasts. Apart from Billy. His gaze lingered. So, he wasn't too fascinated by the tiny font, then.

What was he thinking? Usually, Bre could read Billy's thoughts as though he was screaming them, but honestly, it required a lot of decoding and she was too tired to translate the minutiae of his expressions right now. Physically, mentally, and emotionally, the whole Being Pregnant thing was draining the energy she usually reserved for conversation with Billy, who communicated in a cypher of grunts and facial twitches more than words.

His true thoughts and feelings had always taken energy and focus to decode. Occasionally, he'd offer full sentences, even the odd paragraph, and it was like the sun finally coming out from behind the clouds. He'd always been more open with her than most others, but after the night they'd shared tossing and turning, too hot and horny and with a tangibly growing rift between them, their unsaid thoughts too loud in the too-quiet room ...

"Billy?" Holly prompted, drawing Breanna back to the present once more as he grunted in response. "Doesn't Bre look lovely?"

Bre wanted to strangle her pseudo-mother and was shocked but grateful when Billy offered an appreciative, though slightly dismissive, noise.

Holly's brows crashed down. "Everything okay with you two?"

Hoping Billy would hear the apology lacing her tone, and that Holly would gain an explanation as to her son's darkened mood, Bre said, "Neither of us slept well." The twins only chuckled. "NOT like that, you nymphomaniacs!"

"Breanna, lass, no sex at the table," Nick said without looking up from his newspaper.

Liam added, "Or *on* the table."

"Or *under* the table?" Connor piped up.

"Boys, stop!" Holly poured a round of coffee into familiar mugs.

Bre ran her thumb over the rough, chipped edge of hers,

smiling down at the monstrosity. When they were seven, Holly had insisted they all make their own mugs, dragging clay and paints from one of her many craft cupboards. Each one had ended up wonky and wonderful, delightfully ugly, and frequently used. For years, Bre had tried to glue googly eyes onto hers, but they never stuck.

With a knowing smile, Holly refilled Bre's mug with juice.

"Thanks, Mrs C."

"You are most welcome, Breanna, dear."

"*Anyway*, back to funner things ... Like Seth ..."

"Funner is not a word," Billy muttered as the twins resumed their previous conversation.

"Seth lost the bet. Buck naked *or* butt naked," he shot a look at Billy, "he's been tied to a tree and tanning his jibblets this morning. He's *probably* untied his ropes by now ..."

"Will you lads never grow up?" Nick sighed. "At least you're honest, I suppose."

The word 'honest' had Bre tugging at Billy's Mighty Ducks jersey, thinking of her smashed phone, Revv Ryder, and the numerous details the Carmichaels needed to know, as they'd undeniably complicate the entire family's Christmas plans.

"Well, on to a different topic now ..." Holly started, adding a mountain of toast to the table. Her tall, lean body tucked neatly into the space between her husband and son. She looked so delicate, among the gathered brutes.

Bre wondered, for the first time, what *she* might look like to an outsider – what Piers 'Revv' Ryder might see when he arrived. She knew who he was expecting – the red-headed, grinning, grease monkey he'd seen in the profile picture Billy had snapped last year – the flat-chested, flat-stomached car enthusiast covered in freckles and gunk he'd met all those months ago. He wouldn't be prepared for the lumpy bag of marbles her body now was. And Revv sure as shit wasn't expecting the baby belly she'd carefully neglected to mention when she'd invited him to the farm to stay for Christmas.

"Everyone *except Graham* is here," Holly amended. "How is our first-born always the last to arrive? Anyway, now that we're all assembled–"

"Oh my–"

Hysterical laughter exploded from the twins.

"Seth?"

"I know, I know, I'm late!" Nude as the day he was born, Seth Henderson strode into the kitchen, grinning from ear to ear, and bowed like a damn courtier. Countless red scratches criss-crossed his entire body. A long coil of blue rope dangled from one hand, while the other gently cupped his intimate parts. Pine needles spiked from his reddish-brown hair, and colour was high on his cheeks, blurring the freckles all Hendersons shared. Most late arrivals would have included an apology – but saying 'sorry' was not the Henderson way.

"Bruce." Seth nodded to Breanna, eyes pleading. "Help a fella out and hand me a tea towel? Please, sis?"

Bre leant back in her chair, crossing her arms across her chest with a smug grin. "Tea towel is a bit generous, don't you think?

How about a hankie?"

The twins roared louder, banging the table. Plates and cups jumped with the blows, like they'd come alive and were about to start singing 'Be Our Guest'. Even Billy's mouth twitched upward slightly, though he was clearly not in the mood for anyone's antics this morning. Bre elbowed the twins in the ribs, joining the chorus, at Seth's expense. When Connor and Liam elbowed her right back, Billy's mood darkened further.

"Careful!" Billy snapped, his voice like a bolt of lightning through the room. Everyone quietened, before chiming in:

"Careful? With Bruce? Nah, she's fine!"

"She's one of the boys!"

"She's not a girly girl!"

"She's–"

"Pregnant." Billy said. Simple. Factual.

Bre shuddered. Heads whipped to her, the warm room now feeling so cold and silent Bre could practically hear Seth's pine needles hitting the floor. While the men spluttered, Holly only smiled, nodding with that smug look that said she hadn't need confirmation – she'd known it all along.

"*PREGNANT?*"

"Bre can't be pregnant, she's–"

"One of the boys!" Liam and Connor exclaimed.

Seth, naked as the day he was born, clearly didn't know what to do or say. Standing arse-to-the-breeze in the kitchen, he only stared at his sister. The twins continued.

"And Bruce is so small!"

"I mean, she's put on a bit of weight, but …"

"HEY!" Bre finally protested. "Guys, I'm just pregnant, and I'm not porcelain. I can still kick your arse if I have to. Please don't treat me differently. There's no reason why things have to …" She was getting sick of pleading for things to stay the same. Her voice cracked, and the men's eyes widened at her uncharacteristic display of emotion.

Who was this teary mess? Clearly no one recognised her anymore. All plans for normalcy this Christmas were completely and utterly fucked.

"I couldn't bear it if things were … weird … this Christmas." She looked to Billy, who was once again staring intently at the *Moonshine Gazette*.

"Wanna know what's weird, sis?" Seth offered, finding his tongue at last. "Having my junk in my hands and my arse hanging out at breakfast."

"Not like we haven't seen it all before, Seth," Bre commented. Laughter filled the room and the weird spell was broken.

"Fiends, the lot of you!" Holly scoffed, whipping her apron off and looping it around Seth's bare neck. "Let's get this morning back on track, shall we?"

Seth gave her a quick kiss on the cheek. "Thanks, Mrs C. You're an angel."

"I know," Holly replied with a smile, pulling a chair out for him on Bre's other side. "But leave a butt print on my chair, young man, and you'll see the devil's horns emerge, I promise you that!"

Everyone knew that Holly was a great cook, but she also dished out a lot of empty threats. They weren't required, as history had shown. True power wasn't with the biggest or baddest in the room, it was with this sweet, motherly woman who had each of these towering men wrapped around her little finger, evidenced in the way they each kissed her cheek each morning.

The rose among the thorns, Holly Carmichael did her best with a household of giant males. She gave her rowdy brood room to get into trouble, but she was always there to bail them out. Oh, she'd let them stew a good long while before *posting* bail, but she always showed up.

Seth sat down on the wooden chair with a fleshy slap, Holly and Bre flinching while the twins once again howled.

"Shut up!" Bre chuckled, picking pine needles from her brother's hair and throwing them at Liam and Connor. "Down, you hyenas!"

"*Now that we're all here*," Holly started again, "minus Graham, but we spoke to him last night before they started the trip from Melbourne ... Anyway, your father and I have an announcement to make."

"You're pregnant?" one of the twins blurted, before swinging an apologetic wince to Bre. "Sorry."

"Don't be." She shrugged. "I'm not." Unexpected as the pregnancy was, her baby was very much wanted.

The twins looked at each other before saying, "Can we ask–"

"NO." Billy's and Bre's voices rang out in unison. Their eyes met briefly, then looked away.

Another moment of dead silence hung in the kitchen.

"As your mother was saying." Nick gave each boy his 'settle down, OR ELSE' look. "She has organised for some internet person to come play spotlight on the farm."

"A *social media influencer* is coming to the farm for a *highlight*," Holly corrected. "She is a celebrity stylist and interior designer and I am just so excited!"

Bre looked again at her phone.

"And Breanna organised it for us! All those planners and post-its came in handy after all! Boys, you know Sharee DeLuca?"

"Do we!"

Connor grinned. "Mum, you clever woman! Delivering my future wife right to my door!"

"*Our* door!" amended Liam.

Connor guffawed. "There is no *sharing* Sharee DeLuca!"

"You two barely shared the womb," Nick chuckled. "Kicking and fighting even then."

Bre's phone – what was left of it, with its spiderweb of cracks across the screen – lit up, a pitiful sound attempting to play out.

"Shit."

"Language!" Holly reminded.

Billy's eyebrows rose, but he didn't look at her.

"He's here," Bre said, to no one in particular. "It's happening."

"Who, dear?"

"What's happening, Bruce?"

Tugging at her jersey, Bre stood, and the table fell silent.

"Revv–"

Billy's head jerked up at the name.

"Revv Ryder."

Revv's horn blasted a merry tune down the long driveway, a long line of dust consuming the two large caravans that followed his iconic Chevrolet. The twins, spotting the procession from the window, sprang from the table and bustled out the front door, Seth's bare bum trailing behind.

"Is this Sharee?"

"My wife!"

"No, mine!"

Nick and Holly slowly rose and followed, as whoops and whistles began floating in from outside.

"Bre?"

Sweat dotted her forehead; her ribcage aching from the effort to contain the rapid thudding in her chest. Deafening to her own ears, the beat drowned out all else.

"Bruce!" Billy's grip on her upper arm guided her body down gently. She sunk onto his lap, curling into his broad chest, breaths shallow and quick. He tightened his hold, a silent and reassuring weight.

"Billy, Revv ..." Bre gasped, hot and cold all at once. Why wasn't the oxygen hitting her lungs? "I ..." Her throat closed, chest tight. She may as well have been swimming a marathon in a cement swimsuit, the way her body was flooded with adrenaline and struggling for air. "He ..." She was stuttering, but Billy waited for her words to tumble in longer processions. He listened intently as she managed half-formed phrases about 'plans' and 'fucking up' and more than one 'it wasn't meant to be like this'.

"Bruce." Her nickname sounded too soft and too severe, all at once. "It will be okay. Breathe. You can do this. With me. In, out. In, out. Good."

Fisting his shirt, she fought for control, breathing away the spots that danced before her eyes. Squeezing them shut, she focused on his words, the gentle rumble of his deep voice and the way it vibrated through his chest and straight into her fingertips. She inhaled, her breaths becoming slower and deeper, quelling the rising nausea.

Billy's fingertips drew circles on her back as she melted her weight against him, comforted by the familiarity of tucking her chin into his neck. Where she belonged. Where everything was known and safe. Or was it? After the night they'd just spent, maybe not. *Old habits die hard,* she reminded herself.

She knew how Billy had taken her baby news – the image of him lying on the floor would haunt her for years to come. But Piers Ryder? The celebrity she'd admired for years now, who was here specifically to spend Christmas with *her* ... How would he react to her unexpected pregnancy announcement?

"What ... will he ... say?" Gasps punctuated each word, her small hands tightening on Billy's colourful, heavily tattooed shoulders as tears streamed down her face.

Billy's fingers pressed deeper into her back, circling, and she focused on the pressure, breathing in and out with each circle drawn on her skin. The rhythm, so calming, was hypnotising. Despite all the mess, *this* she knew – Billy's touch, that beautiful, familiar comfort, was exactly what she needed. Without considering her words, or their implication, she told him as such.

"There she is." Billy's smile brushed his tickly beard against her face. "I was wondering where the old Bruce was. My best friend who verbalised every thought." His voice, so low and deep it came from the depths of his soul, was warm against her ear. Something about it changed the rhythm of that too-loud pump in her chest.

"Have you experienced this often? The debilitating panic?" he asked, his voice low and calm, stroking her neck gently.

She wriggled in his lap and he made an involuntary noise she knew well. What would she have given to have heard it last night – hell, even right now. The distraction would have been a welcome blessing. But morning sex with your best-friend-with-benefits in his family's dining room probably wasn't appropriate, especially with Revv right outside, or anyone able to walk in at a moment's notice. Not that her aching core cared who saw them right now. Most of the people in this house had seen her naked in some form or another, over the years.

"Debilitating panic?" She attempted to laugh it off, trying not to squirm against him again. "You mean a minor heart attack? The lack of ability to breathe? Usually, I only feel that way when you do that thing with your tongue–"

Billy's rumbling laughter shook the remaining panic from her veins. It was a welcome earthquake that rippled through both their bodies.

"Bruce. Be serious."

"But that's *your* job. Actually, it's Reece's. I swear that guy was born with a scowl."

Billy pulled back, fixing her with those brilliant light blue eyes. "Stop with the deflection, or I will call Dr Reece Hargraves right now. The panic attacks, Bruce. How long? The truth."

"For a while," she admitted, breathing as deeply as she could, and exhaling slowly. "Damn, it feels good to admit it. I ... I haven't told anyone."

He huffed a noise that sounded like gravel shifting in a strong wind.

"I know, I know. But you know me ..."

"I do." Billy gripped the back of her neck, forcing Breanna to look directly into his eyes. "And right now, Bre, Revv Ryder is here." His fingertips lightly trailed up her thigh, heat and blood rushing to the area so fast her head spun again. "And you," Billy said, eyebrows rising, "are only in your underwear."

Her legs opened slightly for the strong fingers that brushed gently over the aforementioned fabric. Just once. That was all it was. A teasing touch that set her body on fire. Her hips rolled, seeking his fingers once more. He breathed a little chuckle against her ear, and if her underwear had been on fire before, the embers were now drenched.

His fingertips dug into her thigh, the delicious pain of it shooting straight to her centre. "Do things have to change? We have a plan, Billy."

His hand immediately retreated, and she knew, once again, her damned mouth had gotten her in trouble. Speaking or not, she messed it up.

Gently, with only the slightest hesitation, Billy slid his solid palm across the swell of her belly. Deep within, the baby kicked in answer and Billy gently noted, "Nothing is the same Bre. Whatever plans you had ..." His deep voice rumbled into nothingness.

Then she was standing, and Billy slapped her Shit Show Supervisor hat onto her head. Adjusting his prominent erection before heading for the door, he didn't look back as he ordered, "Go get dressed. You shouldn't keep Ryder waiting."

4

Scrap The Plan

Billy

HE SHOULDN'T HAVE TOUCHED HER. In fact, he'd sworn to himself last night that he wouldn't, at least, not until they discussed a few things – like the paternity of her baby, for instance. Perhaps it wasn't a good idea to get his hopes up and assume she carried his child.

He'd lain awake far too long last night replaying each of their encounters and tracking them on a mental calendar. And as fun as mentally recreating their liaisons had been, remembering the way her face tilted upward as she came undone hadn't helped settle his mind, or ease him into sleep either.

She carried the bump well, her body lean and strong, her skin taught over the growing babe within. He could only guess the gestation, based on the miniscule details she offered in the dark last night, when his back had been hard on the floor, despite the air mattress. There were also clues in the size of her stomach and the time she'd started being 'too busy' to see him regularly over the past few months.

Undeniably, there was a possibility that he was the father – a thought that forced his heart to pound double-time – but those dates Elanor arranged for Breanna had muddied the waters somewhat. They rarely discussed their other partners, and while he hadn't had any worth mentioning over the past few years, he wasn't certain the same could be said for Breanna.

Her pregnancy wasn't a consideration in his hesitation towards her. If she was here, he knew, she was here for *him*, and for his family. Tradition. The Plan.

She'd never looked more beautiful in her life, and when she'd shed that Santa Suit ... it had unlocked something primal inside him, taken all his considerable self-control not to press her into the curtains, tie her there, kick her ankles apart, and thoroughly ravage her like the beast inside him wanted to.

No, it wasn't that Bre was pregnant, and it wasn't that he'd lain awake all night pondering the baby's paternity. His hesitations towards Breanna surrounded the fact that she'd inexplicably stopped speaking openly and honestly with him. Communication – her ability to verbalise every thought without holding back, and the truth plainly written on his face, despite often remaining silent – it was the foundation of their entire friendship. Without that ...

Last night he'd been so sure he could withstand the intense tug his body felt towards hers and abstain from touching her, until they'd discussed everything properly. And yet, with her pressed into his lap, in a moment of utter vulnerability, he'd relented. He'd touched her ... and damned if he didn't want to do more.

Shaking his head, Billy adjusted himself again then stepped out into the blinding sun. A tiny mass lurched sideways and he barely managed to catch his frail old grandfather who seemed intent on kissing the wrap-around porch.

"Billy, my lad! Ye scared wits outa me! Thank goodness ye caught me before I fell arse over teakettle. I nearly flashed these people wi' me nethers!" Grandpa Carmichael chuckled, adjusting his kilt, a beautiful tartan of blue and green, with thin yellow, red and black hatch-crossed lines.

Billy searched the vast blue sky for the universal sign he'd clearly missed – today was not meant for pants. Bre, Seth, and now his old Scottish grandfather – who was busily righting his walking cane and smoothing the traditional Carmichael plaid around his knobbly knees – clearly had not missed that pants-optional memo.

"You and Gran just arrive?" Billy asked, trying to blink the vision of a pants-less Bre from his mind. He squinted, struggling to see their hire car on the parking lot that was quickly springing up along the gravel driveway.

"Aye. Barely made it because of these nit wits!" An arthritis-ridden finger waved accusingly over the crowded area, noting the scattering of family and newcomers.

A bare-bottomed Seth flirted shamelessly with a young blushing girl holding a long-armed microphone. His mother and father were engaged in animated discussion with a beautiful lady Billy immediately recognised as social media influencer Sharee DeLuca, who'd made a career from inventing concepts like 'cottage core' and 'celebrity styling'. Sharee, every bit the supermodel she appeared online, gushed with his mother about spending Christmas here at the farm. Their heads bent together, they conspired, until Sharee declared loud enough for everyone to hear, "Holly Carmichael, we will take the online world by storm this Christmas!"

His mother flushed, and a warmth grew in his chest. She worked so hard every Christmas, to provide a magical Southern Hemisphere experience. Now, this beautiful American influencer was going to expand Holly's reach further, and they would indeed take over the online world with carefully framed images of all things festive.

To the other side of the dusty driveway stood Bre's guest – Piers 'Revv' Ryder, car enthusiast and host of *Crank Shaft*, an international TV docu-series that featured rare and vintage cars, their owners, mechanics, and restoration teams. Bre had loved *Crank Shaft* with the same adoration most girls bestowed upon their Barbie dolls, dreaming for years of being featured on the show. Apparently, the universe hadn't thrown enough spanners into their usual holiday works because that plan was finally coming to fruition right now.

Revv wore aviators and a leather jacket, despite the already biting sun of the December morning. He looked bored and disinterested as Connor and Liam swooned over his Chevrolet, yet managed a beaming smile when the cameraman turned their way.

"Breanna!" His grandfather's voice pulled Billy back to the porch.

"Richard! You old fox!" Bre swept past him, sounding much more herself than so far this morning. His old Mighty Ducks jersey was now tucked smartly into stretchy black leggings that left nothing to the imagination and made Billy's cock strain.

Normally, Bre didn't wear form-fitting clothing. All their lives, she'd hidden her body, swathed in baggy-jeans and too-big t-shirts. Bre was baseball caps, overalls and boots. Big jumpers to her knees and generally loose fabrics. Comfortable. He liked that about her, that she didn't feel the need to dress up or put on a show or pretence – not for anyone, or anything. Billy gulped, trying to snatch his eyes back from where they were glued to her arse.

Her ability to get him hard, so easily – and so publicly – was going to be problematic. Normally, they would have already dealt with their body's pent-up frustrations and needs, but ...

He shook the thoughts away as she bent to hug his grandfather. The sight did nothing to deter his imagination. Pressing his lips together, Billy leaned back against the doorframe, hoping the solid weight of the weatherboard house might lend him some strength.

"Love yer legs, lass." Richard patted Bre's rump affectionately, the cheeky bugger. "Ye finally fillin' out, I see." He tugged the brim of her cap down, teasing.

"Love your skirt," Bre shot back, grinning widely as she lifted the hat. "But I'm not going to comment about how you fill it out. Not on your life, old man!"

"Oh, ye do know how te spoil a man's fun." Richard tutted, leaning heavily on his cane. "Once ye get used te the fresh breeze around yer nethers, ye know, ye canna go back to wearin' pants! Plus," he leaned in, whispering loud enough for those back in Scotland to hear, "the lassies like the easy access!"

"Oh yeah? Which lassies? Speaking of, where is your wife?"

"Oh, you know her." Richard waved towards the house. "She's probably already hidin' away in a corner somewhere, bein' the *anti* te my *social*." His voice lowered conspiratorially. "Such a wallflower, she is. Wee Billy gets it from her, I swear!" Richard chuckled, and at the same moment Revv's mirrored glasses slid down his long nose as he eyed the porch and its residents.

Nudging the cameraman and pointing to the wrap-around veranda, Revv called, "Breanna, baby! Are you ready for this?" He opened his arms wide, walking towards her.

Then, without waiting for her reply, he spun on one sleek dress-shoe heel and spoke to the camera.

"Breanna Henderson is Miss Shit Show Supervisor herself. She's also the owner of the acclaimed restoration garage, Rust Busters, here in the small town of Moonshine in New

South Wales, Australia. This Christmas, we'll be highlighting her story and her amazing 1943 Ford Coupe Utility that has become a prominent feature of the town's Christmas celebrations. We'll also join you LIVE on Christmas Eve right here on the Carmichael Christmas Tree Farm for their annual town-levelling party. And as an extra-special Christmas gift to *you*," Revv pointed into the camera, grinning, still slowly making his way towards the veranda, "in this episode of *Crank Shaft*, we'll also be joined by interior designer to the stars, my *very good* friend, Sharee DeLuca!"

The portly cameraman swung the lens Sharee's way. It took her less than a second to react, sliding a practised smile onto her face, but as the camera's attention shifted back to Ryder, Billy noted the confusion ... or perhaps annoyance ... that etched grooves between her eyebrows. It looked like she hadn't expected Revv to be here. In fact Billy, would not have been surprised if they had ever spoken to each other, let alone been 'very good friends'.

Sharee was gorgeous yet understated, in fresh white linen and open-toed sandals that were no fit for a farm in high summer, if she had any intention of heading out into the trees – and why wouldn't she? It was December and this was a Christmas Tree Farm, after all. He'd have to mention the necessity of boots. Red-bellied black snakes, brown snakes, tiger snakes, ants, a host of spiders, and a few rather grumpy wombats called the farm home, and the sharp jab of fresh pine needles to your foot wasn't pleasant, either.

In too-white clothing that danced around her, polished gold jewellery and fashionably large spectacles that framed equally large, lovely eyes, she didn't look like someone used to being around dirt. She might be at home on a smooth sandy beach, with a too-wide brimmed hat atop her head and a cocktail in each hand, rather than here in the Australian bush, just far enough from civilisation to be officially considered The Middle of Nowhere.

Sharee confidently snapped photos on her phone, needing no entourage or concerted attention. In fact, now that Revv was busy, once more talking to his reflection in the camera lens, Sharee was trying desperately to extricate herself from Liam and Connor's conversation. Backing away with a winning but genuine smile, she excused herself, heading into the house where Holly promised breakfast was still hot and waiting.

"Why is it so hot here? Is it always this hot here?" Billy's grandfather complained, eyeing Sharee with soft milky blue eyes and flapping the hem of his kilt.

"Grandpa!" the twins intoned, outraged at the old man trying to steal Sharee DeLuca's attention.

"It's December in Australia," Seth reminded Richard with a clap on his stooped shoulders, arse still visible behind the frilly front-cover of Holly's apron. "Though I could get used to this whole free-balling in summer thing." He swayed slightly left to right, chuckling. "Breezy."

Billy smoothed down another smile. Sharee and Revv had good instincts – Christmas at the Carmichaels' would provide a lot of unique footage for their respective audiences.

"Hush down, Pa!" Nick scolded his father. "The ladies don't wish te hear ... nor *see*... such things. Right, Holly?"

His wife nodded as she bounded past, arm-in-arm with Sharee, chatting about 'Insta-worthy décor' like it was the momentous invention of sliced bread.

"Best. Christmas. Ever!" Holly said as she disappeared into the house with her guest. Sharee smiled with genuine warmth.

She could be a kindred spirit, Billy thought, watching attractive American woman melt into the background, happy to disappear. He wished he could disappear, too, especially as Revv Ryder advanced.

In stark contrast to Sharee, Revv was the embodiment of over the top. Every gesture was bigger than necessary, and his slightly-too-loud voice was too smooth, with the inflections that came with years of media engagement. He had a way of speaking into the camera lens, schmoozing the audience, and forgetting to speak directly to the guests on his show. People were props just as much as the cars were, and with Revv consistently front-and-centre, he saw himself as the undisputed star.

Finally reaching the porch, Revv hinged at the waist in a practised bow, taking Bre's hand with the clear intention of kissing it. He halted, noting the ingrained black crescents around her nails and the dark lines that refused to scrub away, no matter how hard she tried. Each crack and crevice in her rough little hands revealed hard work – something the celebrity clearly didn't appreciate in the way that Billy did. And then

Revv noticed her swollen belly, panic crossing his features for a split second.

Could Piers Ryder be the father of Bre's baby?

Billy shuddered to think of this greasy celebrity's hands trailing Bre's soft skin. Begrudgingly, he had to admit it was a possibility. The *Crank Shaft* host had met Breanna in a preliminary interview several months ago, right around the time Billy estimated she might have fallen pregnant, based on the limited information she'd given him.

As repulsive as Billy found the man, he understood that celebrities held a certain appeal, and Bre's attitude towards the man was ambiguous. He'd seen Bre flirt and fight – the line between the two sometimes obscured by the passionate way she approached both activities.

Could Revv be the father? Bre would share that information with him, surely? Did the father, whoever he was, know she was with child? Thought after thought tumbled through his brain. Running his hand down his face, Billy tried to wipe them all away.

It didn't matter who the father of Bre's baby was. All that mattered was that she was happy. If she was happy with Revv Ryder ... Billy watched her punch their celebrity guest lightly in the arm. Piers grinned down at her upturned face. A growl half formed in Billy's throat.

She didn't need protecting, but that primal side of him wanted to do just that. Rip the sleazy celebrity from where he leaned too close over her, schmoozing for the rolling camera.

Revv's lips aborted their original mission, flicking to the menacing shadow Billy had morphed into, before plucking at the air above Bre's hand. Colour rose high on Bre's cheeks and Billy's stomach twisted.

Another vehicle – an SUV – arrived in the rapidly growing car park. Four children of various sizes and states of excitement piled out, followed by Billy's eldest brother, Graham, who was already apologising for his family.

"Lianne was unable to make it, so it's just me and the boys," he said, temples shining with more grey hairs than last year. "Hopefully she can be here for the Christmas Eve Party."

Hope, Billy knew, was needed with this rowdy bunch.

"UNCLE BILLIAM!" The two youngest bolted from the car and straight for Billy's legs, circling their considerably smaller limbs around him and holding tight.

"Lachlan, Leo." Billy tried lifting his feet, and the three-year-olds squealed in delight as they clung like lead shoes. "My favourite twins."

"HEY!" Connor and Liam protested.

"And Max!" Billy greeted the more subdued boy of eight, who leaned over his siblings to hug his uncle's waist before reaching up to pat his bearded cheek.

"They're your problem now, Uncle Bill," he said with mock seriousness, before adding in awe, "Is that ... are you ... Revv Ryder?!" Flustered, Max spun, burying red cheeks into Breanna's side. "Hey, Aunty Bre!"

Almost as quickly as he dived in for the hug, Max retreated, his amazed expression shifting back and forth between Bre's face, her distended stomach, and Revv. He shot Billy a look of absolute delight before darting into the house, calling for his Nanna Holly.

Revv rubbed his hands together. They were too clean and soft to be a real mechanic's hands, Billy noted. "All that kid's Christmases have come at once with me here, right?" Revv sought affirmation. No one answered, and in the growing silence, his reflective glasses dipped as he eyed Bre's belly once more.

Callum, Billy's eldest nephew at ten years of age, hung back to help his father with the bags, waving enthusiastically up to them.

"Kids," Revv commented between gritted teeth. "Gotta love them."

He made it sound like a question, and Billy felt himself bristle. Breanna, too, seemed to straighten at Revv's tone, her belly pushing further into the space between the three of them, before she exhaled and leaned over the railing, moving her attention elsewhere.

"Welcome home!" she called to Graham, who was clearly relieved to have finally arrived. By all reports it was a lengthy, noisy drive from Melbourne to Moonshine, in an enclosed space with four children, two of whom suffered terrible car sickness. Owning a pub, Billy was well acquainted with the smell of vomit, but by some minor miracle, none of his nephews smelled of the stuff.

"Yeeees, children." Revv's eyes searched the sky for something like strength. "*Wonderful.*"

Billy found himself asking, "You have any children?" The answer was clearly written on the celebrity's photo-ready face – in Revv's world, there had never been anyone but himself.

Billy managed to extricate the squealing, giggling bundles from his legs, chasing them inside with threats of hiding the lollies so high they'd never find them.

"Tis goin' te be a big Christmas this year," Richard said to the TV host and his entourage. "Ye might want te come in an' fortify yerself wi' some whiskey. That's what I'll be doin' ," he added. "Tis so good, this stuff, like an angel pissin' in yer mouth."

"Delicious," Seth grinned, lead the way. The fiercely blushing microphone girl was behind him. The cameraman, already sweating through his t-shirt and wiping his damp face with a hankie, soon followed, Richard tapping his heels, tutting, "Hurry up, man, good whiskey waits fer ne one!"

With his audience gone, and drink on offer, Revv wasn't far behind.

"I'll be there in a minute!" Breanna called after them, leaning heavily on the railing and fixing her eyes on the sprawling fields of radiata pine.

Moving beside her, Billy stood close, bumping her shoulder with his. *I'm here*, he wanted to say. *Talk to me*. Laughter echoed from inside the house, carried away on the same breeze that caught the door, gently clicking it closed.

"So," Bre began with a small smile, "Revv finally realised I needed to be on *Crank Shaft*." It was a safe conversational starting point, if not a bit obvious.

It wasn't a question; she didn't need a response or confirmation, so Billy simply waited for her to continue.

"He's … we're … it's a Christmas Special. About me. And Edsel. Pre-filmed episode, then a live special on Christmas Eve …"

Billy watched Breanna closely as she breathed in and out, a hint of her former panic detectable, though she still seemed incapable of the easy speech he'd taken for granted all these years.

Her breathing changed and she sniffed the air. Once, twice. "Billy, why does it smell like bushfire? I thought all the backburning finished months ago."

With a small jerk of his head, he led her down the front steps and to the side of the house, past the pristine little white Suzuki that could only have been Sharee DeLuca's car, and towards the boundary of the property.

Bre stood with her arms resting on her belly. Billy watched as her hazel eyes widened, surveying the charred boundary fence – or what remained of it. The long, dark line that scorched a clear divide between Henderson and Carmichael land still emitted a faint burnt smell.

"It's *her* handiwork, isn't it."

Billy nodded, seeing tired disappointment, heavy and familiar, wash over Breanna at the thought of Mrs Elanor

Henderson. He knew Bre wanted to apologise for her mother's behaviour, but Hendersons didn't say sorry. And if she, or Seth, started down the path of asking forgiveness for their parents' antics, they would never stop.

The deliberate burning of the fence between the properties was just one incident in a long line of 'neighbourly disputes' that had long ago exhausted the patience of the Moonshine Police Department. The Montague-and-Capulet-style civil war between the Hendersons and Carmichaels was legendary, most of the conflict stemming from Elanor Henderson herself.

Sure, the four Carmichael lads had made their fun, too, Seth planning a lot of the calculated, devious retaliations, but Elanor Henderson had a knack for un-neighbourly subterfuge that would have made a seasoned spy uneasy. The woman was an evil genius disguised as a homemaker.

"It's not smart. Or neighbourly. *OR* festive!" Bre ground out. "What kind of an idiot sets a brand-new wooden fence on fire in the peak of a bloody Australian summer?"

Billy didn't respond, knowing those waters ran too deep to dive into right now. Instead, he cleared the lump in his throat that seemed to lodge there every time he was around Bre, preparing to – somehow – try and bridge the gap their silence had built last night.

"She must've used an accelerant, too. That's malicious damage." Bre exhaled slowly. "Thanks for not holding it against Seth and me. She's our mum, but she's barely family. Not anymore."

Elanor had tried to come between their families for years. Now, Billy was grateful that she might be the one safe topic they could discuss.

"You have always been part of our family, Bruce. That will never change."

She reached for his hand, giving it a quick squeeze. "Thank you." Her voice was watery again.

"Out of curiosity," he hedged, "do you know *why* she burned the new fence down?"

Shrugging, she shot Billy a smirk. "To be fair, it was an ugly fence."

The laugh that erupted from Billy was pure depth and baritone, a sudden boom that sent the birds fleeing from the trees. He mastered himself quickly, surprised at the outburst. He forced himself to mumble, "You always knew how to make me laugh, Bruce."

"Best sound in the world," she told him, her own quiet chuckle dissolving quickly. Her hands slowly roamed her stomach as she thought.

Billy had to admit, he could see why Elanor had refused the fence. If he'd been in her shoes, he wouldn't have wanted to sacrifice the view of the Carmichael home, either. Not that anyone would ever actually *agree* with Elanor Henderson's irrational incendiary actions, but still ... his family home was a remarkable sight, especially from this angle.

Beneath the brilliant, vast blue sky, the sprawling, modern country home, with its expanses of timber and white, was set between tall evergreen trees. A big, red, American-style barn sat to one side, in the seemingly endless landscape of deep green radiata pine trees.

"You know, Billy, I think we–"

"Breanna, baby!" Revv Ryder's voice disturbed their conversation. Billy swallowed a growl at the interruption.

Taking a deep breath, Bre tore her eyes away from the burnt earth – and the small house just beyond it – turning to the oncoming intruder.

"Baby, you going to officially introduce us or what?" Even from here, Billy could smell the whiskey.

Bre blinked. "Oh, yes, of course. I'm a bit ... distracted."

"By me?" Revv grinned, but Bre continued as though she hadn't heard his quip. *Good,* Billy thought.

"Revv, this is Billy. Billy, Piers Ryder, better known as–"

"Everyone calls me Revv," the celeb said seriously, looking up at Billy who was taller by a good few inches, even with the lifts in his impractical shined black shoes. "Cos I go *revv revv vroom* with the cars and the ladies."

Revv flexed his wrists, as though riding an imaginary motorbike up Billy's torso. Torn between a grin and a grimace, Billy slid his hand down over his beard, smoothing all expression from his features.

Clearly, this well-delivered line must have worked for Revv in the past. Women probably swooned and sighed at the celebrity. Men likely chortled deep in their throats with masculine appreciation. Not here. On the farm, Revv's too-reflective glasses, slicked back Danny Zuko hairstyle, always-ready-for-the-limelight charm, and leather jacket on an already thirty-degree day, just didn't work. Not on Billy, at least, and surely not on Breanna, whose bullshit-o-metre was notoriously accurate. The woman could smell a deception – and call you out for it – with just a look. And ... yep ... her shrewd eyes were judging Revv.

He waited for Bre to chew Ryder up and spit him out. No words came, to Billy's surprise and disappointment. She must still be using the same glue she'd sealed her mouth shut with last night.

Waiting, hand outstretched, Billy waited for Revv to give up on his show and just shake his damned hand, while trying to ignore the fact that his best friend had, apparently, received a brain transplant.

When the TV host finally took his offering, Revv shook and squeezed with too much force. The man had just ridden an invisible motorbike up Billy's chest, so how he expected to command masculine respect with assertive handshake now, he would never know.

Clearing his throat, Revv extricated his hand and, lips pursed, subtly rubbed his knuckles. Billy clocked the moment – hell, he'd seen it often enough – when a person realised he only had one arm. So he wasn't surprised when Revv asked bluntly, "How'd you end up one-armed?"

"Revv!" Breanna looked ready to punch him.

Billy gave her a look – *My fight, not yours* – and

she unclenched her fists with a small, begrudging nod, understanding immediately.

Best friends were like that, almost telepathic. Billy was glad to see *that*, at least, hadn't changed.

"No shame, man," Revv continued, sliding his aviators higher up his sharp nose. "No shame. Birth defect? Wrestling a grizzly in these woods?"

Billy's eyes bore holes through Revv's confidence. He enjoyed watching the celebrity squirm. It was rare that he needed to tell his story; everyone in Moonshine had been acquainted with it long ago. But now, standing beside a burnt fence in the blistering sun, with his surprise-I'm-pregnant best friend and an obnoxious celebrity car enthusiast ... This wasn't the time to share his story.

The dinner table always bustled with conversation. Perhaps tonight he'd regale the newcomers with the tale. He'd recount how, at the tender age of five, he and his brothers had been playing amongst the abandoned train carriages in the railyard. How he'd somehow become trapped beneath a large wagon that hadn't moved in years – except that day, when fate cursed him. He'd tell them about the pain and shock, how his three older brothers ran into town seeking help. He'd leave out the part where Breanna, just a child herself, appeared to him like an angel, bravely setting her shoulders and demanding he stay awake and talk to her.

"Don't leave me!" The words echoed in his mind. "No matter what, Billy Carmichael, don't leave me! I'm here. I won't go anywhere. Just listen to my voice ..."

Billy noted the expression on Bre's face, like she saw right through his skin and into his brain ... like she was reliving that day, too.

"There are no grizzlies in Australia, Ryder."

Revv ignored the comment. "I'm just curious," he added, somewhat defensively. "Might be good to get someone like you on the show."

"Someone *like him*?" Bre spluttered, incredulous.

Interesting. He'd never been wanted *because of* his disability before.

"Great for ratings," Revv added. His eyes dropped to her stomach, as though a beautiful woman sporting a baby belly might be good for the *Crank Shaft* ratings too.

"Revv." She was fuming. "Billy should be on the show, no matter what! He helped me with the Ford, he's–"

"If Mr Lefty here was involved with the restoration? He can certainly be involved in the show!" Revv flashed a dazzling fake smile. "C'mon, Breanna, baby!" Revv practically purred before snatching her away. "We have so much to do." He threw this last comment over his shoulder to Billy. "*Crank Shaft* will take a fair chunk of her time."

Billy trailed behind, trying desperately to loosen his tight jaw and unlock his eyes from Breanna's arse and those stretchy leggings he was going to insist she wore forever more.

"Viewers love a chick holding a wrench, you know," Revv said. "Great for ratings. Breanna is perfect for this Christmas

Special. And this place!" He spun on his shiny high-heel dress shoe. "Perfect filming location, man. Thanks for inviting us."

Billy's eyebrows crashed together, but Bre shot him an apologetic smile.

Right, so this was The Piers Show, and they all had to play their parts.

"How long do you plan on staying?" Billy asked, trying to clear the mental image of ripping off Ryder's arm. It was draped around Bre's shoulders, his hand inching lower.

"Breanna knows the plan. You told him the plan, right baby? You, me, old Edsel." Revv's voice had taken on a wistful tone. All his 'baby' talk was making Billy's skin crawl.

If Billy knew nothing else about Breanna Henderson, it was that she abhorred nicknames. 'Bruce' had been her own choice, when they were children, to signify that she was part of the boys crew. A mate. But any other name? From anyone else? Hell, he'd seen Bre break up with a man on the spot for calling her 'sweetie'.

At times, when he was caught up in her, when the world became a hazy almost-there reality he'd departed from, he let the monicker 'honey' slip. At times, Breanna loved it. Occasionally, he'd earned a swift fist to his stomach.

"Baby," Billy growled, low enough that only wild dogs might hear. When had Bre and Revv become so familiar?

"So," Revv practically purred, "that Nick fellow said something about searching for a pickle?" His grin was fiendish. Billy bet he was the kind of man who giggled like a child at crude words. "And in a related matter, how can I get my hands on one of those kilts?"

"You can't." Bre told him, finally shaking Revv's arm off her shoulders.

Billy rumbled. "Kilts are only for clansmen."

5

The Christmas Pickle

Bre

"THE RULES ARE SIMPLE," Nick called to the assembled Carmichael clan, Sharee, Piers, and his crew. "Most of you know the game, but I will repeat and reiterate, for our new friends and guests." He tipped his greying head to Sharee and Piers (who seemed to be watching himself smile in the reflection of the camera's eye), and the few seasonal workers who'd been called to join the assembly. The farm got busy from August onwards, but December was, obviously, the busiest time of the year, work made 'fun' by the search for the pickle.

"We know you love a wee bit of *competition* amongst yourselves!" Nick continued.

Liam, Connor, and Seth laughed, loosing a rowdy, "Aye!"

The children, beyond excited, barely stood still, requiring hand-holding and frequent reminders to "hush now" and "listen to Grandpa."

Nick grinned at everyone and Bre's heart swelled. Where would she be without them? This large, loud, mass of hulking young lads and tender-hearted older people who had basically adopted her and Seth so long ago.

She shot another worried glance towards the little house that lay beyond the trees. What would her mother make them endure this year? Seth must have been thinking something similar. Their eyes locked across the Carmichael crowd, and they exchanged a small, worried glance before turning back to Nick, standing elevated on the wide porch.

"It's no secret we borrowed and somewhat altered this centuries-old German custom, but as a Carmichael family tradition, the Christmas Pickle started back when Holly and I met," Nick told the congregation. "We were meant to be, my lovely wife and I, this farm, and our four strapping lads." Nick waved to the long lines of trees that comprised the farm, and their gathered family.

"Holly found yer wee pickle alright!" Richard called, ducking a blow from his red-faced wife who, despite his previous claims, was not hiding in the house at all.

More hoots and hollers made Nick blush, as he continued. "In the spirit of Christmas joy, last night my lovely wife and I took a stroll through the fields and we left a little bit of joy in the trees for one lucky person to find." The crowd cheered once more, Nick raising his voice above the din. "Now, you all know how hard it is to find the Christmas Pickle ornament, and you know the best way to find it is–"

"Look under yer kilt!" Richard called, to great amusement.

Despite all pretence of propriety, Nick couldn't help but chuckle. "Aye, Father, true. But if you're stringing Christmas ornaments under yer kilt, I'll be a wee bit worried!"

"And I'd be worried if your wee kilt-pickle is *green*, Grandpa!" Graham called across the crowd. Despite her promise to be cool, calm, and collected while Piers was here, Bre couldn't help but laugh along with the Carmichael crew.

As well as those brilliant blue eyes that you couldn't help but get lost in, the Carmichaels were all blessed with a wicked sense of humour. They were fun to be around and found joy so easily, it made her heart ache. The Carmichaels actually enjoyed being around each other. They were so unlike the much smaller, more serious Henderson family.

Bre and Seth would prefer to suck on a workman's sock than spend one sunny afternoon with their folks. The Henderson house was always one of two thigs, Bre thought. It was either too quiet, stifling and oppressive, or a screaming match between her and Elanor. The first option, she rather enjoyed. Billy was habitually quiet and pensive, but his when he did loose his big, booming laugh, the very earth itself shook joyously with him. Laughter like that had never shaken the foundations of the Henderson household.

"The way te find the Christmas Pickle," Nick tried again, "is to pitch in. Work hard. Tell the customers you're searching for snails – God knows ye should be doing that anyway! But all the while, look through the tree for the prized Pickle ornament."

"What's the prize if we find it, Grandpa?" ten-year-old Callum called, so excited he couldn't decide which foot to stand on.

"Whoever finds the Christmas Pickle is proclaimed the champion of the season, and all that entails!" Nick declared to the assembly. "Including – but not limited to – choosing the Christmas Day meal for the family, who MUST in turn, eat it–"

A few moans went up amongst the older Carmichaels, who had lived through their fair share of awful dinners over the years.

Nick continued, "A personal favour with no questions asked from each and every family member ..."

"No foot massages this year, Mum!" Liam called to Holly.

"And no roping us in to be your sexy lumberjacks for Instagram either!" Connor added.

Holly and Sharee laughed, sharing a knowing smile that did nothing to dispel the idea that their coordinated social media blitz would include plaid and bared pectorals.

"AND the best prize of all!" Nick continued, "the person who finds the Christmas Pickle is allowed to inspect their gifts under the tree and can open any one present early!"

The children nearly fainted. Graham had to catch Leo and Lachlan by their shirt tails as they tried to dart off into the fields.

Piers had moved, finally, from the centre of the shot. Nick

continued, straight into the camera. "We used the search to get our boys invested in helping out during the busy season, but I am glad it has carried on. You four lads –" Nick looked from Graham, to Connor, Liam, then Billy. "You have been great sons to your mother, and great friends to me. And for the next few weeks, you'll be jolly great workers as well! Now, to work!"

"Let's find the pickle!"

The kids were off, darting about with no idea that finding the pickle among the acres of trees was the festive equivalent of locating a needle in a haystack.

"Come inside and I'll show you my Australian native wreaths," Holly said to Sharee and Billy's grandmother, who hung back, quiet and observant, as usual.

"I would love that!" Sharee gushed, linking arms with the two women. "And any chance of those sugar cookies you sold out of last year? Thirty seconds flat, I think you said?"

"Three seconds," Holly beamed. "Quickest online sale my store has ever seen!"

"That is amazing! Especially considering the sheer amount of baking you did! What did you call them again, the biscuits?"

"The festive phallus." Holly's voice dropped ever so slightly, her hand moving to her mouth in a mock stage whisper. "We don't mention the festive phallus around Nick. He's a bit of a fuddy duddy sometimes."

Nick's eyes narrowed and his lips pressed together as he pretended not to hear the comment, helping an unsteady Richard into the fields.

"I've got a few batches in the oven," Holly confided. This was nothing new. Holly perpetually had something in the oven. The day Breanna entered the Carmichael residence to find that overworked double cooker wasn't packed like an overstuffed Christmas stocking – well, that was the day the world was officially ending.

"You are a goddess, Holly Carmichael," Sharee said.

"*You* are a goddess, Breanna baby." Piers Ryder's voice slid down Bre's spine like engine oil. "Lead the way to Edsel, and we can start filming, hey? But ..."

Revv drew the word out as he pouted, and she had the sudden, unnerving desire to punch him in the throat. The pout was endearing on TV, and the puppy-dog eyes were cute and all, but on a fully grown man, in real life, it just felt wrong and rather manipulative.

"... we can't take my Chevvy," Piers continued. "Jaxon and Trudy will have to wash her, get the dust off and camera-ready, you know? But we could go ahead and scope out the scenery, prep the sets ..."

Her garage was hardly a 'set' to be prepped, but she supposed Revv knew what he wanted to film for *Crank Shaft*. If she was in his too-shiny shoes, she'd want to do her research, too, before filming began. He'd probably want to make sure the garage was as tidy and presentable in real life as the photos she'd submitted with her application all those months ago.

She knew from experience – and from watching countless years of the show – that not every operational workspace was fit for a film crew. In Bre's experience, many garages, especially in small towns like Moonshine, were disorganised, greasy, and dank places, their walls often collaged with magazine pages featuring naked women.

There were often too many tools in too few toolboxes, and the occasional uninspiring mechanic who'd added a spare tyre to his belly years ago. She'd worked in these places, ignoring the boobs and outrageously fluffy pubic hair of the 70s models, so she could finish her apprenticeship.

At first, she'd expected the male gaze to slide from the walls to her, thinking the men might have issues with a female mechanic in their workshops. Looking nothing like those wall-women – plus having the backing of the four strapping Carmichael lads, and her own brother, if ever she needed them to fight for her – had fixed any lingering unwelcome attention.

Once on the show and under international scrutiny, the cracks often began to show in people and places like those. Piers Ryder was the Gordon Ramsay of the car world. Instead of kitchen nightmares and mouldy disaster-filled cooking spaces, Revv exposed oil spots and transmission leaks, criticising the general mess, and the chaos that busy, careless mechanics allowed their garages to become.

Not Bre. She'd always been a little ... particular. Methodical. Structured. And she'd been preparing for months to showcase her space and restoration skills with her pride and joy, Edsel.

Edsel was a 1934 Ford Coupe Utility, and a central element in Holly's social media presence each Christmas. Edsel, in various stages of restoration, featured in family photos with Santa at the farm, hauled decorations to and from various barns for events, and gave countless kids tours as they bumped along the paths at snail speed, giggling with pure, unrestrained joy from the tray of the ute.

"You want to start now, Revv?" Excitement filled Bre's veins where worry had previously flowed. "We can take the ATVs. I have a small garage in town that's basically just a shop front and servicing space for the locals, but my main restoration work is done out here."

"Which is why you invited us."

"Exactly. Years ago, the boys–"

"Boys?" Piers eyed the hulking, muscled mass that was Billy, before his gaze flicked back to the large house that held even more equally large men.

"– and I," Breanna affirmed, "built a decent garage at the edge of the property. That's where you'll be staying, since all the rooms in the house are full. Plus, it'll give you immediate access to Edsel. It's the best workspace I could have asked for, really. Still on the farm but just out of the way enough that I get privacy and space to work to my own schedule, when I'm not busy with –" she tried not to look at Billy, "– other Christmas plans."

The extent of those plans had been carefully omitted. As had the fact that they'd find her impressive workspace at the end of the long, black line of ash that was the result of yet another of her mother's mood swings.

The Carmichaels had hoped building Bre's garage on the Henderson side of their property might (a) improve relations between Bre, Seth, and their parents, by the sheer effort of proximity, and (b) prove to be something of a buffer between their borders and disputes. They'd been wrong on both accounts.

Thankfully, her memories of the garage were much happier. Heat crept into her cheeks now as she recalled the last time she and Billy had been there, together. Music had blasted from the speaker system Billy had long ago helped her install, the old CD from their younger years shaking the building with each heavy drum beat and screeching electric guitar solo. Somehow, he'd managed to become tangled in a string of tinsel, and she hadn't wanted to waste the opportunity for a fun game.

They'd taken turns to strip each other, wrapping the tinsel around and around each other's bodies, using it to tickle, tease and seduce, until they slowly became aware that the music had stopped. Only shaking, heavy breaths filled the minute spaces between them.

She could almost feel the slightly rough tickle of the tinsel between her legs as he bit gently on her bottom lip – the same lip she bit down on now, trying to suppress the memory. It took real trust to be that silly and sexy with someone, and she trusted Billy with her body, and her life.

God, she'd really made a mess of things.

"I can't wait to hear about these other Christmas plans, Breanna baby." Piers grinned.

Billy's eyebrows drew down.

Billy wasn't a mind reader. He needed her to speak her mind and intentions. She could read him well enough, though, and one thought showed plain as day on his face: *No way in hell, buddy.*

6

The Ties That Bind Us

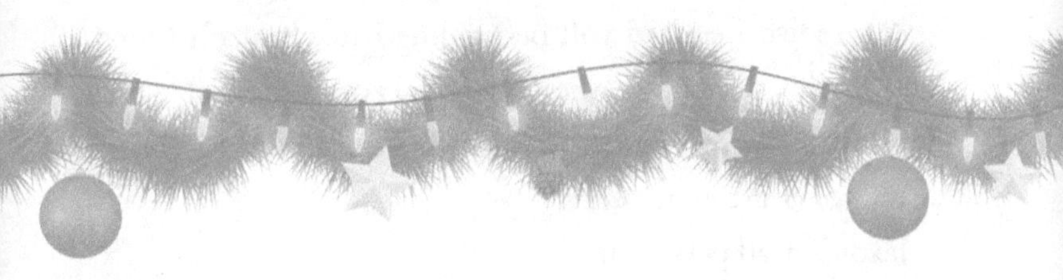

Billy

REVV'S CREW – CAMERA MAN Jaxon and sound technician Trudy – were ceremoniously awarded the afternoon off by a magnanimous Revv Ryder. When they expressed a yearning to sample the old-world, small-town charm of Moonshine, Breanna, businesswoman and best friend that she was, sent them straight to Billy's beloved tavern.

"The Pope is the best place in Moonshine!" she told them, explaining that the pub was conveniently located at the first intersection in town, just a few kilometres down the tree-lined road they'd driven along mere hours ago. "There's a lot of history there, with the bushrangers and the founding of Moonshine on the illegal liquor trade, but it's best told by the publican himself, so you'll want to get the story from Billy tonight."

From the expression on their faces, Billy guessed Jaxon and Trudy were unsure of his ability to do anything except be a giant, menacing presence. He added a mental note to find the energy to discuss both his amputation and his business tonight, clearing his throat as though that would make the task easier.

"Meredith Leonard will be tending bar," Bre continued, ignoring his rumbling. "She's new but extremely capable. Tell her Breanna knows *exactly* how much tequila is in each bottle ... and to rebutton her shirt."

Jaxon's head perked up.

"Speaking of shirts ..." Billy started.

"You're right." Bre nodded, reading his mind the way she always seemed to. "And tell Meredith that Adam's shirt is to stay ON or he's getting kicked OUT. She'll know who we mean."

We. A tiny spark of hope ignited in his chest. Could Billy and Bre still be a 'we'?

With a swift honk of the horn, the crew left for the afternoon.

Revv Ryder turned his practised smile on Breanna. "You ready?"

Of course she was. The woman was a walking, talking organisational savant. Having Revv here, filming *Crank Shaft*, the spotlight shining firmly on Bre's painstakingly restored Edsel, was more than a dream for Breanna. This moment was a huge tick on her most important plan – her life-long Bucket List.

Edsel's restoration had taken her years, and its final stage had occupied much of her time over the last few months. Now, though, Billy began to wonder if it had been a ploy to avoid him more than was strictly necessary ... and to help hide her pregnancy.

He could have kicked himself for not noticing it before, the way her figure curved and swelled so invitingly. It fascinated him, the difference not just in her body, but in how she carried herself as she strode to the line of all-terrain vehicles they used on the farm.

"You know, ATVs are becoming rare on farms these days. Most folks prefer the steering wheel and seat configurations of side-by-sides to these old-fashioned quad bikes. Plus, side-by-sides are safer." Piers grinned, "Not as fun though."

"We're a bit behind the times, I suppose." Bre's clipped tone went unnoticed.

"Can I drive?" Piers asked, already moving to where the ATVs waited.

An engine roared to life before anyone thought to respond. Clearly used to getting his way, the man spoke only to hear his own voice, and was full of frustratingly unnecessary rhetorical questions.

"Sure," Breanna responded as Piers revved the vehicle, raring to go. "I'll take–"

Billy slid into the seat of the second quad bike, patting the seat between his long legs. The end of Bre's sentence was swallowed by Piers' almighty revving. Bre shot a frustrated glare towards the celebrity, clearly remembering why his nickname had stuck.

Wiping the smile from his beard with a quick swipe of his hand, Billy watched Breanna's bun of red hair wobble with each shake of her head. What he wouldn't give to dive his fingers into her tresses and tug her close. Just the thought of it sent a hopeful tug straight into his trousers. Trousers he might have to abandon altogether, if only he knew where he stood with Bre ... or if his mother got her way and forced the clan into their kilts.

Billy patted the seat once more, shifting slightly.

"Billy, I–"

"Bruce." His voice left no room for argument. "We were in this together, remember?" *We.* His words held the weight of layered meaning, and she knew it. Plus, there was no way Billy was going to leave Breanna Henderson alone with the infamous celebrity slimeball. She'd have Revv's balls cut off and worn as earrings if he wasn't careful.

Sleazy as the celebrity was, he didn't deserve to be defiled by the short, freckled redhead he had clearly underestimated. Lavishing her with almost-kisses and winks and the repeated, coquettish moniker 'Breanna baby' wouldn't get Ryder far, if Bre's usual biting honesty had anything to do with it.

Despite his charm, it could be dangerous for Revv if Billy left them alone. It was the chivalrous thing to do, Billy told himself, to act as an escort. He conveyed all this silently through blinks and raised brows and small shakes of his head, knowing Breanna would read him like a book, while she, arms crossed, flung equally pointed looks back.

Piers turned to watch their heated, silent exchange before clarifying, "He's coming?"

The rhetorical question grated on Billy's last nerve. "Correct." The word was a deep rumble. "I am not leaving."

Billy patted the seat again, sliding back and allowing her room to swing one leg over. With a loud exhale she settled on the ATV, hands on the handlebars, scooting her backside into the most comfortable position. He felt the moment she froze, having rocked her arse back and against his groin, noting the length of him there. She paused, clearly considering, before pressing her weight back once more. Clutching just below her ribs, Billy fisted her shirt – *his* shirt – before bracketing her hips, noting they were slightly wider than he remembered them feeling between his long legs.

"You are a temptress," he growled into her ear. Her body shook with one silent laugh before relaxing beneath his touch.

"You're riding dink?" Revv huffed a laugh.

Dink. The word wasn't uncommon, but there was something about his tone that locked Billy's jaw tight. Perhaps it was the implication that he was less of a man, abdicating the driver's seat to allow a woman control of the vehicle. Or perhaps it was years of dealing with the casual judgement and (usually) well-meaning bias he faced for his physical disability.

Whatever it was, Piers Ryder had firmly jabbed himself under Billy's skin, a leather-jacket-wearing splinter that had gone too deep.

Bre must have felt the stiffening of his entire body. "*Men –*

honestly! Everything's an excuse to measure your dicks. C'mon, this way."

An awful, exquisite echo of something like hope rekindled in Billy's stomach at her cutting words. It had often been noted by Jillian, Bre's best female friend, that Breanna had no shame and was too honest for her own good. A bit of that old spark was back, and after a long night of her refusing to effectively communicate about her circumstances, her wishes, and how he might support her through this time of transition, here she was, letting those blessedly blunt opinions loose.

Billy's moustache tickled his lips as he forced himself to untense his pinched expression. "Go, Bruce. Leave him in the dust."

Piers laughed and revved the engine yet again, gravel flying as he waved to the full windows of observers.

"Just follow the line!" Bre yelled over her shoulder, zooming away from Ryder, who had turned his reflective aviators and winning smile to the children and phone cameras now demanding his attention. Quite literally leaving him in the dust, Bre's muscles loosened beneath his fingers with every metre gained.

Piers called something about catching up, but Billy refused to hear the words, instead shrinking his entire world to the feel of his legs around Bre and the sight of the thin, loose tendrils of her hair as they whipped back and forth in fiery flashes.

Rumbling along the worn path, faintly scented with charcoal, Billy revelled in the warmth of the sun, the fresh pine on the breeze, and the heat of Breanna, solidly planted between his thighs.

After a long while, he shifted his chest forward to prop his chin onto her shoulder.

"We need to talk, Bruce." He pressed the words into her neck, hoping the shiver rolling down her spine was one of pleasure, prompted by his words, and not a cold wave of abhorrence at his proximity. "We are open books …"

He'd thought long and hard about the words he wanted to say, and now finally had the time and courage to voice them. "And best friends, besides. There is nothing you could do, no one you could be, or anything you could say, that would ruin our friendship."

Bre increased the throttle, and the ATV accelerated to full speed. Crunching his abdominals and squeezing his knees, Billy managed to stay upright.

Having no right hand seemed a small infirmity most days, but when matters of balance were involved, Billy had to be quiet and concentrate – and Bre knew this all too well. Hanging on with only five fingertips, he determined to wait, nodding as they flew past rows of trees, past the blurry shapes of his brothers, one wayward child, and the occasional farm worker.

He vaguely noticed the chains adorning numerous pines that indicated pre-orders, as charcoal and sun-bleached grass crunched beneath the tyres. He'd spent less time at the farm than usual this year, having been too busy at The Pope.

The dump of a pub became his business and primary

residence at the tender age of twenty. Restoring it to its former glory had taken a few years, with the help of friends and family. Billy preferred to move his own mountains, but at times, the simple sincerity of the word 'please' and admissions that he required help had made a vast difference.

Just months into his ownership, Moonshine's favourite watering hole had begun to flourish once again. With its new staff and old drunks, he'd been so engrossed in the business for years now that he'd missed the subtle changes in his best friend.

Simply having her close by was a comfort he'd taken for granted, whether she was at her garage or at the tavern. Hell, even when they worked together at The Pope, he rarely saw her. She was too busy managing birthday parties in the attached bistro, hosting events in the courtyard whiskey bar, or whirling around his bulk, behind the bar serving patrons.

They'd been so busy ... *too* busy ... and somehow he'd missed the signs – the tiredness and her sudden aversion to certain smells. The cravings she'd had for pizza every night they ended up in his private rooms resuming their friends-with-benefits relationship. The frequency of those liaisons had increased over the past year or so, then all but stopped when she'd become 'too busy' prepping for the arrival of Piers Ryder.

It hadn't seemed strange at the time, but now, as he slid his hand gently around Bre's belly, he pondered how he could have ignored so much, for so long.

Billy had never considered himself a self-obsessed man, but perhaps he had more in common with Revv than he'd thought, if he hadn't been able to see two feet in front of himself these past few months; if he hadn't really noticed her. "Bruce ... Breanna. Can we talk about-"

His words – and Bre's sudden engagement of the brake – had them skidding to a halt outside the garage. Dust clouded around them, briefly obscuring the solid wooden building and its cheerful red door.

"What do you want from me, Billy? An apology?" She turned, eyeing him over her shoulder, and the kookaburras fell silent at her outburst. The dust drifted slowly downwards, much like Billy's jaw. Hendersons did *not* apologise. Sliding his hand from her stomach, he ran it instead through the length of his dark hair, unsure how to proceed.

"I'm sorry, Billy," Bre continued, "for not telling you the truth straight away. I'm sorry that I didn't want to ruin our friendship. And I'm sorry for not telling you about Piers ..."

Her gaze wandered down the scorched boundary line before drifting over to the Henderson side, then back to him. Hell must have been freezing over as she spewed her frustrated requests for forgiveness.

But as swiftly as the words came, they left, and Hell heated back up to its typically fiery Christmas-Down-Under temperature.

"I just ... I don't see why things have to change ... between us, I mean ..." She moved to grip his forearm as he dismounted from the ATV, but he managed to evade her. "Wait, Billy! Hear me out. I think I've ruined everything – ruined us. But all I want is for things to be normal. We had a plan, and I know I'm fat and not exactly fuckable right now ..." She reached for him again. This time, her fingertips seared his skin, marking him deeper than the tapestry of tattoos spread across his body.

"Don't touch me, Bruce –" Billy's voice was strained, "– because if you do ..." If his voice got any darker, midnight itself would spew from his lips. He knew how threatening he sounded, but couldn't stop himself from grinding the words out, deep and low.

They both knew he wanted her touch more than a kid wants presents under the tree, but he needed to warn her. "It is taking all of my control not to grab you, to press you up against whatever hard surface is closest and rip your clothes off because you are ... always have been, and always will be ... completely fuckable." He ran a shaking palm down his beard. "I've only got one hand, Bruce. Literally HALF a chance at managing to hold myself back. Don't make this harder than it has to be."

"What's hard? This?" Her hand dipped indecently, fantastically low. Despite the barrier, his body knew her touch. Craved it and responded immediately. What he wouldn't give for the damned kilt now, to flick the fabric back and feel her, skin to skin.

She moved, watching him suck in a sharp breath as she told him, "I *want* you to touch me. I want things to be normal between us. And you want it too ... right?" She pressed her hand harder against the seam of his jeans, and he nearly growled like the feral he was.

He'd always been feral for her, hungrily gobbling up whatever scraps of affection she offered, insatiable, and unwilling to ask for more than whatever she offered in the heat of the moment, for the same reason she shared now – for the sake of their friendship. But what was a friendship, whether it included naked liaisons or was completely platonic, without honesty? She used to give him the courtesy of truthfulness. Now ...

"Wanna know what the absolute worst part of being pregnant is, Billy?"

He grunted in response, unable or unwilling to say more and shatter this fragile, surreal moment in which Breanna was expressing regret, possibly for the first time in her life, with the hard weight of his cock pressed into her hand.

"The worst thing is ... I'm *horny*." The words fell from her lips to his as she pressed further into him. "All. The. Time."

He should be more mindful of what he wished for. He wanted truth from her, but this admission might just force him to burst. Inhaling sharply, Billy forced her hand to still, gripping her petite fingers in his own larger ones, holding tight.

"Bruce ..."

"Billy ... Please ..."

Who was he kidding? He could never deny her, deny them. His hand still circling her wrist, he led her with long strides to the cherry red garage door. Ripping it open, he stalked past car after car, Bre matching his pace with two quick steps to his one. He pulled her past Edsel and through the little door that led to her office, whirling to slam it closed as soon as she'd entered behind him. Hand propped on the frame, he dipped his forehead down to meet hers, deftly sliding the latch he'd personally installed. It warned in bold red font: *Occupied*.

The soft, hope-filled curl of her lips was so familiar and warm, he nearly melted at the sight of it as he pressed her against the locked door. The freckle on her top lip disappeared as his mouth eclipsed hers. Longing, strong and pure, surged through him, the remaining space between them banished from existence. Curling into her body, he cherished the weight of her, admiring her new curves, and loving how readily she responded to him.

Bre hadn't been lying about her physical state. He'd seen her lustful before, let her take out those frustrations and needs with free use of his body, but he'd never seen her quiver like she did now, or demand more from him, quicker, harder, now, now, now. Words – blessed words – nonsensical as they were, tumbled from her lips. He wanted to bathe in them, soak them into himself, feeling everything between them finally click from wrong to right.

His old Mighty Ducks shirt lifted easily over her head, discarded somewhere in the room beyond as his teeth bit at her bra, tugging it southward.

Bre moaned and whimpered, each roll of her body against his begging for more. The ghost of his right hand reached for her, caressing and gripping. Billy's brain filled in every gap between them, real or imagined. Frenzied didn't come close to describing it, the way their bodies sought each other like the night drew out the stars.

A half-opened box of Christmas decorations lay open on the end of her desk. Pushing it aside, he swung Bre bodily from the door, sitting her at the edge of the worn industrial bench as baubles and glittery things raced around his feet, covering the floor in festivity. Finding a length of tinsel, he dragged it slowly across the table.

"Hands." The word was guttural.

Her wrists, held out in offering, were quickly bound.

"I meant it," he said, wedging his thigh between her legs. "No touching, or else." Dragging her mouth closer once more, he luxuriated in the taste of her, sharp orange juice and sweet oat biscuits. He could have basked in the sweetness of her mouth all day. But her body wasn't sweet. It was needy and savage, a carnal beast with its own mind.

She rocked against him, seeking friction, writhing, kissing, needing, wanting.

Gripping the tinsel tied around her wrist, he dragged her arms up slowly, before looping them over his neck. She gripped the base of his skull, the shaggy hair she found there, hauling him closer.

"God, Bre." The words escaped like a prayer. A thanks for bounty he was yet to receive, but desperately wanted. For the return of the person he recognised, not the strange, stuttering woman who'd stood in his room last night, then lay in his bed, consumed by a silence he'd never known from her.

Uncertainty flashed over her face, so briefly he nearly missed it. His throat constricted. Would that stranger return? They needed to talk, yes. There were questions that needed answering and plans to be made – if she hadn't already constructed elaborate colour-coordinated, dot-pointed enumerates.

"Take what you need, Bre." He kissed her nose, her cheek, the corner of her mouth. "I've got you, honey." *I'll always have you.*

Now was about her, the way her eyes glazed and her mouth hung open. Now was about all the ways they didn't need words, their bodies communicating in a language of their own, perfected over years.

Her soft whimper was pure delight, hips rolling as she surged forward, straddling his thigh. Bre's mouth had always been a fascination – the way her truth flowed freely and she didn't hold back. But when she let her body do the talking ... He loved that even more.

Bre's hands clutched at his neck and his hair, fingers digging in, swirling through the dark strands and over tattoos that disappeared into his shirt, spreading to places her hands couldn't reach right now. The sensation thrilled him as she rocked higher and higher.

"Billy, I ..." Her nails dug into his scalp.

He watched, awed. She was close. So close, so fast. Whether it was the long, wiry hairs of his beard she tugged, or the shaggy brown hair that fell into his eyes, her hair-pulling was always a precursor to climax.

"Use me, honey." *Don't overthink this now, not when everything seems to be back on track ...* "I've got you."

The bench protested as they moved, desperate and

demanding, needing to be closer. The tinsel binding her hands scratched at his neck, but he didn't care. Another time, he'd strip her bare and use this tinsel as a sexy feather boa, slowly tugging it across her shoulders; he'd watch it fall over the tips of her breasts, just to see her nipples perk in response. He'd make her stand, legs apart, and run the sparkling string between her thighs just to watch her squirm ... at least, if he had two hands, he might have accomplished that. Perhaps he'd need his teeth ... again ...

Bre's nails dug deeper and with a wicked little grin, he mentally filed all the wicked thoughts were filed away. Gathering Bre closer, he dragging her higher up his thigh. The damp warmth that lay between her legs was a blessing and a curse as her fingers tightened in his hair. She clung to him, writhing, maddening in those thin, stretchy pants that barely existed between them, existing only for blessed friction.

The round ball of her belly pressed firmly against his abdomen, and he marvelled – as he always did – how such a vocal little person could become so quiet in the midst of passion.

He wasn't a monk. He'd watched porn, much of it with Breanna right beside him. He'd seen women pant and scream on screen, full of lewd sounds and foul words, but Bre wasn't like that. He'd always appreciated how she kept their liaisons quietly and wholly theirs.

Screaming sounded hot on screen, but no one wanted their neighbours from three farms down bursting in, rifle or axe in hand, assuming someone was being murdered.

Billy, on the other hand, wanted to roar. He needed to let loose the wildness inside him that was usually firmly leashed. He wanted to shake the gates of Heaven with his pleasure, whenever they entered the 'benefits' part of their friendship. He didn't, though, for fear of scaring this fierce, beautiful creature. Also, because most of their trysts occurred at his parents' home, during a busy, family-friendly Christmas, where roaring sexual releases were, thankfully, uncommon. He did have three older brothers, however, plus his father and grandfather. When they were all under one roof, accidents occasionally happened, resulting in incessant teasing the morning after.

"Where are you?" Bre's voice broke through his thoughts about the more primal aspects of manhood, hands on either side of his face as she locked eyes with him. "Come back to me ... Please, Billy." Her voice warbled. "I need you."

"Here, Bre." He gripped her neck, pulling her close. "Here. Always. You need me? Use me, honey."

Weaving her hands through his hair, she dragged him closer, before letting out an almighty grunt as, in one hard tug, she broke free of the tinsel ties, dragging her hands down his neck and chest, fumbling at his crotch. "Clothes off."

Chest heaving and lips swollen, the way she switched speeds – the slow tug of the zipper rolling down while grinding herself against him – might have been one of the sexiest things he'd experienced.

Why hadn't they done this already? He struggled to

remember. He could watch her all day, flushed and panting, moving against him. His cock strained for freedom as the zipper finally stopped and she worked to release his length, greedy, needing.

Seizing her hand he brought it to his mouth, kissing her palm before urging her hips higher. There was only her and him and now, push and pull, kissing and –

Bre near pulled the hair from his scalp as she spasmed and shook, teeth digging into his shoulder as she rode out wave after wave, soft little sounds filling his ears, just for him. He marvelled at her blushing cheeks, heaving breasts, the way her dazed hazel eyes found his, startled, like she hadn't anticipated any of this, but refused to apologise for it, either.

"Damn, Bruce," he murmured, "that was …" He gripped her chin between two fingers, breathing heavily himself, as she extricated her hands from his hair, slowly, staring at her fingers as though they'd suddenly turned into candy canes.

She shuddered once more against him, mouth opening and closing, eyes wide, lost for words – a state Breanna Henderson rarely found herself in, until recently.

"Hello?" Revv Ryder's voice demanded an answer, as if this wasn't the first time he'd called.

"Piers!" Bre called too loudly, snapping back to reality. "Just a sec!"

Billy lowered Bre to the ground as she hastily fanned her face and tugged her shirt – *his* shirt – down over her flushed skin.

"Just getting the lights!" she called, flicking the dodgy switch.

The fluorescents flickered once, twice, before crackling to life, bathing everything in harsh, too-white light that deftly snatched him from a dream-like state.

Casting a small, bewildered smile over her shoulder Bre unlatched the door, the lock now proclaiming: *Vacant*. That was how he felt, as she pressed her forehead against the doorframe, eyes squeezed shut.

He saw her struggle, forcing herself to continue, the woman he'd known all these years slowly returning before his eyes.

"I know we still need to–"

"HELLO?"

She shook her head in Revv's direction.

"If I'm going to survive this, I need you, Billy ..." Her words trailed off as she slipped into the main garage.

At the last second, his hand caught hers. Turning slowly, she offered a shy smile.

"Tonight," he told her. "We can talk tonight." The tone of his voice brooked no argument.

With a tiny nod, she left the room, walking towards another man.

Billy watched through the half-window, manoeuvring his painfully hard erection into the band of his underwear, hoping to hell he could get his body under control before he had to join them.

Revv Ryder's voice floated through the door. "So, what's this Christmas Pickle all about?"

He didn't hear Bre's response, but he did hear Revv's

too-loud, too-confident reply, dripping with implication: "So you can unwrap any present?" His laugh filtered through the door just as Billy had finished composing himself. "Breanna, baby," he drawled, "if I find the ornament, can I unwrap *you*?"

7

Some Damsels
Don't Need Rescuing

Bre

PIERS RYDER WAS NOT what Bre had expected. Sure, she knew
he had a reputation as an egotistical flirt, but she'd assumed the
celebrity stereotype was just that – a charming façade, or some
overexaggerated typecast. Her friend Adam James had a similar
reputation, but Bre knew for a fact that gossip was just that
– especially in a small town with a long memory and people
who didn't know better. But with Revv, every scandalous photo
montage and outrageous interview quote was proving to be
true.

The man had the haughty manner of a mob don in a crime
thriller, and more self-importance than a ditzy heiresses in

one of those rom coms Jillian used to make her watch. Bre had hoped this special episode of *Crank Shaft* might turn out that way – Reality TV car show turned romantic comedy, with a slightly festive Christmas-Down-Under theme. Piers would be a charming knight in shining armour riding his noble six-horse-powered steed into the small town of Moonshine, AKA Middle-of-Nowheresville, Australia. She'd be swept off her feet and feel so in love (with the cars, not Piers himself), and they'd all live happily ever after – Bre in Billy's bed and Piers curled up beside whichever supermodel he was dating this week.

Now, Bre could almost imagine the theme song of this episode of her life – it would have a thumping bass and lyrics about summer sunshine and how you should never meet your heroes, because the disappointment will surely kill you.

"Edsel Ford, right? Named for Henry Ford's son?"

She saw Billy's eyes roll slowly skyward, his lips disappearing into his beard as he bit them, trying not to comment. He hated rhetorical questions, and Piers Ryder, in his element, was positively full of them.

"1943 Utility, yeah? Isn't she a beauty?"

"Edsel's a *he*." Breanna said.

Piers ignored her. Again. It wasn't uncommon, this feeling of being pressed to one side just enough that she felt like she couldn't quite step into her own limelight. Her mother had so thoroughly pushed her into the dark, Bre hadn't known anything else for a long time. It was easier with the Carmichaels.

They were pure sunshine, every one of them, and no matter how many were around, they seemed to share that light and brighten each other's day.

The boys had accepted her and Seth as their own, saving her from the constant menacing shadow that was Elanor Henderson. But here, Piers wasn't just hogging the spotlight, he was the entire stage, leaving no room for anyone else to breathe while he was basking in his element.

"And the cameras aren't even here," she whispered to Billy, whose beard twitched, just slightly, cool blue eyes twinkling with the silent mirth that generally refused to register in his facial features. Stoic was the perfect word for Billy, but she saw through that façade and could almost hear the thoughts buzzing around in his head.

"Later," she promised in a whisper. They could talk later. She owed him that much, after embarrassing herself so thoroughly in the office. She'd never had so much fun with her pants on. She was still tingling from their encounter, the throbbing in her body refusing to be ignored, which only made being forced to entertain Piers and his non-questions even more irritating.

"And this is an original part, yeah?" Piers continued, pointing, already knowing the answer. "Don't you just love it?"

Piers had his phone out, snapping shots of her clean and orderly space, the perfectly polished cement floor, the three other vehicles in various states of restoration, and her prized Ford, Edsel, who had lived here for as long as she had. Edsel, who had cohabitated with ping-pong tables and looked on stoically as teenaged parties raged around him, witnessing sneaking ins and sneaking outs, before finally claiming the spotlight he deserved. Edsel, named for Henry Ford's son, who deserved to be featured on *Crank Shaft*. Edsel, who had seen and heard too much over the years, including her earlier encounter with Billy.

"Is it always this hot?" Piers flapped the studded collar of his leather jacket. Bre couldn't help but slide her eyes Billy's way.

"Usually," she told him, warmth still pooling in places she'd prefer not to consider with Piers so close. "It's *very* hot here."

"Tell me again why one half of your business is in town and the other half is here?" The upward infliction at the tail end of the sentence felt like a cheese-grater against her bones.

Billy's nod encouraged her to respond.

"Well ..."

Fifteen years ago, Seth had quietly confided to the Carmichaels that Breanna needed space from their mother. When Elanor and her hormonal, teenaged daughter clashed, it was near biblical. Seth could stomach living with his parents, but Breanna, he said, couldn't stay under a roof where World War Three broke out every few minutes – especially when his sister was too stubborn and opinionated to back down from a fight, with anyone.

Angry at her mother, Breanna would storm over to the Carmichaels' and take her frustration out on whoever she found – usually one of the brothers, who gallantly took it in turns to bear the brunt of her wrath. They raced through the fields, rough-housed and boxed, wrestled, and ensured she spent all her energy until black eyes, bruised knuckles, and scars became so commonplace that Holly and Nick forcibly intervened. Enough was enough, they'd said. New strategies were needed, for the sake of their sons and the Henderson siblings alike.

Bre was a fearsome adversary and had always been one of them, but everyone had admitted things needed to change. So, one afternoon, Nick drove all six kids to the far end of the property, to this very spot, where they'd set out sticks and string, measuring and planning, working little by little each day until a modest, barn-like building had been erected.

She called it an office, but in reality the room was a small, open-plan studio with an attached six-car garage that they had all built for her.

Breanna found the pickle that year. She'd chosen to open the biggest box under the tree, as she always did, somewhat disappointed to find it contained only a small set of golden keys, dangling on a pine-cone keychain with googly eyes. When she discovered what those keys unlocked, however – her freedom, her space, and *peace* – she moved in that very day.

Piers barely listened to her story, not caring enough to inquire about current relationships between Bre and her mother. *He's not here for you,* she lamented, watching him drool over Edsel. Billy, was there, however, solid and comforting. Placing his palm on her back, his thumb gently rubbed circles as she answered question after question about her vintage car.

Sunset burned oranges and pinks through the trees as they finally arrived back at the house. 'Tired' didn't begin to define the way she ached, and how her skin seemed too thinly stretched over her body, like she was an overfilled water balloon, threatening to pop.

From the heartbeat that had taken up residence in her swollen ankles, to the pounding in her head, she was more than ready for a shower and a decent sleep. That was, until she remembered *where* she'd be sleeping and how she *wanted* to sleep – slightly sticky from summer sweat, with Billy's big cock buried deep between her legs, and his large body curled protectively over hers ... just like last Christmas, and many more before that.

The thought sobered her up, fresh agony and energy flooding her system all at once. She promised they'd talk. Tonight. But what could she say that wouldn't ruin their long-standing friendship and the tentative, albeit sexually charged peace she'd literally thrust upon him in the garage?

"Meet you inside!" Piers said, slicking back his hair before following his nose to the elaborate dinner Holly inevitably had waiting inside. He hadn't bothered to park the quadbike in the line of farm vehicles. Bre made a mental note to move it, and take the keys from the ignition, lest he get any ideas of riding off through the trees for some moonlit fun.

Her own ATV engine died and Billy dismounted before turning, offering a hand. Bre batted it away, but after a teetering moment on her feet, she gripped him tightly and dismounted on sore, wobbly legs.

"My calves are screaming like I've run to Darwin and back," she mumbled. His fingers gripped hers tighter, answering,

I'm here. Those brilliant blue eyes patiently waited for her to continue. "I'm pretty sure my calves are rivers of lava right now. At least, that's how they feel. It reminds me of that time we ran that marathon with Adam and Jillian, remember? Like, six years ago?" A grunt escaped as she curled and uncurled her toes, stretching her legs, one at a time, now she was back on solid ground. His thumb brushed her palm.

"I remember," he said. "Are you terribly uncomfortable?"

She slowly withdrew her touch, tucking her hands under her armpits as they walked towards the house. Music, laughter and light flooded from the huge windows, bathing the farm beyond.

"Growing a human? Uncomfortable? Nah, it's a breeze, if you're into heightened senses and never knowing if you're going to vomit or nap. So much fun. I can totally see why Lianne lets Graham talk her into another kid every few years. In fact, she's probably due for another one soon." She grinned wickedly. "I might have a pregnancy buddy to join my lament about the lack of wine and ham." She read his question before he even asked it, shrugging, "The books and apps all say I'm not supposed to eat deli meats. You're not the only one who's been reading a lot."

Their attention drifted to the strings of lights illuminating the trees. One path led from the main house to the huge red barn that housed the annual Carmichael Christmas party. The other, lit with additional solar candy-canes, wove a shorter path to the cabin-like guest house Billy's grandparents used to occupy when they stayed in Australia from December to March, before jetting back to Scotland. But with the children needing more space, and Billy's ageing grandparents needing to be closer to the main house, the cabin had been re-allocated to Graham's rowdy brood.

Standing still for a moment, she soaked it all in – the joy of the large family, their guests, and the way their laughter mingled with the heavenly scents of sun-baked pine and cinnamon that hung like a mist in the air.

She sighed, feeling Billy's solid warmth press against her spine. "I love this place." Leaning back, she closed her eyes and tipped her chin to the purpling night sky, as the weight of his arm wrapped around her shoulders, a small comfort above her aching chest.

"Home." They said at the same time, voices warm as the breeze.

"Breanna." Her full name rustled through her hair, reverberating through his body and into hers. "I am sorry."

"For what?" She spun to face him, looking up, up, to the bearded face she knew so well. Hendersons never asked for forgiveness, but Carmichaels? They'd said enough sorrys to fill an ocean, even when they didn't need to. Hell, she'd seen them all apologise when someone bumped into *them*, more often than she could count. "Billy, you don't have to apologise. You haven't done anything–"

"I'm sorry for him. His attitude." Billy nodded to the house, where Piers stood in a window, clinking the neck of a beer bottle with Seth who – thankfully – had exchanged Holly's frilly apron for pants and a shirt. Bre squinted. No, not pants ...

The tartan pattern circling his waist was clearly the Carmichael tartan.

"Seth's fine, though I wish he'd quit freeballing around the farm. Surely that's a workplace health and safety hazard." Bre earned one of Billy's notorious scowls. "Okay, okay, I know you don't mean my brother. You're referring to the B-grade celebrity whose ego is larger than the house. Still, there's no reason for you to apologise."

"I am sorry he treats you as less than his equal. You shouldn't let him speak to you the way he did today," Billy said. "You never let us treat you that way, and we are better for it. Even the Bumstinger Boys–"

"Those schoolyard bullies!"

"– knew not to push your buttons."

She shrugged it off, another thing she was too exhausted to discuss in the depth it required right now. "I can handle Piers."

Billy grunted in assent. "I don't worry about him, necessarily. I'm worried *for* him, if he continues in the same manner."

The *Crank Shaft* crew wouldn't be here for long, so she would just have to remember to keep calm and in control, and remember Piers Ryder wasn't one of her brothers-in-arms, but an actual television celebrity who planned to showcase her and Edsel on his show. That alone, the exposure it would bring to her restoration skills and to Rust Busters, made it worth putting up with Piers' annoying habit of directing all conversation and questions to either himself or to Billy.

He may as well have been speaking to a brick wall, in both

cases. At least Piers didn't speak straight to her chest, now that she actually had breasts to speak of, though she was sure that her swelling midsection was contributing to an impression of femininity she preferred to avoid.

Piers asking Billy questions wasn't unusual. Men talked to each other – that was normal. What irked her most was the casual sexism implied by the lack of directed attention. Many men in male-dominated industries or environments were the same. For instance, she'd call a plumber, and they'd ask, "Can we speak to your husband?" as though she couldn't comprehend how water and pipework operated. Other typically male-dominated industries were the same.

Whenever Bre contacted a manufacturer for car parts, they'd assume she was a secretary calling on behalf of her boss, rather than the lead mechanic herself. She'd learned years ago how to deal with this unintentionally demeaning behaviour – by calling it out. Nowadays, the Moonshine locals knew her temper and tended to avoid her wrath, though she still had to assert herself occasionally, especially while overseeing the renovations at The Pope.

No, it wasn't the way Piers directed all queries and comments to Billy that upset her. It was the way she was made to feel completely irrelevant, when she and Edsel should have been the stars. Months of pregnancy and a beach-ball belly hadn't made her a big enough presence in the room to be truly seen, beyond his flirtations.

It all felt too familiar, reminding her of her mother's attitude, and the way she'd grown up being either ignored or told to be something less sharp-edged than she was. Something softer and more feminine. She'd hated it. Another reason to adore the Carmichaels – in their house, everyone was treated as both unique and equal. Everyone rode the bikes. Everyone cut trees. Everyone wore a skirt – though they much preferred the term 'kilt'. Everyone had a place and a purpose that wasn't hinged on having been born with or without a penis. Bre's 'running wild' with the Carmichael boys was still, to this day, Elanor's biggest complaint about the devilish, corrupting influence of their neighbours.

"Kids will be kids," the Carmichael's had said.

"Unruly, immoral, unsupervised brats!" Elanor had spat back, for years.

Piers hadn't noticed his faux pax, hadn't seen Bre's too-tight lips or the way Billy shrugged those broad, muscular shoulders before looking pointedly at Bre, who took her cue to answer with the swiftness of a relay runner. *Baton passed, thank you William Carmichael.*

"I appreciate you, you know," she told Billy now, unable to keep the gratitude bottled up. "Can we stay out here for a while? It's nice, and the stars are just coming out."

Billy mumbled a deep sound of approval, arm tightening around her shoulders.

Richard's voice wafted out through an open window. "Dinnae come in here, you two!" The scent of roast meat and vegetables hit her almost as soon as the words did, assaulting her senses. Bre's belly flopped. "Not unless ye wish te be postal all over the internet!"

"Posted?" Bre wondered to Billy, whose mouth quirked up on one side.

"If I were ye," Richard added, "I'd go find that pickle! Try the fields closest te the house this year," he added with a wink. "Might even get lucky!" He gave a wicked little chuckle, closing the curtain and extinguishing the shaft of light that had spilled across the grass.

Billy smirked. "C'mon, lass." His grandfather's accent was thick in his mocking tone as he took her hand. "Let's become nemophilists for a wee while."

She loved it when he took on the Scottish brogue his heritage allowed, easily imagining this large, hairy man back in time, as a clan chieftain, leading a band of men into battle against the Red Coats, or perhaps engaging in the more familiar visions of war that took place on a sporting field.

"A nemophilist? Tell me what that means, you walking dictionary," she teased, loving the easy way he spoke to her in the dark, walking through the trees, fingers entwined. This was so easy, so familiar, she almost forgot the throbbing that had started in her feet and continued to her temples. Billy squeezed her hand, smiling down as they strolled into the increasing darkness of the fields.

"A nemophilist is a lover of forests," he said, his voice low and husky, "of timberlands and woodland scenery. A person who haunts the woods."

"Oh, aye."

"Yer accent's terrible, lass." He chuckled, the sound so deep it could have been the earth itself rumbling.

"I know. But I can't let you have all the fun. I mean, I already had more fun than you in the garage, before Piers interrupted ..."

Billy nodded slowly, eyebrows drawing down as they strolled past long lines of trees.

"Before you say anything, or storm off like the big brute you are–"

His eyes cut to her, scolding.

"Okay, not a brute exactly, but you are a huge, hulking human and ... just hear me out, okay?"

He said nothing, waiting for her to continue as they strolled.

"I need you, Billy. To help me see this thing through with *Crank Shaft*, and to survive Christmas. Don't look at me like that, because yes, it *is* survival. It's life or death and-" she swallowed those lingering reservations. "Alive is how I feel around you, Billy. I need that more than ever. My old life is slipping away, and I don't know how to feel about that just yet. What I do know is that I want things to be normal between us, because I need this Christmas ... my last Christmas before everything changes forever ... I need it to be as perfect as possible."

The expression on his face said too much, asked too many questions, so she rushed to add, "I don't want to talk about the pregnancy or the baby. Call me crazy, but I don't want things to change, and I have it all mapped out so it will be fine. I have lists and plans and schedules upon schedules to get everyone through it all–"

"That sent you into a spiral this morning with the arrival of Piers Ryder," Billy interjected, his tone full of warning and worry.

"I know. I … didn't sleep well. You know I cope a lot better after a solid eight hours."

"Not an excuse."

"Fine. You want the truth? I'm worried I'll scare you off."

Having wandered deeper into the fields, Billy, more shadow monster than man, froze. Bre rushed on, all the things that went unsaid last night rushing out, unbidden, under the cover of rapidly encroaching darkness. The rustle of the trees swallowed most of the noise in the field, making her braver, knowing the words would be gone on the breeze.

"I'm so worried I fucked up our friendship, that I'm fucking it up even more now, and I don't know what to do or say to make it better. I broke our deal, Billy … I took a chainsaw and shredded a line through our regularly scheduled naked time by showing up with a plus one." She motioned to her belly, but wasn't entirely sure if he saw the movement in the darkness. After another deep breath, with Billy silent and still, she soldiered on.

"I never wanted things to change between us, Billy, but they have. I changed them, and it's all my fault. I asked you last night how you could want me like this, all round and sweaty and–"

"Breanna, you are more beautiful than ever."

"So why did you sleep on the floor?" The warble in her voice caught her off guard. "I wanted you in bed. Needed you."

"I need you too, Bruce." The warmth of his embrace surrounded her all at once and she pressed her face into her favourite spot beneath his chin, nuzzling into his neck, trying not to cry.

"Hormones," she sniffled, the tightening of his embrace saying the words his mouth didn't. *I'm here.* "You don't deserve this, Billy. You deserve uncomplicated and planned, like we always have been. I feel like I'm grasping at straws in both those areas right now. And I know we go together like ugly Christmas sweaters and festive bloating, but I won't let you marry me, and–"

His laughter shook through them, echoing into the night. "You won't let me marry you."

He tried the words on his tongue with the same hesitation you might use to lick a spider – like something you'd never considered before. His hesitation offered ... relief? Somehow her body had loosened and tightened all at once, a cold, hard slice of disappointment cutting too deep while somewhere deeper down, a tiny foot kicked her in the gut at his response.

Maybe she had been wrong about Billy's White Knight Syndrome, after all. He'd always let her fight her own battles, watching ringside, and encouraging, but this ... well, she'd thought it'd be different, somehow.

"Elanor?" Billy asked, that one word so densely layered with meaning. "Attempting to brainwash you again?"

"You mean about unmarried mothers being outcast and labelled as town harlots?"

"You do not need a man to complete you, Bruce."

"I know that!" She sniffed. "And who says *harlot*?"

"People who read," he commented casually.

"Yes, well, *The Scarlet Letter* and *Le Grinch* are vastly different books, Billy. And no, it's not my mother talking here. It's me."

"Finally."

She ignored the jab. "It's just – you're such a good guy, and we've spent a lot of time watching movies, yeah?"

Billy's silence betrayed his confusion.

"All the movies say that men like you – good men – will try and rescue the damsel–"

"Bruce." His voice held no room for argument. It was the same tone he used on too-drunk patrons at the pub, demanding they leave the premises or face the wrath of both the Carmichael clan and Constable Keneally.

"Bre," he started again, his tone somehow softer, but just as gravelly. "A few things. One, you are no damsel. You're more than capable of rescuing yourself. Two, stop telling me what to do, or *not* do, feel. Thirdly, you are wrong." He paused, cupping her cheek. "You are unbelievably and absolutely incorrect about me being a good guy."

She scoffed. "I'm really not. You donate to all the causes, and go to church with your mother, and you're such a great uncle to Graham's little feral amazeball kids and ..." she swallowed.

"Earlier, you said you didn't want me to touch you, and–"

A finger touched her lips, the impact so soft and sudden in the dark, she startled into silence.

"I don't want you to stop communicating, Bruce, but..." Her breath hitched as his warm breath fanned across her skin. "Stop talking now. I most certainly, beyond any doubt, want you to touch me." His grin lit up the night. "You think I'm a good guy?" His fingers roamed, the broad palm of his hand sliding lower. The ghost of his lips met hers. "Let me show you some of the bad, *bad* things I have been dreaming about."

"UNCLE BILLIAM!" The unmistakable sound of trouble approached on swift, tiny feet. "AUNTY BRE! WHERE ARE YOU?"

"DINNER'S GETTING OLD!" a second voice yelled. Torchlight flicked this way and that through the trees.

"YOU MEAN COLD NOT OLD, YOU NINNY!"

"BILLIAM!?"

His fingers tightened; hand splayed wide across Bre's arse.

"Kids," she mumbled. "Always know how to interrupt the world's best snog session."

Her lips tingled, skin flush and prickling from the thorough way his lips explored hers, his beard scratching across her skin.

"I could get drunk on your kisses," she told him, struggling to steady herself as he reluctantly stepped back. He was intoxicating, a drug that altered her entire perception of where reality began and dreaming ended.

"THERE YOU ARE!" Torch light blinded as Billy – and the tent in his pants – stepped behind Breanna, the hard warmth of his body pressed close.

"Children," he said in a tone that demanded above her head, "who sent you?"

"Granny Holly says she needs everyone at the table," Max said, all eight years of maturity weighing heavily as he eyed his younger sibling.

"I don't think we'll fit," Lachlan huffed, crossing his arms, torchlight cutting the tops of the trees. "But that Sharee lady says it'll be 'picter perfect'?"

"You mean PICTURE perfect, you ninny!"

"Stop calling me that!"

"CHILDREN." Billy's warning had the boys' spines straightening. "Tell Granny Holly we will be along presently."

"Okay!" Lachlan turned, satisfied, towards the house.

"Lachlan! Wait!" Max ran off after his charge, clearly frustrated by his lack of ability to control his younger sibling. "Dad said we needed to stay together!"

"C'mon, lass," Billy said, their boots shuffling through the grass. "There is always time."

Later. That one word was becoming a prayer as thoughts too loud remained unsaid between them.

"My chin and lips are tingling." The words tumbled out

before she'd registered the thought, adding, "You know I'll be mercilessly teased about 'pash rash' from the twins and Seth, spurring a million questions from Graham's brats, right? And we didn't find the pickle, not that we could in the dark, anyway."

Billy's sigh threatened to shake the nearby tree as he drew back, tipping his face to the stars.

"Later," she promised, not sure what she was referring to. Resuming their heated snog session? Moving the delicious tingling friction of his beard to places much further south of her face? Finally stripping down and getting into their regularly scheduled clothing-optional evenings?

"I think we need a contingency." The words drifted absently as a re-drawing of lines began in her mind, their original plans torn up and re-written with new rules and boundaries.

Catching her hand, Billy spun her back to face him, so close her nose almost hit his chest. In the light from the house, he ducked his head and she noted the arch in his eyebrow.

"Later," he echoed, his thumb running gently over her heated cheek. When her stomach growled, Billy drew back, marvelling at her midsection like it was the first time he'd heard such a sound, or noticed her big belly, pressed firmly to his smooth, flat stomach. "Come, Bruce."

"I would have, in two more kisses," she told him honestly. "This pregnancy thing is a trip!" Her stomach grumbled and rolled once more.

A laugh hid at the edges of his voice as he said, "Let's get you … both of you …" his hand skimmed her mid-section hesitantly, "something to eat."

"See? You're a good guy. Taking care of me and everything."

"Breanna, whatever you want from me, whatever you need, I will make sure it is given."

Taking the stairs two at a time, Billy launched himself up onto the veranda. Propped against the screen door, he struggled to maintain a bland façade as she curtsied, whacked him in the stomach with a roll of her eyes, then disappeared inside with a curt, "whatever, nice guy."

8

Words Said ...
And Things Unspoken

Billy

BILLY WASN'T ONE FOR PLANS. Rosters and schedules, sure. Business objectives and goals, necessary. Life Plans, meticulously detailed into actionable and tickable checklists like Breanna insisted upon? They made his mind boggle. The strangeness of this big moment in her life, this baby, unplanned, as far as he could deduce from what limited information she'd offered, didn't seem rational. Over the years, she'd proclaimed quite frequently her detestation of 'snot-nosed ankle-biters' and how, based on her own mother's efforts, Bre thought she would also be a horrible mother.

Marriage, children, a large, loud home of his own like this

132

one, set on a few acres ... these were all hopes that Billy had considered at one stage or another, but never thought he'd obtain. It was a pipe dream born of too much alcohol and the presence of his nephews, whose sticky hugs and thoughtful stick-figure artworks warmed his soul.

But as Breanna entered the bustling house – chin high, dodging zig-zagging children and the teasing of his brothers at her flushed face – Billy couldn't help but wonder once again ... to hope ... was the baby his? Was this potentially the start of those dreams coming to life? It wouldn't be the first time Bre had made anything seem possible. He loved it when she took the reins, urging him to take an opportunity when it presented itself ... which was exactly why he hadn't hesitated when his best friend suggested they spice up their friendship.

Was the baby his? Perhaps 'later' he'd find out.

His fierce little spitfire took it all in her stride as his family and their guests dragged her into conversations while he followed behind, a brooding, hairy shadow. She threw words back at the teasing twins, witty retorts and easy laughs, while Billy tried to keep his eyes on the back of her head, all so he wouldn't stare at her perfectly rounded arse.

He wanted to – *needed* to – rip those stretchy, tempting abominations off her as soon as possible, or he might well explode. He'd never had to daydream about tearing her clothing from her body before, but now ...

"Finally!" Holly sung, grinning wide as she ushered everyone into the formal dining room.

If he hadn't known the furniture could withstand the combined weight of his brawling brothers, Billy might have fretted that the old dining table would fail under the smothering presence of the brimming plates. His mother's preparations were often sufficient to feed an army, but tonight she seemed prepared to end world hunger altogether, and her efforts were beyond decadent. Billy couldn't have imagined the perfection that his mother and Sharee had created over the past few hours.

Arrangements of native flowers dotted the table, pops of yellow wattle muted between green-grey eucalyptus branches. The glow of battery-operated candlelight cast a warm glow over the scene. Billy loved the flickering fakes; his mother refused to incorporate naked flames in her plans, thanks to an accident involving all the brothers, a stuffed bear, and inactive smoke alarms. With the inherent risk of bushfires in an Australian summer, and Graham's little gremlins, it was still a well-considered choice. Thankfully, cool air blasted down from vents in the ceiling, stealing the humidity and all thoughts of fire, replacing it with a blissful chill.

Pulling his mother's slim figure closer, Billy squeezed her tight. "This is amazing," he told her, dropping a kiss on her temple.

"Isn't it?" Sharee beamed. "I wish I could take the credit for this gloriousness, but I really can't. How Holly and Breanna arranged all this–"

"Breanna?" His eyebrow quirked at his mother.

"She has become invaluable around here. How she manages

to do everything is beyond me, but I think she must have the power to stop time!"

She sure does, he wanted to add, but didn't, as memories replayed of countless hours lost in a world where only the two of them existed, and time had indeed seemed frozen, somehow prolonged.

Returning his hug, Holly added, quietly, "Luckily we have no intention of letting her leave, right, William?"

Hope and warning echoed in her whispered words, her meaning clear – *Don't let her go*. The implied threat '*Or Else*' was added to the dictionary of Words Unsaid he'd apparently begun compiling this Christmas. Thankfully, Breanna had started to open up.

Finding the words was the first step, and that task needed to be initiated by Breanna. Despite everything that had transpired today, how could they move forward together and survive Christmas? The birth of her – their? – baby? What then? Then, perhaps, he could approach the topic of Breanna never leaving.

He had never considered it a possibility before. But she'd made it clear she didn't want change, or the permanence of marriage. In fact, the thought of him dropping to one knee essentially repulsed her. Adding a baby into the equation ... how might he convince her, them, to stay? To become 'us' and 'we' more permanently?

"Sit! Sit!"

"Is the air on?"

"It's set to freezing!"

"Hurry up, food's getting cold!"

"Dad, do I have to eat Grannie's peas?"

Beneath the table, Bre's hand found his and her smile damn near melted his heart.

"Holly, Sharee, I don't throw my words around lightly," Bre began, but the twins, claiming the seats to either side of Sharee, howled with laughter. "Well, not my compliments anyway," Bre amended, "but this is divine!"

"*Divine*, Sharee!" Holly beamed. "Did you hear that?"

"I completely agree," the interior designer agreed, already snapping photos as the children sat at the table, eyes as large as saucers and smiles so wide their back teeth were gleaming.

"Grace!" Piers shouted, leaning over little Lachlan and helping himself to the chicken drumsticks.

Holly's mouth opened to protest, but the spell had been broken, and all hell broke loose as the children launched for the food.

Shrugging, Sharee laughed, continuing to click the camera on her phone as she captured the scene.

Bre squeezed Billy's knee as she reached for the pile of sliced ham, diverting at the last minute with a grumble towards the pyramid of sausages nearby.

Taking the carafe from the centre of the table, he poured Breanna a tall glass first, then his mother, who beamed at him. He filled his own glass last.

"Shit, sorry!" Bre said, her elbow too close to his nose as she re-knotted her hair atop her head.

"Don't say shit, Aunty Bre!" came a serious scold from a small child whose plate of mashed potato was so full of tomato sauce it looked like a murder scene.

"Sorry, kid." She grinned, snapping the hair tie in place. "What?" She threw a demanding look Billy's way.

Two apologies!? he wanted to say. Spoken from Bre's lips, the words were a foreign language. Luckily, he loved languages, but this change in Bre ... all her changes ... he struggled to keep up. Billy dropped his gaze from her hair, his mind still reeling as he shook his head.

"Nothing." It was nothing. Then again ...

He didn't remember tugging her hair loose, but Billy learned long ago that whenever Bre was around, his brain wasn't in control of his body for long. Plus, he loved her hair, the smooth texture, and the way it was red or brown or gold, depending on the way the light played with each strand. Now, for instance, it glowed almost copper in the moody atmosphere the candles created. The low lighting sedated the children and provided lovely images for Sharee, he was sure, but it also felt a little too ... intimate.

Bre laughed, pitching forward, the copper of her hair filling his field of vision. He wanted to reach out and touch it. Examine it in the flickering shadows. The feel and sight of the fine strands sliding through his thick fingers had transfixed him for years.

"So, Billy Boy." Revv Ryder's voice boomed through his ruminations, shattering the delicate mood Holly had so carefully curated. "You never answered my question. How'd you end up crippled?"

♠ ♠ ♠

Revv's crew squirmed in their seats, shovelling food into their mouths. Sharee, on the other hand, let her delicate mouth hang open, eyes flicking between Billy and Piers like they were playing a tennis match. The adults at the table all seemed to slow, the din muting.

Bre was going to kill Piers. Billy knew it, just like he knew she preferred pants to dresses and orange juice to apple.

"Piers." The word hissed from Breanna, laced with poison.

"We don't use that word," ten-year-old Callum said around a mouth full of tempura prawn. "And, honestly, it's not your business, right Uncle?"

Billy winked in acknowledgement at his nephew, and the entire table seemed to sigh. The clinking of glasses and general noise resumed once more. Sliding his hand beneath the table, he squeezed Breanna's knee.

She shot him a look, a silent conversation striking up between them.

I'm okay. Let it go.

He's such an arsehole!

You need him.

I despise him!

Piers was oblivious to the ripple effect he'd initiated through the family. Many around the table seemed to be holding their own quiet conversations about him. Respectfully, they waited for Billy's story.

Clearing the lump of words in his throat, Billy spoke of the old train yard where rust, echoes of laughter, and playtime away from their parents had ruled their childhood. How the Carmichael brothers used to explore the giant, rusting playground. How their game of hide-and-seek had gone terribly wrong.

"Having four boys, Mum knew trouble would always find us, but that day, I found trouble first."

Soon came the usual jokes about learning to do everything with the opposite hand, the tension breaking.

"Ever tried te wipe yer arse cack-handed?" Richard asked, slapping his knee. "My grandson's a legend for his perseverance."

Perseverance is right, Billy thought, eyes drifting to Breanna who chuckled along with his brazen grandfather.

Humour often helped dissolve the awkwardness of a situation, and while everyone laughed, he could retreat from the conversation, becoming the taciturn shadow on the wall once more.

"Many situations only require the one hand, Grandpa," he said. "Some men have the full set and don't know how to use them properly. A waste!" Billy smirked, scratching his bearded chin as laughter peeled from the adults, and confusion grew among his nephews.

"I'll tell you when you're older," he heard Graham explain to his children, wiping at his eyes. "Off to bed, the lot of you."

"AW, DAAAD!"

"Don't forget," Nick added, "you'll want all your energy tomorrow to find the pickle and win the game! I know all of you are dying to open a present early ... and think of the favours you'd be able to get from everyone!"

Sufficiently enticed, the children went round the table saying goodnight and offering hugs to most, before racing each other out the front door and towards the cabin.

"I'll get them organised." Holly stood, taking her leave. "Be back soon." Shooting a look between Graham, Billy, and Piers, she added, "Behave yourself." Graham offered a tight-lipped smile.

"He always does. Graham's the good one, eldest son and all that," the twins chimed on either side of Sharee DeLuca, who had finally placed her phone face down on the table and was enjoying the meal with the family. Billy noticed his eldest brother shooting venomous looks towards Revv Ryder whenever the TV show host opened his mouth to toss in a tedious observation or rhetorical question. Or when, as happened frequently, Revv's too-loud fake laugh attempted to draw attention his way. Catching Graham's eye, Billy raised an eyebrow.

You okay? Graham's look queried, followed by something Billy could only interpret as: *because if you're offended by this guy, Bre and I can take him outside and flog him. It's no trouble.*

Billy nodded appreciatively. *All is well, brother.*

Good. Graham nodded before indicating with a thumb jerk then a quick flick of his wrist in Revv's direction: *Wanker.*

A chunk of sausage lodged in Billy's windpipe with alarming speed.

Bre stood, pounding his back as tears flooded Billy's eyes. Revv eyed them suspiciously. Graham, smug as ever, silently offered a top-up of water from the carafe.

Communication isn't difficult, Billy mused, gulping cool liquid. Especially when two people spoke the same language, whether that was verbal or otherwise.

"So," Nick said a few moments later, "anyone find the pickle today?"

Revv looked scandalised as Liam joked, "Pretty sure Bruce did!" and Connor's red wine sprayed all over Sharee's fine white outfit.

"Shit, Sharee, I am sorry!"

"Language!" Nick scolded as Connor dived for a napkin. Ripping it from its surfing koala holder, he waved it in front of Sharee, clearly unsure if he should dab at the stains or abstain from touching her altogether.

After a few clicks of her camera – did the woman document everything? – Sharee swiped her hand in dismissal.

"It's no trouble, honestly. Connor, it's fine." She took the napkin and threw it on the table, ignoring her stained clothing and his flushed cheeks as she dug her teeth into a corn cob, its juices spraying the twins. Running her mouth along the back of her hand, Sharee DeLuca, with all the grace of pig in mud, snorted a laugh. The twins just about melted in their sets beside her, completely smitten.

"You know, Sharee," Bre said, smirking at the designer across the table, "You're not what I expected at all!" She meant it as a compliment – Billy knew she did – but he saw Breanna's spine stiffen then her shoulders fall as Revv mumbled from the end of the table, "Seems to be a bit of that going around."

Excusing herself, Breanna stood and headed towards the bedroom. Revv watched her stomp up the stairs in her Doc Martens and those tight, stretchy pants. Not once did she cast a glance over her shoulder, and not once did Revv's eyes leave her arse as she disappeared from sight.

Billy resisted the urge not to growl, *Mine*. Because she wasn't his. Not really. Breanna Henderson belonged only to herself, and only shared what she wanted, when she wanted. She was his best friend, Bruce, though over the years he'd come to think of her less by that name she'd insisted upon as children. And calling her Bruce was becoming increasingly difficult the more she flaunted her growing femininity, in those damned stretchy pants. She didn't want marriage – she'd made that clear – or anything more than what they usually shared at Christmas. That had to be enough.

"Night!" the D-grade celebrity called, heading out the door. Seconds later, loud revving indicated he had borrowed one of the farm vehicles to head back to the garage, where he'd sleep in relative comfort away from the loud, large family. With the

Crank Shaft host absent, Billy breathed a little easier.

"Off te bed, grandson?" Richard asked, "or off te coddiwomple through the trees fer a while?"

"I need ..." *To think. Breathe. Soak in some silence.* His eyes flicked to the ceiling, and the second storey above, where Breanna would be climbing into his bed.

Richard nodded. "Well, I'm off to scandalise ye grandmother." He hitched up his plaid, near skipping down the hall, despite the walking cane. "G'night, ye wee gomeral!"

"Gomeral? How am I a fool, grandfather?"

Richard didn't respond, shaking his head vaguely at the tinsel-framed family photos that hung in the long hallway.

Boots thumping on the wooden floorboards, Billy examined the images, smaller versions of himself, Breanna, Connor, Liam, Graham and Seth all beaming back. His mother called them all 'her pride and joy', every one of the six people whose lives were chronicled throughout the house.

A mud-covered Bruce, having just beaten Seth in a wrestling match, beamed out from the wall. It was his favourite image of her – an explosion of summer freckles and red-dusted cheeks, brilliant hair that shone like a gold halo around her head, wild eyes and that too-gappy grin children present to a camera right after losing a tooth.

She was strong. Fearless. Brilliant. Those things hadn't changed. Everything else? He'd wanted it to change for so long, for Breanna to see the true depth of his feelings for her, and to finally admit those same feelings to herself, but now ...

Gently closing the door, he shut the cool air inside and stepped into the humid night. Crickets and cicadas sung to each other from leafy places that retained the summer heat. Staring up at the Milky Way, he blinked up at the millions of stars scattered above, trying to swallow the ache in his throat and the words he wanted to say. Phrases such as 'I love you' and statements like 'I want to be your baby's father'.

There was no arguing these facts, despite how she'd likely try.

The ladder, propped against the side of the house, had his eyes trailing upwards to the open window of his bedroom, where he hoped she was waiting for the 'later' conversation she'd promised. Would she be ready to talk tonight? To explain? To free her tongue and let the words flow, unabated, as they always had?

Billy longed for Breanna to be around him, to fill his nostrils with her scent and to feel her presence, but just for a moment, he needed quiet. To think through everything Breanna had said – and what she still refused to discuss. He needed space, and there was no chance of finding it inside his family home.

Space, Billy knew, was not infinite. The acres of farm could often feel very crowded, not just with the surrounding, stoic evergreens, but with the sizeable, loud-mouthed Carmichael clan, their guests, and soon, the customers who would begin wandering the fields with their families.

Piers and Sharee would increase their content creation and officially begin filming for their respective audiences soon, causing massive waves in the wider digital world, which could all be very good ... or very bad ... for them all.

It was no wonder Bre was struggling to manage it all, and why that tight leash she'd kept on her many plans was slipping into anxiety.

"Frustrating woman," he growled at the Southern Cross, remembering the look on her face only this morning when sheer panic had turned into a debilitation. How long had she been suffering? Nothing had ever seemed to phase Breanna Henderson ... until now.

He took a moment to consider the years of overstuffed planners she'd kept, how she consistently added more to her calendar, and the lists upon lists she insisted on keeping, just to vigorously scratch items off. The way she'd helped his mother contact Sharee, orchestrating and organising their social media takeover this Christmas, before hesitantly giving them the reins. Piers and *Crank Shaft*, the spotlight on her and Edsel, and she'd managed to coordinate a film schedule and TV crew without anyone's assistance or knowledge – all while anticipating she'd continue to work as usual on the Christmas tree farm.

And the baby! Was it his? Or someone else's? The desire to know was a fishing hook in his heart, tugging sharply every time he considered it. All this, plus the ever-present threat that Elanor Henderson posed, from the property next door.

Many times over the years, Bre told him she didn't want to be a mother, fearing she'd replicate Elanor's mistakes and turn her children against her. It was no wonder she was scared to reveal the truth ... and with the outdated notions her mother imposed,

Billy could see why Bre had been worried he might drop to one knee and propose.

Not to mention their own personal Christmas Plans, laborious physical work during the day followed by equally hard, but much more enjoyable, sweaty nights. There was no way Billy would let her work the farm this season. Not because she couldn't – hell, Bre was an excellent employee, chopping the trees, hauling them onto the ATVs, utes and trucks, netting and assisting to load them into cars, mount onto roof racks, or in trailers. She was capable, but after seeing today how quickly she tired from being on her feet, he knew she couldn't carry on as usual this Christmas.

Bruce had always been strong, but there was no denying she was more 'Breanna' these days, and she'd wither quickly. Her ankles were bound to swell to the point of pain before 10am and she'd melt faster than ice in the inferno of an Australian Christmas. Breanna was pregnant during the hottest Australian December on record – but weren't they all? – and she'd been completely overwhelmed.

Reconsidering the list of To-Do's, or, at least, the tasks he knew about, Billy kicked at the ground. Any *one* of those agenda items alone was enough for him, but for Breanna, managing each of these matters, with their unique subtleties and considerations, was too immense.

Somehow, he needed to get her out of her head and speaking freely once more. Glancing up at his window, Billy felt that familiar knot clogging his throat. Later ...

He was used to working to her timeline, but perhaps that, too, needed to change. Her health required that she slowed down. How the hell would he convince her to apply the brake? No one bossed Bruce around. The woman was a freight train, always heading somewhere at full speed, and unstoppable, He'd need a plan ... and help ...

A rock flicked from the toe of his shoe, a soft *tink* coming from low in the tree as it hit something solid. Kneeling down, a green line of light shimmered within the branches.

"Clever," he mumbled towards the house, watching his parents dance in the light of one window. They'd never left the pickle so close to the house before. Doubtless everyone would bustle past it, delving deeper into the trees to work and play. He considered pocketing the trinket, but ultimately decided to leave it for someone else. Someone who needed it.

"I have all I could want," he told the pickle ornament, his eyes returning to the window, half-formed plans and thoughts swirling as he climbed the ladder.

Perching on the sill, he watched Brenna's chest rise and fall as she lay on his bed, already asleep. She was gorgeous, one arm curved above her head, her exposed skin glowing in the low light. He loved seeing her like this – so relaxed and oddly still. It was a rare sight and he soaked it in.

"Later," he whispered, planting his long legs inside the room and gently shuffling inside. Eyeing the air mattress, he pursed his lips, weighing options, before shucking off his clothes. Brushing dark hair from his eyes, he considered Bre, her long red hair swirling across his pillow, his shirt barely covering the curves of hip and belly. Her nose periodically crinkled as she snored lightly.

"Beautiful," he told her, hoping the praise permeated the veil between them and seeped into her dreams.

9

Hell Hath No Fury
Like a Woman Needing
an Orgasm

Bre

"Hey, Bruce. Find the pickle yet?"

"No!" The word snapped out like she was a piranha, and they were fresh meat.

Connor and Liam, infuriating as per usual but additionally so when her hormones were this heightened, accepted their cuss-outs with all the dignity of five-year-olds. Five-year-olds as wide as mountain ranges, which was the exact image they portrayed now, working shoulder to shoulder.

Mountains or not, she was ready to strike them down like

skittles if they looked at her the wrong way. She was tired. She was hot. And she'd woken in such an intense state of arousal that she'd needed a long morning stroll, on ankles too willing to inflate like balloons, just to alleviate some of the tension that buzzed beneath her elasticised skin.

Two days on, and nothing had changed. In fact, the last forty-eight hours had been almost identical to each other, except for the absence of Billy's thigh hard between her legs. That one frenzied moment in the garage was almost as embarrassing as the way she slipped into coma-esque sleep every evening, exhausted from days spent indulging Piers Ryder.

'Later' with Billy was proving to be as elusive as a snowflake in a Southern Hemisphere Christmas. The tight line of her lips seemed to grow more solid with each day that the promise of 'later' didn't materialise. They needed to talk. To kiss and make up. To make out! How a man could be so close and yet so far was the greatest paradox of her life.

These last few mornings she'd woken nearly nose-to-nose with her best friend. She'd stare in the dark, willing him to wake, to grumble about something, and get this ball rolling. But no. She'd inevitably have to rise, thanks to an overfilled bladder and churning stomach, and he would stay safely tucked on his side of the very mature and highly effective pillow wall he'd constructed ... and which she destroyed to pad around her aching hips and slide between her knees. Pillows had never stopped them from touching before.

Before, however, she hadn't been a whale, and he wasn't jaded about their usual plans to screw each other's brains out.

"Hell hath no fury like a woman needing an orgasm," she spat at Connor and Liam, whose exploding laughter made her nostrils flare.

"Sorry to hear that, Bruce!" one of them called.

Sorry ... Carmichael apologies wouldn't win any friends today. Her middle finger gave a salute over her shoulder as she barrelled past, hell bent on this morning's mission.

Graham, handsome in his Carmichael tartan kilt and pressed white shirt, brushed past, chasing his kids into the fields, walkie-talkies amplifying their excited chatter between infrequent static. Thankfully, they didn't stop to chit-chat, or to get their heads bitten off for simply existing.

"Morning, sis." Seth eyed her, wary as a man happening upon a snake in the bush. "Who's shoved a bee into your bonnet so early this fine morning?" His eyes flicked to the neighbouring property, the question *Our mother?* on the tip of his tongue.

Bre shook her head. "No one. Nothing." She didn't want to talk to her brother about her raging case of whatever the female equivalent of Blue Balls was. Blue ovaries? Whatever the name for this condition, she was suffering. Who knew growing a human could make you so desperately want to practise the art of reproduction?

Knowing better than to interrupt one of Bre's moods, Seth stood aside, letting her storm past before joining the line of full-time and seasonal workers, and the extended family, as Holly and Sharee read from Bre's plans, allocating each worker their various assignments for the day.

Dipping his worn baseball cap at the ever-white-linen-clad Sharee DeLuca, Seth bowed slightly as she told him, "You are today's Greeter!" handing over a clipboard and water bottle from the trestle table.

Connor and Liam narrowed their eyes at Seth as he told the designer, "Have a great day, gorgeous," before running the few hundred metres towards the open candy-cane-striped gates of the property to take up his place as the Carmichael Christmas Tree Farm's official welcoming committee.

The Greeter was the first – and last – line of defence in the tradition of the pickle. Nick hadn't explained the role of the greeter when the *Crank Shaft* crew had been filming, but everyone knew that if the prized ornament left the farm, Christmas would, officially, be ruined. No pickle meant no presents opened early and no bragging rights, no ridiculous demands that made the family holidays memorable. If the Greeter let the pickle leave the farm ... it was all over.

Waving from the gate, Seth threw a kiss across the space to the twins.

"Bruce, don't say it!"

"What? I wasn't going to say anything!"

"Yeah right!" Liam scoffed, as Connor chimed in, "Don't say whatever it is that you're thinking! Just close your mouth and keep it to yourself for once."

Breanna feigned ignorance. "Do you mean Sharee and–"

Both twins flung piercing blue glares her way before hopping into a ute and rumbling away down well-worn tracks.

Stepping into the shade, Bre rolled her eyes to Holly and Sharee.

"Men," they agreed in unison.

"Their words might bruise at times, but at least they don't bite," Holly said.

Bre tapped her shoulder where a faint trail of scars circled her skin. "They used to, years ago. Sharp teeth, little buggers." Winking to Sharee, whose mouth hung open, she added, "It's quite useful to remind the patrons at The Pope that the twins aren't all bark. And don't worry, I got them back."

Holly explained that her middle sons often worked as security at The Pope, but to her, they were as harmless (and often as annoying) as gnats.

Leaving the women to chat, Bre eyed their long lists of tasks for the day. After yesterday's interior photos and the dinner shoot, today Sharee and Holly were focusing their festive social media content creation on the tree farm itself, and had a long list of carefully curated shots they wanted to capture, including the Carmichael clan in their kilts.

Piers wasn't nearly as organised, but, she supposed, *Crank Shaft* was an entirely different beast, and there was only so much influence Revv allowed over his programming. According to the scrawled schedule Trudy and Jaxon had shoved into her palm last night, Piers wouldn't be ready to film until 11am, after an hour of hair and makeup and when the sun was bright enough to glimmer perfectly off Edsel's Christmassy fire-engine-red paintwork. They'd break for lunch at 1pm and then finish filming at 3pm so the fading sunlight didn't impact the wingback-chairs-in-the-tree-fields interviews Piers demanded.

Never mind that sundown began around 8pm, there were no wingback chairs, and she rather thought *Crank Shaft* viewers would prefer to see a more relaxed chat in the lovingly restored tray of Edsel, but ... whatever. At least Piers had listened when she suggested the bright red of Edsel's paintwork would contrast nicely against the deep green of the trees for promo shots. In fact, all morning he'd been insisting it was his idea and that it was the only way to film the three-minute episode trailer.

Shoving a whole pig's worth of bacon into his mouth, Piers' imagination had grown into a beast that further demanded these shots would be cut with extreme-close ups of Bre's hands and dissolved with footage of her slowly rubbing a cloth over the cherry panels, fading to Piers' winking into the rear-view mirror as he adjusted it.

"It's all very cinematic," he'd explained, as though she were a child, unable to understand. In truth, she didn't comprehend how such a popular show successfully operated on a team of one camera man, one sound technician, and a Dani Zucco T-Bird wannabee with an overinflated superiority complex.

Bre really wanted to kick him in the kneecaps, eternally grateful he was staying in the garage rather than the main house with the other guests. Piers seemed like a five-star-minimum hotel kind of guy, but the best accommodation in town was above the tavern, and on the farm at least, he didn't have to pay for his bed, laundry, or meals.

Born an Aussie, he'd spent so long overseas cultivating what he loved to define as his "CAReer" that his accent was more American than Ocker, and he'd clearly forgotten what Christmas Down Under entailed. Among Breanna's growing list of frustrations with Revv Ryder was the fact that his plans were ridiculous. He failed to understand that his schedule meant they'd be filming outside, in the hottest part of the day. That, and his penchant for leather jackets, despite the summer sun, would have him melting in seconds. He'd be hot in every sense of the word.

She, on the other hand ... Bre looked down at herself, at her Doc Martens, the heavenly stretchy pants Holly insisted she learn to love, and her oversized shirt, and began to wonder if she was ready for her TV debut. Normally, she gave zero considerations to her appearance. Comfort was her singular goal when dressing.

"Things are so different now," she muttered to her belly. A fluttering reply pressed beneath her skin. "Morning, little shit. Sleep well?" Again last night she'd completely passed out while waiting for Billy, sprawled on top of the sheets like the ungraceful watermelon with limbs that she was.

Waking up to him beside her, his hair falling across his brow, his quiet breaths, the way his large body made the mattress dip, encouraging her to roll into the bare, tattooed chest that rose and fell beside her ... it had taken considerable restraint not to brush that hair back, to nuzzle closer and touch him. Everywhere. Anywhere. All at once.

But she didn't. Instead, while warmth grew down low in her body, the chilling realisation of 'get-up-now-and-vomit-or-else' spurred her body into an entirely different course of action. After her now-habitual morning chunder, she dressed quickly and escaped down the stairs for breakfast, helping Holly prepare for the imminent onslaught of hungry male mouths to feed.

"May as well work until eleven," Bre mumbled as she passed Holly and Sharee, whose discussion had turned to the various photos they 'needed' of the kilted clansmen, to get the most hits on their respective social media pages. "Maybe I'll get lucky and find the pickle. Make them all give me a massage while feeding me grapes and fanning me with golden palm fronds or something." The idea had merit.

Fifteen minutes later, however, she regretted her decision to search for the ornament while working.

"Have you found it?" Bre shifted on throbbing feet, the sun stinging her face as she rounded a row of trees to where the twins' dual chainsaws were cutting through arm-thick trunks.

"Ten thousand snails and a corner of one field infested with aphids, but no Christmas Pickle," Connor sighed. "Assuming that's what you meant, Bruce."

"You might not have a special pickle –" Liam grinned, shoving his brother's shoulder, "– but *I* do ..."

The twins erupted into a familiar series of vulgar gestures and jokes about size, girth and how one should most effectively use it. Having heard variations of this discussion countless times over the years, Bre returned to the trees. Maybe Graham and the children, with their many eyes and variation in heights, would have better luck.

Legs aching, she mentally ticked and crossed things off her to-do lists.

- Make a mess of things with Billy? Tick.

- Swallow nearly all her pride and apologise? Tick.

- Resume naked festivities with best-friend-with -benefits? Ba-bow. Nope. Not able to tick that one off. No ticks, no crosses, no nothing.

Well, not nothing. She couldn't discount one clothes-on orgasm that he'd encouraged her to take, not from him, but from friction alone.

Take what you need ... Use me, honey.

He'd been so accommodating. His remembered words flooded her system with heat, adding more discomfort to her current swollen, overheated condition.

She'd hoped that escapade might have opened the doorway to more starlit recreational fun, but the only thing that had seen any action at night had been Billy's damned air mattress that first night, then the Great Pillow Wall of China built between them every evening since. Any other time, she would have smashed through that construction with a wrecking ball, but lately, finding the energy to do anything other than making herself comfortable was proving difficult. She'd been so fatigued from her days, in particular:

- having Revv's huge presence in her garage

- the epic family dinner Holly put on for the entire assembled clan and guests

- playing board games with Graham's kids before Billy read to them from *Le Grinch* and helped carry them to their beds

- the nervousness of going to his room, with so many baby-blue Carmichael eyes watching her retreat up the stairs ...

She went down the list, analysing it, examining each moment to see if there was any tiny moment Billy had given her that look, the 'come hither' or 'I want my face buried in your breasts' look she'd sometimes caught on his face. That tiny spark of hope didn't exist. Aside from The Incident in the garage, Billy seemed to have no intention of remaining anything other than platonic. There'd been no reason to battle with her exhaustion once they closed the door to his room each evening.

In the morning, she'd find him beside her, having crawled into bed like a giant cat, without tipping the mattress at all. Her balled up clothes would be neatly folded, her discarded boots suddenly standing side by side at the door. This morning, she'd even woken to a glass of water and crackers beside the bed. He'd wasted a cracker by gluing two googly eyes to the salted upper face. That one thoughtful gesture near made her heart burst, and gave her hope. Luckily, she'd fished the plastic eyeballs from the masticated mess in her mouth before swallowing.

Awake before dawn – again – and gripped with the now-familiar morning sickness that she never quite managed to get rid of, even with Billy's crackers, she snuck out of the room. With nowhere else to go and ponder, Bre made her way into the fields searching for the pickle, because what else could she do to alleviate her frustrations about Man Number One while Man Number Two took his sweet time getting camera-ready?

At least Piers wanted and needed her, in some way, though it made her skin crawl every time he opened his mouth. That hadn't always been her immediate reaction to the TV star, but this Christmas was *all* about change.

With gritted teeth she'd tried to ignore the item currently top of her mental agenda – unleash righteous justice upon Piers' perfectly sculpted nose job. But Constable Keneally had made it very clear, many years ago, and reiterated often, that continued callouts to the Carmichael or Henderson properties would result in swift arrests, and she didn't want to be locked in handcuffs – unless William Carmichael was the man circling them around her wrists.

Billy had always been a great friend, and she didn't want to ruin that or push him into a situation he wasn't comfortable with, just because she wanted more. She held out all year for this, and he humoured her. That's all it was. That was The Plan – They were Friends with Festive Benefits.

Plan B had been ... a misstep. Okay, if she was being honest, Plan B had been a series of hot, sweaty, clothing-optional missteps that had occurred with increasing frequency over the past year. Still, each encounter had: a) been communicated, with b) clear expectations set – orgasms and nothing more, and c) nothing – ever – would compromise their friendship.

She didn't want Billy to expect anything more than that previously arranged Big O moment. He didn't need to look after her needs and those of her baby, too. And he probably didn't even want her in that same way, not if there was a dependant relationship at play. They'd always been so independent, then she'd been greedy. She knew it was the hormones, that it was unfair to ask him to change their plans yet again, but she couldn't help it. Billy made her that way, and damned if she wanted him more than ever. So why did she feel so desperately alone?

The Carmichaels had saved her from loneliness and sorrow. They had taken her from the clutches of Elanor, offering her safety and comfort. The excited squirm in her stomach registered that someone was listening. Absently, she stroked her stomach. "We'll be okay, little shit."

The increasing fluttering deep within her both amazed Bre and freaked her out. Not once had she imagined what having a foetus inside you might feel like, but if she had, she wouldn't have imagined these gentle, intermittent butterfly motions.

Every time she felt movement inside, she couldn't help but think of those gory extraterrestrial scenes in the 'Alien' movies.

After a year of demanding she wasn't "too girly" and could handle it, the boys had finally let her in on their horror and sci-fi movie sessions, so Bre had seen more alien spawn slice through human abdomens than she cared to admit.

"Doc said you're definitely human, though," she murmured. "Even though you look exactly like a comma in a snowstorm. Actually, I'd welcome a blizzard right about now." Wiping at her damp forehead, she began to doubt the sanity of her plan to work until Piers was ready to film.

The summer sun blazed tirelessly down, adding more freckles to her fair skin. "More constellations for Billy to discover, eventually ... hopefully."

The tree rustled as she quickly checked it for the pickle, head spinning as she stood up too fast, too soon. "I'd love to win this year," she confided to the pines, wiping at her face once more. "I need a foot rub ... badly! Bring down the swelling. I can't believe I've had to loosen the laces on my Docs. And I need Billy to barge through the pillow wall like a fucking pillaging Viking!"

In fact, one of her favourite sights in the entire world was Billy Carmichael descending on her, eyes blazing and mouth quirked, his large body hovering above hers. The calm after the storm was a beautiful sight, too. Billy splayed out across his wide bed, sheets rumpled and their noses pressed together as her hair cocooning them in their own little world where nothing else and no one else existed.

"It's part of the magic of the season," she swore to the nearest tree, rustling through its greenery with quick fingers, coming up empty. "Where did they stash that damned pickle this year?" If one of Graham's kids found the ornament and made her do something ridiculous, she was abandoning Christmas at the farm in favour of working double shifts at the pub through to the new year.

"Next year ..." She trailed off, already trying to make plans in an unknown future where she was a 'we' – just her and her baby a big question mark on next year's calendar. She wiped again at her forehead, her breaths shallow as her mind wandered, stretching between past and present like a tinsel-wrapped bungee cord.

The thought occurred to her that she still needed to have a decent conversation with Billy. He deserved her words. Not another apology – hell, one of those rarities was enough! But still, she should say ... something. A lot of somethings, if she was being honest. He needed answers to:

- who her baby's father was

- why she refused to discuss it

- why she wanted their friendship to stay the same.

This new list grew longer with every step.

Perhaps they should discuss the future, and how – if – Billy might remain a part of her life, once she became a single mother. She was under no illusions that this was one of the most difficult choices she'd ever made, but she refused to trap a good man like William Carmichael in a bad situation. He needed to have all the facts, and to make up his own mind. They needed to discuss options, though if history told her anything, she'd be the one doing most of the talking while he nodded occasionally, offering the occasional grunt.

If she tried conversation soon, everything she'd been trying to deal with would tumble out, jumbled, confused, and angry. Not at Billy, but for Piers and his behaviour. She'd invited *Crank Shaft* here, and yes, Revv Ryder was a celebrity, but that didn't give him a licence to carry on like an ignorant arse, particularly around the dinner table, and the children.

The kids looked up to their uncles. Billy in particular, seemed to have infinite patience with Graham's messy offspring. Yet even Billy was bristling more and more as the *Crank Shaft* host flirted and insulted his way around the family. Revv's crew, rolling their eyes and muttering frequent apologies under their breaths, gave the impression that yes, unfortunately, this was how the celebrity always acted.

"It's just a few more days," she assured herself. Billy didn't need anyone to stand up for him. He was a big boy – in more ways than one – who could take care of himself. "If he's okay with Piers slinging around old-fashioned ableist language like 'cripple,' that's his business." She shuddered, fury and disgust mingling into a hard knot, mirroring her curled fists.

She needed to hit something. Over and over, until her anger died down. Usually, she'd drive straight for Fit But, her friend Adam's gym. He'd hold the big black punch bag hanging from the ceiling, encouraging "more, harder, faster, Bre!" while she belted it until her arms ached, her knuckles bled, and her legs gave out, completely spent. Adam would pat her shoulder, pick her up, and bandage her wounds, proud as punch. He'd whisper encouraging things and turn her pain into battle scars, healed with his delight in her efforts.

Boys were good at that – praising aggressive release. Jillian would probably break her wrist if she even thought about throwing a punch. Her closest friend was delicate, and would find healthier ways to work through her emotions.

Breanna had always found it harder to befriend girls than boys. 'Those With Penises,' as Bre had called them through school, didn't mind her crass loud mouth and generally dishevelled façade, yet these same endearing qualities were frowned upon by her vagina-wielding cohort. Bre had tried to make female friends many times over the years, but inevitably she would upset the girls with her too-blunt opinions, insulting one girl or another. Then they would band together, excluding her – all except Jillian Maitland.

Jillian was a soft 'girlie girl' who almost exclusively wore floral prints. She was a kind-hearted romantic, and Bre was pretty sure that when she sang, forest animals and nearby birds would probably flock to her. Jillian left the singing to her own sister, however, who had long ago flown the coop and moved to Sydney.

Bre thought of her smashed phone, mentally adding it to her shopping list. She really needed a new one, and to contact Jillian, who had a knack for seeing the potential in people. She would offer Bre a silver lining.

Maybe she should be more like Jillian, Breanna thought absently, bending again to search a new tree for the pickle ornament. Maybe she could become the woman her mother wanted her to be? The thought was brief, before the urge to hit something manifested even stronger than before.

Punching pine trees, however, didn't have quite the same effect as flogging the bag at Adam's gym. Here on the farm, Bre could only lose herself in the hard, physical work that a busy business like this required, turning her negativity into productivity.

"Even if I had a phone right now," she told one tree, "Jillian's grieving right now. She's locked herself away in that huge house with her moody jerk of a cat. Poor Jill ..." The toe of her boot dug deep in the grass as she continued talking to herself. "She doesn't need my drama on top of her own issues right now. But what else can I do?" If there was some magical solution to the problems of Piers, the baby, Billy – problems that she herself had created – she needed to find it.

"I am going to find the pickle," she told the butterflies in her belly. "Then I'll unwrap my present like a queen on a throne! And as the Pickle Queen of Christmas, I'll make all kinds of outrageous demands from my subjects, as per the rules of the game. Demands like every time Piers says 'crippled', or 'impaired', or 'disfigured', the nearest Carmichael can punch him in the dick." Hell, they'd gladly oblige her.

The tension had been at brawling point last night until Piers wisely slunk off to bed, nursing his wounded pride. Billy's half English and half Scottish grandmother, of all people, had been the one to give him a solid scolding. Normally quiet as a church mouse, her explosive condemnation was full of anger and disappointment, a combination only seasoned parents could dish out so effectively.

"But right now …" While hunting for the ornament, she would find the most beautiful tree for the Carmichael's home, drag it into the house, and decorate it however Holly and Sharee instructed, for their 'trending' or 'viral' media and marketing goals. She had until 11am after all. Plenty of time to finish a few tasks.

"Piers is such a jerk," she told the nearby pine, "but I'm so glad I put Holly in contact with Sharee, who is a genuine ray of fucking sunshine."

Everything about this Christmas was her doing – even this unplanned pregnancy. She could only blame herself, really.

Her shaking hand wiped absently at yet more sweat. "I need a tree." Somehow, that would make things better. Remind everyone she wasn't the fragile porcelain doll they'd begun to inadvertently treat her as. "No longer 'one of the boys' when the baby in your womb is a swift reminder that you have lady parts down there!"

The trees rustled gently around her, and with a swift mental pivot, she decided to practise the spiel about the Carmichael Christmas Tree Farm she would present on *Crank Shaft*.

"The Carmichael's property is approximately sixteen acres,

quartered into smaller farms of four thousand trees each," she told one tree, inspecting its limbs for a glittering green, camouflaged ornament. "The radiata pines, planted in rows and fields, take four years to grow, with one quarter of the farm cut and replanted each year to cycle the growth. The trees are regularly pruned and of various heights, depending on which farm and field you're standing in."

Taking a shallow breath, Bre pushed on, reciting, searching for the pickle, and for the perfect tree.

She knew how to select a strong, healthy pine that she could manage to take to the house. Still, as her breathing became more shallow and her feet began to throb, Bre wondered how much of an impediment the baby might be for this task.

The creature within her squirmed and she stopped for a moment, gently resting her hand on the fabric that stretched the face of Grannie May, a local bakery icon, wide across her midsection. She'd won the shirt years ago and it had always been too big for her slight frame.

Now, the old baker's nose seemed to be the size of Bre's entire right boob, and it hugged too tight, as though she'd eaten all of the delicious pastries the bakehouse had to offer.

Without her phone and planner, a new list began in her mind:

- Buy new clothes.

- Thank Holly for these seriously amazing stretchy yoga pants.

- Wash said seriously amazing stretchy yoga pants.

- Have gherkins and ice-cream for lunch.

- Lure Billy into the barn and flip his kilt up ... if he lets me.

But no, there was no time for that.

- At eleven, take the perfectly preened Piers Ryder and his crew to the garage once more.

- Film a few scenes there.

- Drive Edsel to prearranged spot. Film some more.

- Lug wingbacks to field, arrange the set, then more filming – Q&A as Piers requested.

- After 3pm – Help Holly with the internal decorations for her own shoot with Sharee.

- Sweep the Big Barn for the famous Carmichael Christmas Eve Party.

- Organise the barn decorations for party.

- Send the open invite to the Moonshine Gazette.

- Put flyers up around town for the event.

- Visit my parents?

- Buy presents for all the Carmichaels ... and probably the Hendersons, too.

- Buy presents for guests – Piers, Jaxon, Trudy, and Sharee.

- 'Later' ... Find time to talk to Billy – properly.

A sharp pain stabbed through her chest.

Billy deserved so much better than Piers, and better than her, too. Some friend she was turning out to be. She'd added a sweet celebrity interior designer and a motor-mouthed TV show host AND a growing foetus into the already busy mix of a Christmas Tree farm during the festive season. It wasn't fair to the Carmichael family, and Billy–

The drum in her chest pounded, hot air, so thickly pine scented she could taste it, refusing to enter her lungs. Doubling over, world spinning, feet unsteady, she crashed to her knees.

No, No, No, not again!

As she dug her trembling hands into the dirt, sweat beads trailed down her cheeks. Hot and cold all at once, she forced herself to focus on the solid ground beneath her hands and knees, the small flutter of her growing baby, and the rustling of the trees as the wind played with their evergreen branches ... to no avail.

Gasping, Bre squeezed damp eyes shut, gulping what should have been air – but wasn't. Adrenaline flooded her system as the panic, burning as the summer sun, set her body aflame.

The edges of the world softened with her unsteady vision, the heat fading rapidly as a cold wave rolled through her body.

No.

Stop.

Her body wouldn't listen. No matter how much she fought, her racing heart refused to slow.

"Bruce?" Dust flew around her as a large body slid in beside hers. "Bruce!"

Vaguely, she became aware of gravity, holding her tight. A large body curled over hers, gravity heavy but comforting, a human blanket, hazy but familiar.

"Breathe," a voice commanded, its edges rough from worry. "Just breathe."

10

InterMENtion

Bre

THE SERIOUS, SCOWLING FACE above her was so unlike the man she'd been having a semi-lucid fever-dream about. This man was stern, the set of his jaw too severe for such a handsome face. With dark lashes, a straight nose and even straighter set of his mouth, there was only one person who had those Mr Darcyish sideburns framing his face.

Still groggy from an afternoon nap such as she never let herself indulge in, because they simply wasted too much productive time, she mumbled, "Don't start, Reece."

"Breanna Henderson." He ground out her full name without moving the straight line of his lips – she must really be in trouble. Bre fixed her eyes on the google-eyed poster of Pamela

Anderson, avoiding Doctor Reece Hargraves like the adult she was.

With a small roll of his eyes, he turned from his perch on the edge of the bed, addressing the many faces who peered in from the doorway. "She's fine."

The collective sigh from the stairs implied the entire Carmichael family was lining the curve of steps between the kitchen and Billy's room.

"Reece." She tried to sit up and failed, immediately dizzy. Blinking it back, she forced herself to smile. "Small world, seeing you here."

"Small town," he countered. "Haven't managed to get rid of me yet."

"Lucky for me." The sarcasm in her tone broke the tense lines around his mouth.

"There is another option, you know. I can call Dr–"

"NO! You are my doctor. And my friend. Hell, we survived school together and have a standing date every four years for my cervical cancer screening."

The twins made a vaguely disgusted noise and thumped down the stairs, freeing space for other faces to press closer.

This time, Reece offered a genuine smile and a half-formed chuckle. "You've always had a way with words."

"So I'm told."

Ripping the black band of the blood pressure monitor from her upper arm, the doctor's voice rose, addressing the crowd once more. "Her blood pressure is still a bit low. Low blood pressure could explain the dizziness, especially if it dropped suddenly. Around one twenty over eighty is normal, so I want to stay and keep it under observation for a while longer."

"It?"

"If I said I was keeping *you* under observation, I'd probably end up with a bag of mint peas on my eye, am I right?"

Smirking, she wriggled down into the bed, unwilling to try sitting up any time soon and losing face in front of this crowd.

"That's what I thought." Raising his voice again, Reece addressed the faces, young and old, who waited with deep-set worry etched into their faces.

They looked rather like a parliament of blue-eyed owls, she mused as Reece absently handed her a tall glass of water, the firm thrust of it into her hands demanding: *drink*.

"Owls in tartan," she mused into the glass as she gulped, watching Reece's eyes flash over her in assessment at the outlandish comment.

"With rest, she'll be absolutely fine." The doctor's words were at odds with the lines of worry on his face. "Go on now, I'm sure it's a busy day." His tone brooked no argument, and it was with some sense of tired amusement she noted Sharee's bubbly enthusiasm leading the way down the stairs – followed much less enthusiastically by kilt-adorned Carmichaels, heads hung. Holly hung back, concern wafting from her like the scent of gingerbread from the ovens downstairs.

"Holly, I promise, she's in good hands."

With a nod, Holly told Reece, "Take care of my daughter."

Salty water caught in the curve of Bre's lips.

"Damned hormones!" Gulping down the rising lump in her throat, she finished the glass of water, shoving it back at Reece who'd fixed her with THE LOOK. Shrinking down, she bit the inside of her cheek, waiting for the lecture she knew was coming.

"Breanna," Reece bit out once they were gone. "You need to take care of yourself … and this baby."

Rubbing the lingering wetness from her eyes, she sighed, "Long time no pee on a stick, Reece."

"Yes, that pregnancy confirmation was the last time I saw you, over six months ago! You're in your third trimester now, Breanna. Where the hell have you been hiding? Moonshine is a tiny town, and besides that, I thought we were friends. But you've been too busy avoiding me, your mate and your doctor, and now here you are, pretending that everything is normal?"

"Not true. Nothing about this Christmas is normal, except the surface-of-the-sun heat outside and the way my calves scream at me all day. That's new. And so much fun." She laid the sarcasm on thicker than Vegemite. "Reece, *normally* I'd be coping. I'd have this all under control. I'd be out there," she pointed to the window, and the trees beyond, "helping the guys cut trees and cart them to–"

"No. Not this year."

She tried a different tack. "But there are guests – *Crank Shaft* and–"

"No," Reece repeated, crossing his arms, the annoyingly crisp white of his overly starched shirt crinkling. "Not this year,

Breanna."

"Reece, listen–"

The grumble – like gravel on rocks – came from the corner. "No buts, Bruce."

"Billy?" She must've been dazed, to resort to rhetorical questions. Of course the massive shadow somehow scrunched into the crevice near the bookshelf was Billy. With that strange grace that men his size simply shouldn't possess, he rose, towering above them both. The tattoos of his forearm shifted back and forth as his fist curled then opened at his side.

"Look, no offence, guys," she said, squeezing her eyes shut, "but I don't need one man – let alone two – telling me what to do."

Neatly folding the blood pressure monitor cuff, Reece said from the side of the bed, "It's not telling, it's *advising*. You need rest. You'd hate for me to *advise* Billy to tie you to the bed now, would you?"

"That's nothing new," she commented, without thinking. Billy's ears went pink, the rising colour wiped away with the hand dragged down his face, but Reece only soldiered on.

"Breanna, I've spoken to Billy. The panic attacks, that's another one of my concerns. I know you had them during high school, and we were working on techniques –" His eyes shot to Billy, conscious of the professional boundary he had to walk between friends and clients. "If you don't look after yourself, we'll have to get creative about how we can make you slow down. Stop, even." He thought for a moment, Bre protesting the entire time. Holding a hand out, he demanded in a tone that was more statement than question, "Where is it, Breanna?"

"Where's what?"

Reece exhaled slowly, eyes on the ceiling. "Your planner."

"What planner? Hey!"

Billy handed Reece the thick journal, bursting with colourful Post-it notes, to-do lists, and receipts, all slightly smudged. Many of the edges had been worried from the crisp and starched parchment it once was into thin, soft paper.

"Give that back, or I'll ..."

Reece flipped the fat little diary open with a crisp efficiency she admired for a second. Tsking and tutting, the doctor shook his head as though it was packed with lewd drawings. Those things *did* exist in there, of course, but they didn't grace every page, and even Dr Super Serious should have laughed a bit when he saw one of her creative little doodles. He should have turned the paper from portrait to landscape and quirked an eyebrow, like Billy had.

"I'm sorry, Bre," Reece said finally, flipping the journal closed and standing to pace around the bedroom. "I'll admit, I should have sought you out sooner. You never come to me, except for your aforementioned smear." His eyes shot to Billy once more. "Anyway, I want to say sorry. I've been busy with the practice, and Sam. He's a bit of a mess right now, as you both know, having seen him so often at the pub ..." Reece shook his head. "But these are terrible excuses. I'm here now. I can see that you're struggling with your body and your brain. Mental health is a big priority for me. Statistically ... well, you know the stats. You both always attend my fundraising events and actually listen to my speeches. Honestly," he paused, "I am worried, Breanna. I need to know what happened out there this morning. What's going on?"

He absently picked up a sprig of dried wattle sporting several googly eyes from one of Billy's shelves. A few yellow bursts fell from the twig, floating to the floor, before he set it back down. Billy, on the other hand, stared straight at her, waiting for more explanations.

"I had a panic attack." There was no use lying now, not when she'd resolved earlier to try and communicate more effectively, especially with Billy, like she used to. "I've been ... a bit swamped –" she pointed to her planner, "as you can see."

"It was lucky you were around, Billy," Reece said. "Looks like she's been pushing herself to exhaustion."

"I'm not exhausted! I can do everything the boys can."

"Normally, yes," Reece agreed, "but right now? You can't. Not because you're not able, but because you shouldn't put yourself into these dangerous situations, for the sake of your health and the baby's. Do you want to go to hospital?"

Bre folded her arms over her chest.

"Didn't think so." Reece smiled kindly, the severe lines of his face cracking. "You don't have to ... IF you listen to me and take a few steps to get this weight off your shoulders." He weighed the planner experimentally in one hand, shaking his head at its heft. "From what I can surmise, your blood pressure skyrocketed

– panic makes the blood pump faster around the body, and you have potentially fifty percent more blood pumping through your system right now. Too much, too fast, then a sudden drop …" Reece spoke more to himself now, nodding as he worked through the symptoms, diagnosing. "Low blood pressure or hypotension isn't uncommon during pregnancy, but mixed with the need for a reduced mental load …. These are all reasons for continued observation, for a while at least."

If anyone had ever had the balls to stand up to Bre – really stand up to her – it was Dr Serious himself. "That high peak from the panic, combined with hypotension coincides with hormonal shifts as your body adjusts to support the foetus. Yes, I'm confident this is a blood pressure issue, Bre."

Bre huffed, trying to sit upright without causing the spinning gremlins in her head to whirl their dizzy dance yet again.

Reece dutifully focused all attention back to his patient, waving the planner in his hand.

"Was the panic attack because of this? The increased stress and worry that this ridiculously detailed Christmas planner contains? I mean, Bre …" He flipped it open to a random page and ran a finger down it. "You've allocated toilet breaks on a rotating roster, including the three-year-old I met downstairs who I know for a fact isn't properly toilet trained yet!"

Billy's eye quirked. Bre's face flushed. Crossing her arms, she opened her mouth to dispute the facts, but Reece got in first.

"Bre, you *know* I can out-stubborn you, but if we need to bother with the traditional arm wrestle, I'll haul that milk crate over and we can get it over with. We've tousled before, and if we need to, I'll do it again."

He was right, of course. Reece Hargraves didn't know what it felt like to be wrong, or make a bad choice, or mess anything up. He wasn't just Mr Serious, he was also Mr Perfect, and for some reason, all this labelling of Mr's brought Bre's mind right back to Billy's Mr Happy jocks.

"Thanks for not treating me like some wilting princess, Doc."

"Even the wilting princesses are strong, Bre. Don't confuse femininity for weakness, or toughness as something more masculine. We all know you're strong. And now, you need to focus all that power into telling me the truth. Is your anxiety the result of this overstuffed planner?"

She nodded weakly, irritated, flattered, hungry, needing to pee, and trying to quell the rising desire to cry. She sniffed, cursing the way her own body was leading the revolt against her. Both men patiently waited for her to elaborate. She couldn't outlast either in a staring contest, so the words came out rushed, hot and angry.

"I don't need you and Billy staging an inter*men*tion right now. I need more hours in the day. There's just so much to do!" she bellowed, arms crossing tighter over herself. "And it's all my own doing, I'm fully aware of that. I have plans upon plans, lists and every minute planned some days, and yet all I needed, *really* needed, was a contingency for ..." She trailed off, eyes on Billy's bare feet. Eyeing the little landing outside Billy's room, she saw her favourite black Doc Martens there, neatly tucked to one side of the stairs, right next to his much larger work boots. Something about them, organised so neatly and regimented, made her eyes prickle all over again.

"Breanna, *this* –" Reece waved her planner before her eyes, snatching her attention, "– is too much for one person. In fact, it's probably too much for several people. *Plus* you're pregnant, so the amount of time and energy you need to complete all these tasks is, more realistically, time and energy your body is using to growing an entire human being! That baby should be your focus right now, for the health and safety of yourself, as well as this child. There are people who need you, Breanna. They need you to be safe and happy, and for your mental and physical health to be stable."

Reece's hand slid over the swell of her stomach, and one hot, defiant tear rolled down her cheek.

"These things are finite, Breanna. You can't stretch a twenty-four-hour day any longer. And while you're the toughest person I know, now isn't the time to keep proving yourself. Stop pushing, for once in your life. You need to slow it down."

"Delegate."

"Billy makes an excellent point. Delegation is a good start. So much of what's in that planner could be completed by someone else, and I know you can delegate. I saw the lists Holly and that woman, Sharee, were working from. It was all in your handwriting." Reece sighed, pouring another glass of water from the pitcher, downing it in two gulps, before refilling it and offering it to his patient. "Now isn't the time to have a death grip on your independence. It's a time to learn how to let that go, because soon, there will be a *dependant*." He motioned unnecessarily to the mound of flesh that had attached itself to her abdomen. "And whether you like it or not, you'll need to learn to ask for help."

Lips pressed tight, she wiped hastily at her cheeks, nodding slightly. She knew all this, but letting go, when she'd orchestrated so many of the moving parts, was like building an engine from spare parts then refusing to slide in the key and test the ignition.

"Billy." She finally met his gaze. "Can you give us a minute alone?"

Wordlessly, the big friendly giant who was her best friend exited the room, leaving a vacuum in his wake.

"Reece," she confided, gripping the glass tighter, so her hands would stop shaking. "I've really messed all this up."

"Nothing is beyond repair." Reece threw her planner to the foot of the bed where it landed with a heavy thunk. "You need to forgive yourself, Breanna. We all love you, even though you're a pain in the arse. Let us help. All you need to do is ask, and I know it'll be hard, but now's a good time to start practising, because when you have this kid ..."

"I know," her voice warbled.

"Postnatal depression affects one in five Australian mothers, and one in ten fathers."

"I know all this, Doctor Serious. I just wanted this Christmas to be the same as every other. A last hurrah, you know?"

Reece wrapped her hands in his. "Now is the time for contingencies. Plans B, C, D. We'll all help, okay? The Carmichaels will do anything you ask, *Bruce*." He chuckled at the nickname he so rarely used. "You know it. You only have to ask. I know that's hard for you, and you're used to doing everything on your own, but you need to communicate what you need. Panic attacks are born on fear. So think, Bre – what is it that you're most afraid of?"

"Billy hating me," she shook out. "Him feeling trapped. He's been trapped, Billy – beneath that train carriage, then later, in his own body and mind. He retreats there, waits for me to seek him out, because I think he's scared, too, to make the first move, you know? ... I can't add an extra layer of resentment in his life."

"I don't think he's capable of resentment, Bre, but you need to tell him that you feel this way. Explain it to him, like you just did to me."

"I did ... Kind of. I told him he couldn't be the white knight, and he wasn't allowed to marry me."

A genuine, beautiful smile transformed Reece's entire face. "That is not nearly the same thing. Out of curiosity, what did he say to that?"

Bre's heart sunk. "Doesn't matter."

"Clearly, it does. You've got too much going on right now to add Baby Daddy Trouble to the list."

"Reece, he's–"

"Communicate. Sort it out," he advised, collecting his

medical bag and heading for the door. "Slow down. And when you feel ready, join us all downstairs. Everyone's in the kitchen."

"That's typical," she grumbled.

"True. But I mean *everyone*. Billy's grandmother has come out of hiding and even Elanor came over, though I think she disappeared as quickly as she came. She worries about you, you know."

Scoffing, Bre studied the many googley-eyed memories lining Billy's shelves. "She probably just came over to plant a wasps' nest in a kitchen cupboard or something. Or to set a bomb in a box under the Christmas tree, ticking down to Christmas morning ..."

Reece's smile was full of sympathy. "When you're ready, come downstairs," he repeated. "Holly's cooked for the entire farm, and everyone from the full-timers to the seasonal workers, to the families who started arriving today ... anyway, they're all awaiting orders. Willing to share the load. Because they love you."

"Really?"

"Really. Billy rallied them."

"Of course he fucking did. Such a white knight."

Reece gave her a pointed look. "Cut him some slack. He might not want to marry you, *Bruce* –" He used her nickname like a weapon, but his growing smile held genuine warmth. "That doesn't mean he doesn't care deeply. You've been best friends forever." He swept a glance over the room, taking in the remnants of their childhood littering every surface, before landing on the googly-eyes mistletoe. One of his rare smiles tugged at the corner of his mouth. "He deserves to know the truth, Breanna."

"He does," she agreed weakly. *Later.*

"Take your time getting up. Don't go too fast. If you feel dizzy, too hot, or too cold, sit down immediately. I'll be downstairs ignoring that tool of a TV show host and discussing Pantone colour choices with that gorgeous woman in white."

With a wink, he slipped out the bedroom door that saw much less action than the window, and Breanna marvelled at just how odd this Christmas truly was turning out to be.

As dusk approached, pinks and purples kissing the tips of the pines, Bre leaned against the veranda railing.

"What a day," she told the Evening Star, the first celestial being to greet her each twilight. Closing her eyes, she inhaled deeply – 'box breathing' as Reece had taught her after lunch. When the racing car in her chest slowed, she opened her eyes, using her listing powers 'for good', like Reece had taught her by listing:

- Five objects she saw:
  A koala with a Santa hat ornament

Bright banksias
Beer bottles in red and white shawls
A pair of thongs in the grass
The tongs hanging over the railing of the barbeque.

• Five things she could touch, and how they felt:
The hard wooden deck beneath her feet
The smooth, sun-warmed wooden railing beneath her
curled hands
The light breeze as it licked at the back of her neck
The lingering warmth of the sun that sighed from the
house as the cooler night-time approached
The fluttering of the baby deep within her,
encouraging her progress.

• Five scents that hung in the air:
The thick pine of the trees
Her renewed spray of deodorant only a moment ago
Cinnamon, from whatever Holly was whipping up in
the kitchen
Sweat and man, the official scent of hard farm work
And ...

Reece called it 'Grounding', a way to quell panic and remain
in a calm present instead of the troubling future by listing in

fives.

Keeping her eyes closed, she thought back on the day.

Lunch was better described as an 'intervention'. Her plans and schedules had been dissected and redistributed so Breanna's entire workload from now until Christmas Eve was to deal with Revv Ryder. Truthfully, it'd take all her remaining energy to accomplish this one task.

Piers had grinned and said, "You can focus all your attention on me now," to a multitude of rolled eyes. She hadn't responded, instead taking the opportunity to nap the afternoon away. It felt indulgent and entirely lazy, when Bre was accustomed to a faster pace, and harder work than being pregnant.

Turned out, growing a human was taxing. Her body needed rest – not that she would ever admit it to the boys.

Reece *finally* drove back into town, leaving Sharee, all soft cotton and softer smiles, to confide that evening, "What a hunk that doctor is!" before adding, "I don't understand why I was on your list, Bre. You put Holly and me in touch, and organised everything between us, however, now that I'm here and we're working together, there's really nothing else you can do."

Bre had moved to interject.

Of course there were things for her to do!

- Confirm everyone was happy with their new arrangements.

- Guarantee the house stayed spick and span for the

millions of photos, videos, and social media content they planned to create.

- Keep Sharee away from the alien slimeball who was Piers Ryder.

"Really, Bre, we're big girls. I am here to work with Holly, and Piers is here for you."

"Piers is only anywhere for himself."

Sharee considered this. "Possibly true." Her manicured hand waved all thoughts of him away. "That's not the point. Holly and I, we love you, but we don't need you. That sounds harsh, but I promise I mean it in the best possible way. Christmassy World Domination Via Social Media is our project. We'll take it from here, okay?"

It was hard to disagree with the woman, when she was so damn nice all the time.

"And unfortunately," Sharee added, "Revv was right – you should focus your energy on *Crank Shaft*. You're the perfect person for this Christmas episode they're filming, and I know Jaxon and Trudy are excited to work with you."

"But what about the Christmas Eve Party? You've never seen it, Sharee, it's *epic*! It's like Christmas vomits itself over the entire farm, like what you see in here, but for acres outside, and the whole town comes out to the farm to see it, and to feel like they've left Australia and entered this magical world Holly single-handedly creates. Sharee, that's exactly why I wanted you here. Why I connected you two. Christmas here is the second of two community events on Moonshine's social calendar. The Wattle Time Festival and Christmas at the Carmichaels' are what these people live for!

Holly's creative flair makes it beyond beautiful, but behind the scenes it takes a lot of planning. That part I do – taking the boxes of decorations from the barn for her to string up, liaising with the external caterers, once Holly's all baked out, calling the band, buying and wrapping all the gifts for the children who come, booking the photographer and scheduling family photos with Edsel and Santa ..."

"You take on too much," Holly had said, with a shake of her head. "I didn't realise you were the one behind all that. I can't believe my sons didn't help you!"

"They do. We all pitch in to move the heavy boxes, and–"

"They should help with the mental load," Holly said. "My boys aren't just muscles for hire." The disappointment in her voice was exactly why Bre had taken on these extra responsibilities over the years. She hated letting this woman down, her pseudo-mother who'd always been there for her.

"And moving forward, we will help to manage it all, under your express direction." Sharee slid a thin arm around Bre's shoulders, squeezing tight.

"But–"

"But nothing. Tomorrow is a day for editing, as Piers decreed, so the *Crank Shaft* crew will be busy. That means you will be free. So ..." Holly and Sharee exchanged wide smiles. "We have something planned for you."

"You're organising me?"

"We are. And it's a surprise. So tomorrow morning, when you're ready, you're coming with us."

"Am I icing white swirls onto Holly's infamous festive phallus biscuits all day? Glueing googley eyes onto all those felt kangaroos whose personal space was invaded when you shoved candy canes into their pouches?" Rhetorical questions, Bre was learning, could be fun – just not when Revv posed them. Then, they made her want to punch something.

"Nothing like that," Holly had smiled. "Trust me."

"Trust me." Bre repeated the words, said with such warmth earlier today, and brought herself back into the present, plucking at the damp clothing that clung to her skin. Exhaustion rolled over her in waves, and for once, she gave in.

Sneaking into the house, she made for the bedroom, curled around Billy's pillow, and fell fast asleep.

The next day, Holly and Sharee refused to discuss their plans, until Sharee rather ceremoniously announced, "We're going shopping!"

"IT IS TIME!" Holly's head perked up from where she was icing a red G-string and thongs on cookies that were roughly Santa shaped. "I need those pants back."

Bre looked down at herself, at Holly's life-saving,

bump-hugging yoga attire, the grass stains and dust hiding under a festive smattering of glitter from an art-and-craft session that had ended up resembling the carnage of a war between rival fairies. She loved Billy's nephews, but wherever they went, destruction followed.

After this morning's sparkling massacre, she knew she'd be finding glitter in her bra for weeks. The idea of shimmering nipple covers might entice Billy, but each tiny sparkle shard would make her sensitive, stretched skin itch.

"I hate shopping." Bre crossed her arms.

"You should go into town and get your phone fixed," Holly reminded her gently. "That Meredith woman who is working the bar at The Pope has started calling here, and she calls me, a fifty-year-old-woman, a 'girl'! I know she doesn't mean to be rude, but it is–"

"– frustrating. And not your problem, Holly. It's mine."

"I'm not adding to your list, Breanna darling," Holly added quickly, "but the phone is an administration line for Christmas Tree Farm business, you know ... But back to shopping. I need more flour for the festive phallus cookies. And you're with us, today, dear. No escaping our clutches."

Sharee beamed. "We'll go slow, of course! And while we're there, if you just happen to find some clothes that fit ..." The end of the sentence dangled above Bre's grunted response.

"As cute as you look in my son's old shirts and my yoga tights, Breanna Henderson, I think we can do better than that," Holly insisted.

"Plus, you'll need something for the Christmas Eve party you just mentioned!" Sharee practically sang, with an excited wiggle of her shoulders. She already had her bright pink handbag over her shoulder, car keys in hand. "When was the last time you treated yourself to new clothes?"

"New clothes?" Breanna thought hard as they gently herded her towards the car. "Does new undies count?"

"No," Sharee and Holly insisted in unison, each taking an elbow and leading her out of the house.

"I'm not a girly girl, you know. A few big shirts and shorts are fine–"

"Get in," Sharee ordered, pointing to the already open car door. "I'll get slip-on shoes for you. You just sit."

"I'm not an invalid!" Bre immediately felt like an ogre for snapping at the lovely lady, but Sharee didn't seem to notice, practically skipping to the veranda and extracting a pair of sandals from the large basket. They were Holly's shoes, but she didn't comment. Neither did Sharee comment on Breanna's already swelling ankles.

"We're going to treat you to some proper maternity wear that will be comfortable and keep you cool during this damned inferno of a summer. No arguments!" Holly held up her finger as Bre began to protest. "Or I'll invite your mother along. I'm sure she'd love to join us, given the opportunity."

"That's low," Bre spluttered.

"Aaand we're back to mono-syllabic answers." Holly beamed. "Lovely. Let's go."

11

A Filthy Wee Thing

Billy

He hadn't intended to avoid everyone, but it had been a blessing to spend time away from the buzz and noise of his family. Preparing the set for the family photos had him driving between the big barn that warehoused a North-Pole-sized collection of festive items – all of which needed to be set up for the upcoming Christmas Eve party – and Bre's pre-designated 'Snapshot with Santa' area.

With his body hard at work, his mind wandered to yesterday. Billy's old friend Reece Hargraves was an excellent physician. Bruce was in extremely capable hands. However, the overprotective caveman urge to throw his best friend over his shoulder and carry her to safety had been strong this morning.

She was safe, he had to remind himself. He'd seen Holly and Sharee drive off with a grumpy-looking Breanna in the back seat of the car. Being chauffeured around wasn't her idea of fun, but there was little about her current situation that was ideal.

Thank God he'd found her yesterday. He'd bundled her into his lap, willed the breath into her bit by bit. Instinct had driven him, with little thought to his actions. Without knowing why or how or what exactly was happening, he trusted the urge to hold her, staying with her until he knew for sure she – and the baby – were okay.

Two hands to touch Breanna Henderson with was a constant dream Billy endured, but when he found her in the midst of her panic attack, he'd wished even more for those hands to hold her, stroke her hair, and tell her that everything would be fine.

The god he'd cursed often for taking his hand was the same god he thanked for sending his brothers in that moment. The Carmichaels descended at once through the trees, a wild pack of tartan-wearing wolves whose instincts – and worried call from Billy's radio – sent them searching for their missing pack member.

No one asked ridiculous questions like, "Is she okay?" *Clearly not.* Or, "What happened?" *Doesn't matter, does it?* They knew better.

Hands came from every which direction, helping to lift a too-tired Breanna, carrying her to the truck, shifting gears and spinning the wheel, driving too fast across the gravel, skidding to a stop at the house. Hands offered reassuring squeezes of his shoulder and pats on his knees. Small hands held his much larger one, paint-splattered fingers curling around his square, dirt and dust crusted ones. Trembling hands dialled the doctor.

Once he'd stopped shaking, he made it up to his room, only to collapse into a corner, staring as she lay white-faced on his too-cheery childhood Rudolph quilt, her breathing shallow but steady. Her freckles blazed across her skin – constellations he longed to trace – but he didn't want to disturb her. She slept, ate a meagre lunch, then slept some more. He'd sat for a long time, keeping watch, monitoring the steady rise and fall of her chest, and the intriguing way her stomach rolled, the movements of the little being inside mesmerising him. He wanted to know how she could sleep with a child practising karate in there, adding it to the growing list of conversational topics he'd eventually address.

This morning, she appeared much improved, and his own breath came easier at the sight of it.

"Lunch time!" Seth said, wiping sweat from his brow, before, "Hey, Doc! You're back! Bre just went into town–"

"I passed them on the way." Reece smiled, his eyes flicking to Billy. "Came for this one. Thought it was time I caught up with my mate. Brought some home brew, too."

"Best doctor ever!" The twins beamed, heading for Reece's BMW and extricating several milk crates filled with brown bottles.

Large hands quickly passed around mugs of the beer. "Reece's best batch yet." The twins raised their glasses gratefully.

More men gathered around, Reece pouring healthy slugs into whatever mug, bottle, cup, or recycled jam jar they were drinking from.

"Take your medicine, son," Nick suggested, tipping his own pint down his throat.

Then there was his grandfather, whose arthritis-curled fingers dug into his sporran and produced a rabbit's foot.

"Ye dinnae need luck, grandson, but here. Just in case. Took me all night te find the damn thing in my suitcase. Eyesight ain't what it used te be."

It wasn't Billy who needed a disgusting amputated rabbit's paw, it was Bre, but mumbled thanks anyway.

"It's a good day to be here on the farm," Reece said, slapping a hand on Billy's shoulder as he took a seat beside him in the shade. "Breanna Henderson. Shopping! In town!"

Billy's voice was gritty and deep. "May God help Moonshine."

"Amen." Reece chuckled, raising his glass to the sky, drinking deeply. "So, what's your plan?"

Billy had to admire the irony. Plans, plans, plans. Where would he be without them?

Alone, a voice told him. *Without a best friend. Without a lover. Without a ... baby?*

Is the child mine? The recurring question beat through him with Bre's promise of *later* echoing in every pulse of his heart.

"What can I do? Reece, everything is ... different now."

"That happens, my friend," the doctor said, scratching at a sideburn. "We grow up, grow older, grow families ..."

"What can I do?" Billy repeated, voice thick. "For her."

"What you've always done, mate. Be there. Listen to what she says and hear the things she doesn't."

"There is nothing she doesn't say," Billy scoffed into his beer. "Blunt as a butter knife, that one." And he loved it, which made this new, suppressed version of his best friend even more confounding.

"That's not entirely true." Reece sat back in his chair, crossing his ankle over one knee. "She'll never say she's scared. She'd never admit that she's terrified this baby will change everything forever, especially between you two. And most of all, Breanna Henderson will never let you know just how much she cares about you, Billy. Don't look at me like that, I can see it – we all do!"

Billy scoffed again. Bre cared about their status as Best Friends with Festive Benefits remaining intact. She had already indicated her fears that the baby would come between them and their very casual, very naked plans. As for how much she cared for *him*?

"Bruce is a locked door at the moment. And I love her, Reece. I always have."

The doctor was nodding, absently. "I know. I think even Bre knows, deep down, though I'm sure she denies it." Reece's hand gripped Billy's shoulder. "I'm sorry, mate. I keep hoping she'll open her eyes and see this thing between you two that's always been there. Billy and Bre ... you two have always been great together. Solid, you know? Complementary. Hell, I wish *I* knew how that felt ..." Reece trailed off, finishing his beer and nodding thanks to the men as they finished their own drinks, fanning faces as they returned to work.

"She's due in February," Reece told him. "Just a few more weeks of trying to get her to see reason, and take it easy on herself. And you may need to get creative with strategies to keep her as physically and mentally at ease as possible. I'm worried, Billy. She keeps pushing herself, she's so worried about being seen as weak or needing help from anyone."

It was nothing Billy didn't know.

"We are planning a coordinated attack." Billy shared a few ideas from his family discussion last night, when she'd been in bed. "Everything in that planner has been re-allocated. Piers –" Billy ground out the name, "has been ... warned." Billy smiled at his three older brothers as they went back to work. "What will happen if he expects too much from her."

"Good plan. That guy is an insistent slimeball if ever I saw one. And, speaking of difficult customers, I want to speak with Bre's mum ..."

Billy grumbled, the reverberations loud in his chest.

"I'm no stranger to difficult people, Billy." Reece chuckled. "Still, Elanor's immaturity and lack of remorse is astounding. Your parents must've done something to really upset her, back in the day. The twins told me she stole all the fairy lights from the veranda last night. Also something about ladder theft and painting hairy warts and scars on dwarf statues?"

"Elves."

Reece shrugged. "So, Christmassy dwarves." The doctor's laugh lightened Billy's mood, just a smidgeon. "Those Henderson women." Reece reached for the rabbit's foot, nose crinkling as he ran one finger over its grey-white fur. "You'll need luck, my friend."

Absently, Billy scratched the stump of his right arm. Having been scarred by Lady Luck once before, he wasn't taking any chances.

Reece nodded, standing to leave. "I'll have a word with Piers Ryder. Surely between the Carmichael brothers' threats and a doctor's orders, he'll change his schedule for Breanna."

Billy had no doubt that Trudy and Jaxon, would be accommodating, but Revv himself?

He'd just been considering the extent to which they might need to stroke the celebrity's considerable ego, and how to play the macho-man game in just the right way, so the *Crank Shaft* host would consider the medical needs of his pregnant, honoured Christmas guest.

"Let me join you." Billy clasped wrists with Reece, who hauled him to standing.

In the end, when Piers started to sulk about Breanna's need for schedule changes, one swift look from Billy's petite Grandma Carmichael was all it took for the celebrity to do a 360-degree attitude spin, becoming full of accommodations and subdued smiles.

Despite the schedule saying he was editing, Revv spent the majority of the day by the pool, downing Reece's beers – a peace offering he'd eagerly accepted.

For once, Billy was glad to be separated from Bre. A day spent shopping was sure to stoke her fires of frustration, but it was a necessary evil. Billy knew she would have been wearing rags in mere weeks if an intervention hadn't occurred. Removing Breanna from the farm, from everything she considered an obligation or linked in some way to her lists and plans, had been as necessary as purchasing clothing that fit properly. He passed the day spraying weeds and cutting the grass between the trees on the ride-on mower, his thoughts returning often to her body's new curves, and how new clothing – while necessary – was far removed from the bare skin he'd rather see.

Weary, covered in perspiration and grass clippings, he eventually made his way up the stairs, stopping to tidy Bre's iconic Docs on the landing, scooping up a sock. How typical of Bre, leaving a mess like a tornado. *Typical me,* he thought wryly, *cleaning it up.* Perhaps she was right – he did have White Knight Syndrome, needing to fix and save everyone and everything, from a discarded shoe to a lost sock. Could he 'save' his best friend, too?

Stroking the rabbit's foot absently, he stood outside his bedroom door, wondering if she'd already be asleep. A day spent engaging in her absolute *least* favourite activity was sure to tire her quickly. Moonshine's Main Street was a long, wide, old-fashioned promenade of individual stores, different to the expansive multi-storey shopping centres found in the major cities. Bre would have been on her feet a lot today, though he had no doubt his mother and Sharee would have taken good care of her.

Pausing at the closed door, he listened.

She'd been snoring quietly these last few nights, hair strewn across his pillows like a blown flame, and dead to the world. He'd enjoyed gently sliding into bed beside her, watching the moonlight play in the lighter places between the freckles that cascaded across her shoulders.

Pushing the door open, he turned to the bed. Empty. Closing the door, he turned fully into the room, eyes roaming briefly before he froze, utterly stopped in his tracks, every thought in his head extinguished.

"Hi."

Unable to respond, he simply gulped at the fact she was entirely, completely, fantastically, nude.

"Wanna know the weirdest thing about being pregnant? Aside from causing a family of insanely huge males to go into full-on Papa Bear panic mode?"

Bre looked down over herself, hands cupping engorged breasts that sparkled with ... glitter?

"And aside from the massive case of raging hormones ... I don't think I can ..." she exhaled shakily, "I can't wash all the important bits – like my toes. I can't reach them anymore. Honestly, if something is on the floor, it's dead to me."

The laugh that burst from him filled the night, a too-loud

explosion that seemed to fade slowly into every memory-laden item in the room. She was ridiculous. Hilarious. Alluring, and with no idea just how deeply her very existence affected him.

"Seriously. Pregnancy is THE WORST. Wait, what ... is that Richard's lucky rabbit's foot?" She sniffled up at him, eyebrows drawing down, her head tilted when he tossed the rabbit's foot to the bed.

"Bowfin wee thing," Billy acknowledged, brushing a stray tendril of red hair behind her ear as he checked her over.

Goosebumps raced across her skin, each tiny prickle sending a wave of pure need over him. The need to touch her. To hold her. To wipe the remarkable, odd sight of free-flowing tears from her face. To roll the curve of a candy cane around her belly button then lower, lower, licking away the sticky trail it would leave behind. To lick and suck her labia while her fingertips buried themselves in his hair.

Peering straight down between their bodies, he allowed himself to look, to really see her. The supple mounds of her breasts, bigger than they'd been before, and the skin, tight and smooth, around the large curve of her belly. A darker line ran down from her belly button along the exact path he'd been imagining only moments before.

She was beautiful, radiant, and driving him completely insane.

His cock throbbed, probing towards her. "I believe that you feel bigger than you are, Breanna ..." His voice was thick and heavy. "What I see is beyond lovely."

"Not bowfin then? This ball with arms and legs? I feel like a skin-coloured Violet Beauregarde."

"Not an inflated Wonka blueberry. Not at all," he confirmed. "Not bowfin."

"That's a Scottish word for gross, right? The kids say it all the time when they're told to eat vegetables, so I'm kind of assuming from context. And would it kill you to use a contraction? Australia is the land of truncated speech, you know!"

Billy chuckled, the deep noise echoing from his broad chest. "I use contractions; however I endeavour not to. They make me sound like my Grandpa, all clipped words and *braw Scots*." He let the tail end of the sentence slip into the accent she openly adored and had, on more than one occasion, described as 'seduction in sounds'.

"I like your Scottish accent … and your kilt." Head down, she peered between their bodies, eventually resting her forehead against his chest and inhaling deeply. Aside from it being the traditional uniform of the Carmichael Christmas Tree Farm, Sharee had insisted they all take photos this morning, before travelling into Moonshine.

"I'm sorry, Billy. For yesterday. For everything."

The apology lingered between them, sudden, strange, and rare.

"Bruce." He lifted her chin, forcing her to meet his eyes. "I need to ask something."

An eternity passed before she looked up and met his eyes, but once she did, he saw it – the determination. She was ready for the question he needed to ask, and the conversation they needed to have. This was his chance.

If he inquired, *Am I the father?* she'd answer with honesty. He knew it. But …

Her tone was soft, slightly resigned when she said, "What do you want to ask, Billy?"

Swallowing the ball in his throat, his voice too gravelly and harsh, told her, "Let me wash them. Your very neglected 'important bits'."

Clearly, this wasn't what she'd anticipated. Blinking rapidly, her eyes flicked across his face, trying to understand.

"May I?" Billy softened his gaze, plucking tendrils of hair from Breanna's misted forehead.

"Let you … what? Shower me?"

Let me take care of you. Show you how much I need you here. How scared I was when I found you hyperventilating in the grass. Responses thought but never said. She didn't want him to say those things, didn't want his truth. His Bruce didn't need him to admit the depth of his feelings and change their friendship after all this time. Not right now, at least. What she needed was comfort, and to rest. Doctor's orders. She needed quiescence, and to realise she didn't need to work so damn hard for other people all the time. He saw her eyes flashing, reading the lines of his face and the set of his jaw, searching for words unsaid and trying to read his mind, as only she could.

Running his hand down his face, he nodded, fingers weaving through hers, tugging gently towards the ensuite he'd restocked with mouth wash and chewing gum, so she could freshen up after her bouts of morning sickness.

"I can wash the important bits for you."

At the door to the bathroom, she tugged her hand back, just slightly, eyes dropping.

"Do not get coy on me now, Bruce," he teased as a light steam filled the room and he worked to remove his plaid. Her hands were already at his hip, making fast work of one buckle, sliding from one hip to the other.

"It's amazing how you manage this on your own." She allowed the fabric to fall to the floor and brazenly looked down. Mr Grumpy stared up from his boxers, the evidence of Billy's arousal elongating the cartoon character's face in strange ways.

"Any man worth his salt only needs one hand, Bre," he murmured into her ear before rising to his full height.

Checking the water temperature, he nodded once more, taking Bre's hand and tugging her into the glass stall.

"Billy! You're still in your Mr Grumpys! Which, by the way, you shouldn't even be wearing under the kilt. Isn't it customary to free-ball?"

"This is not about me, Breanna." He removed the shower rose from the holder, waving it over her shoulders and arms in a smooth arc. "You're filthy."

"You are, too!"

"The only filthy part of me is my mouth." He sprayed water onto his tongue before spitting it playfully at her. She squealed, threatening retaliation, grabbing at the hose. Tsking,

Billy dropped quickly into a squat, directing the spray of the water directly at her feet. Jumping to her toes with a squeak, she pitched forward, hands coming to rest on his shoulders. It felt … right; on his knees before her, Bre's hazel eyes and wide smile beaming down like pure summer sunshine.

From this angle – hell, from every angle – she stole his words, leaving only primal noises that made him feel like an evolutionary regression.

Dropping the hose, he held her eyes as he closed the distance between his lips and her stomach. With a slow, gentle hand on her stomach, he pressed slow kisses to her skin, noting the way her eyelids fluttered closed and she rocked closer to his mouth, her hands gripping his shoulders tighter.

"Billy–"

"Don't cry."

"I'm not crying!" she snapped, clearly losing the hormonal tennis game within her. "It's just … You don't have to. You don't need to be okay with all of this." At his raised eyebrow, the brush of his nose down that darker strip at her belly button, she added, "We should talk. Create this Contingency. And I should …" she breathed deeply. "Do you want me to say it? To tell you?"

The paternity of the baby, she meant. Did he wish to know? *Yes. No. Did it matter?*

"Not here for that," he mumbled against her skin, handing her the shower head, ordering her to run it across her body as he stood once more. "Turn around."

For once, she complied, no arguments. Perhaps that was

easier for her, turning her back to him, ignoring the way his eyes bored into her, full of longing. Reaching for the body wash, he cupped his fingers, thumb pressing down to pump the perfect amount.

Shoulders first, Billy smoothed the foaming gel across slight and freckled shoulders, down the curve of her spine, then around the globes of her arse.

"Filthy," he chuckled low, delivering a light slap that reverberated around the shower stall.

"Tease," she said, stiffening and loosening all at once. This was so familiar. The teasing, the talking, the state of expectation. Comfortable, welcome, and so overdue.

"Turn."

Bre caught his eyes as she spun; he refused to loosen the hold as he pressed his flat palm across her collar bones, down the centre of her chest, resting between her breasts, where her heart raced.

They'd showered together before, of course, over the years, but he'd never washed another person, never rolled soapy fingers over skin that wasn't his. His hand shook, barely within his control. *Grab her. Hold her. Make her come undone.* Billy swallowed the rising tide of need that coursed through him.

Clearing his throat, he asked, "Alright?" He didn't need her anxiety to spike and her blood pressure to plummet while she was slippery in his arm. If she collapsed, he'd have no hope of getting her up with one hand. And there was no way he wanted to share the lusciousness that was a naked Breanna

Henderson with any of his blood relatives ... or anyone else for that matter. As far as they were concerned, she was *Bruce*. A mate. A non-sexual entity. *Breanna* was his. Bre was ...

"I'm perfect," she finally responded.

"I know." He cupped one breast, eyes closing so he could narrow his world to the exquisite softness of her skin and its weight in his palm. "May I admit something?"

"I always want you to be honest with me, Billy." The cringe that screwed up her face indicated how much hypocrisy there was in that statement, considering her lack of admissions. "And in return, I promise to answer all your questions honestly and without reservation, like I normally would. Fair?"

He could only nod, the closing of his throat complete as his heart swelled into the space where words should have been. Swallowing hard, he took a long moment to move her arm, angle it higher, so the showerhead she still held sprayed onto her chest. For a long moment, he scrubbed every soapy bubble down her curves, watching.

"I love how lush you are."

"Lush?" She snorted. "You mean fat. I'm a beached whale in the middle of an Australian summer, and I'm a mess in all sorts of ways, and–"

Gripping her palm he flicked her wrist, spraying water into her open mouth.

"Hey!" Coughing and spluttering, she dropped the shower head, wiping at her face.

"*They* are filthy words. Do not speak about yourself that

way."

"So bossy." Her teeth flashed as she grinned widely.

"You." He gripped her chin, dragging her damp face closer. Her hands fell to his hips, holding herself there, captured. "You are not fat. Not a whale. Not a mess. Not a disappointment or anything else you claimed that first night. You are a fantasy, Breanna."

She laughed, wryly. "The old Breanna is back, Billy. And she wants to remind you that she never shuts the hell up, and never holds back. So, I have to say, there's a difference between a fantasy and a fling."

"You are no fling, Bre. You are ..." *Everything.*

If he expressed the depth of his adoration, how every moment with her was heaven, and how there was absolutely no way he would ever let her out of his grasp, how would she react? There was no denying that the distance between them was down to his reaction to the surprise pregnancy. Their festive plans had forced Bre to reveal the truth, in all her naked glory.

She read his concern, smoothing the brows that had crashed together in the centre of his face. Closing his eyes, he relished her touch.

"It's fine. I'm under no illusions of what I am, Billy. What we are. I'm Bruce. Your best mate. I just also happen to have a vagina and adore screwing your brains out occasionally ... okay, Mr Eyebrows ... maybe *more* than occasionally. But still, that isn't fantasy worthy. We're a fling, Billy. Opportunity. Need. I thought we were on the same page about that, but ..."

He captured her hands in his. "No."

"No?"

"Bruce ..." Every child knows that being good means you receive well-deserved presents at Christmas, and Billy couldn't help but wonder what he'd done to deserve the gift that was Breanna Henderson. Why she wanted him, allowed him near her, he'd never know.

"Bre," he started again. "You have a knack for making me feel like I'm whole and complete, despite my disability." He didn't need two hands to touch her, two arms to hold her. They made it work, compensating for each other, exploring, experimenting, unafraid, together. The night she'd broken down that final barrier between them, proposed they become Friends With Benefits and followed him to bed ... it had been heaven on earth.

"You are my best friend, and when you moan my name," he groaned, voice so rough he wondered at her ability to hear any warmth in it, "I turn manic. Covetous." He was a man possessed. He silently vowed every time to worship her forever more, whenever she wanted. However she wanted him, he was hers. Completely.

"You are no fling." Billy cupped his hand beneath the shampoo bottle, pressing down with his thumb before nodding for her to turn once more, forcing his vocal cords to work as he massaged the foam through her hair. "A fling isn't when you can't stop thinking about someone, Bre." His body ached to be closer. To press against the curves of her arse, slide against her, force her silence as he plunged into her. His blood roared with the need.

"A fling is forgetting. It isn't constantly imagining ... constantly *remembering* ... someone's touch when they're not there." Tracing her ribs to her breasts with his wide, greedy hand, Billy pulled her back against the hard wall of his naked chest, and she huffed with the pressure. "A fling doesn't make your heart race so fast, so frequently, you are honestly concerned it will explode from your chest."

His hands roamed her breasts, pinching at slippery nipples, and she melted against him. Unable to stop himself, his hips rolled forward, Mr Grumpy's elongated nose grazing the curve of her lower back. Amazed by her, and himself, he continued to test the words he'd wanted to speak aloud for years.

"Flings aren't the desire to spend all your days and nights just being in the same vicinity, breathing the same air." He noted the way her breath became shallow, and how she pressed back against him, her own hands roaming her swells and curves right alongside his. "What we have between us, honey, it's ..." He had to clear his throat, to loosen the words around the grunts that her presence often reduced him to. Their damp skin slid together and against each other; the stall was too confining, too humid, all at once.

"This is not a fling, Breanna." *This is lust. Longing. Love.* Resting his chin atop her head, he was glad she wasn't facing him, seeing his thoughts with that magical power she had to read him like a book. She didn't want to hear those words, his true feelings. She'd made herself clear on that point.

"By definition, it is," she argued, her breaths quick as she writhed against him, wanting more friction and unable to source it. "You deserve not to be used." She was referencing the garage. *Use me, honey,* he'd said. *Take what you need.*

"It's unfair of me to hold you to any plans, or contingencies, Billy. I am not that bitch. I won't make demands on your time or your body. You don't deserve that."

"Whatever you give me, Bre, I deserve exactly that. Nothing more."

Whatever she offered, he'd take, like always. He was nothing if not smitten. Some 'Best Friend'. All he ever wanted to do was waste their days, lip-locked, curled on the couch, casually touching, feeling out each other, finding where the lines were, and where they blurred. Now was no exception.

He wanted to push her to the brink. Break her remaining barriers down. Prove he could last and go the distance, that he was never going anywhere, no matter how much she tried to deny that what lay between them wasn't just fling or fantasy – it could be forever.

It might have started as fun. Just fucking. The casual liaison and release they both needed. But over the years, their explorations of each other, blunt conversations, and obliterated inhibitions had paved the way for something so tender and raw he could only label it as love. He'd given up denying it.

"You're phenomenal."

She chuckled softly. "Phenomenal? Who even says that?"

"People who read." His touch was leisurely, every stroke

unhurried and luxurious, building the depthless well of need within him. "Whatever the way forward, Bre, we still have time to figure it out." *I'll always have time for you.* "Rinse."

Dutifully, she brought the shower head higher, the hose sliding between them. Pushing it out of the way, Billy pressed Mr Grumpy back against her, dragging his hand down her rich ruby hair.

"This is so nice." She told him, receiving a grunt of assent. "And I love this shampoo."

"That's why I buy it." He thought the words remained safely locked in his head, but when she turned to look at him over her shoulder, wide eyed, he knew they'd escaped.

"You buy it because it's my favourite?"

"When we were seventeen," he said eventually, quietly, eyes fixed on her skin, "you told me you liked coconut. It reminded you of that holiday we took the previous year ..." he paused briefly. "It reminds me of something, too – the first time you let me touch you, rubbing in that coconut-scented sunscreen, remember? You wore a green polka-dot swimsuit. The twins teased your lack of bikini, but that one-piece ..." He adjusted himself, clearing his throat once more. "So, I started buying the shampoo. For you."

Taking her other hand, and the shower head she still held, he slowly dragged the water spray across her shoulders and down the centre of her chest. Together, they swirled it slowly twice around her stomach, then dipped further. Wet red hair fell back onto his shoulder as he left her there, helping herself. She bit her bottom lip and he cupped her breast, grinding against her glorious arse.

"There's nothing I wouldn't do for you, Bre. Nothing."

She squirmed against him, her free hand arching up to twist deeper into his hair. Gripping her hip, he held her still, rocking forward. Gasping, she begged him to do it again.

"No, Bre."

"No?" The spray fell to their feet. Sliding his hand down her arm, he repositioned the jet between her legs.

"Not until you say it."

"Say what?" she breathed. "You want to know–"

The father. Hope swelled in his chest, his throat tense and tight. He hoped, prayed, that he'd been the one to create that baby growing deep within her. He'd never wanted anything with such instant clarity in his life. But ...

"I want you to tell me what is between us, Breanna."

Her voice wavered at the edges as mist rose and her legs started to shake. "Billy ..."

"Say it, honey. You promised to be honest, remember." Billy released his grip on her wrist to slide his palm across her wet breasts.

"This ..." Her words puffed out as her arse ground against him. "This isn't a fling." Her fingers dug deeper into his hair as he gripped and pressed, while her other hand directed the jetting spray, squirming. "It's ... something else. Something more."

She turned, dropping the showerhead. Gripping her chin, he dragged her mouth to his. "Precisely."

The kiss was savage and immediately deep. No more dragging this out, he stole the words from her tongue with practised sweeps of his. Grinding against her, his soaked underwear and a few explanations were the only thing between them, and it felt … normal. The resumption of normal, at least.

"Billy, I need – oh!" Before she finished the thought, his fingers resumed the shower's work. Bre fell instantly silent, her mouth fused to his once more. She thrust against his palm, and he could have sworn his missing fingers gripped her hips, dragging her body closer. She pressed against him until his back hit the tiled wall, or had he pulled her back? His middle finger moved inside her, while his thumb circled her clit slowly, pushing with the exact pressure he knew she loved. Years of fooling around and somewhat awkward honesty – 'a little to the left' or 'I don't like that' then, 'oh, god, fuck, yes! That's it!' – had been excellent practice.

She writhed and breathed, fingernails biting into his scalp, his hand, her own breasts as she moved and sought the release she needed.

Billy watched her, entranced, hard as stone against her soft curves.

"Clean yet?"

"N-never!" she panted, her inner muscles clenching around his fingers.

"Good. Because now you've been medically retired, I have plans, Bre."

Billy kept his gaze down, sliding his fingers free of her slick warmth, reining in a moan. The things he wanted to do to this woman. The way he wanted to worship her body, the changes in her, the way she was so strong, so resilient, so .... *Mine.*

Locking eyes, Billy brought his hand to his mouth, sucking those fingers like a starving man.

"Plans." And she knew exactly what he meant. "I may not have a ring, Bre, but you're right about one thing, I will take care of you. And right now, if you'll let me, I need to bury my head between your legs because you taste so fucking good."

He punctuated the last few words with deep kisses that made him forget why they'd taken so long to get here. She was warm and wet, naked and willing. It was a minor miracle he hadn't blown his load yet.

He ached to push his cock inside her, thrust deep, go slow, touch her everywhere, lick every inch of her skin, trace the thin stretch marks that had grown among freckles that had always been there. If ever there was a list he wanted Breanna to create, this was it – their Sexy Bucket List, a long line of dirty deeds and filthy words organised in whatever order she desired. A long, meticulous, dot-pointed catalogue sure to land them both firmly on Santa's Naughty List for years to come.

He'd do all that, and more, hoping and praying that maybe one day she'd want him with the same terrifying ferocity.

"This isn't a fling, Billy." Her words echoed, aftershocks to the tremor that had steadily built in her body. Trembling hands circled her bump.

"Woman," he growled, nipping at her neck, "you're my

undoing, and I'm here to tell you that I will undo you, too."

"Promise?"

His wide smile caught him by surprise. "I swear it."

The gushing water trailed off to a trickle as he directed her from the shower. Throwing towels to the floor, he created a path out of the ensuite, mumbling, "Don't slip, honey."

Something changed in her expression, and her body.

"What is it, Bre? Are you okay?" When she didn't respond, he gripped her cheek. "Bruce. Talk to me. Never stop talking to me. Please."

12

Something ... More

Bre

What she liked about Billy the most was the story his body told. The thin scars that intersected his many, many tattoos, memories of a childhood lived rough and outdoors with a band of unruly brothers. The art itself, sprawling lines of colour and shape so intricately designed that she had spent days, years ago, exploring.

He'd added a mass of smaller works to the collage, each individual image telling a story. They were a collection of moments and memories, he'd explained long ago, permanently inked on his skin, seeming to emphasise the magnificence of his body. Covering so much of him, they added texture and depth to muscles defined through hard, physical labour, ignoring the things he couldn't do to focus on the numerous things he could.

She stroked the little coconut she found in the collage, and something deep and sentimental clicked into place.

Was it for her? This tiny tattoo among the artwork spanning his skin? How many other tokens would she find, if she looked closely, now she knew.

You have a knack for making me feel like I'm whole and complete.

She entirely understood that sentiment, so boldly spoken. He was so much braver than she was. He always had been, even that day at the train yard, when they were only five. She'd held his hand, her palm slick and clammy, awaiting the return of the brothers, who she'd ordered to find help. Billy had been valiant, stoic. Her hero, even then.

Lifting her eyes, she marvelled at his mouth hidden in that dark shadow of a beard, lips so soft and perfectly shaped to hers. Yet another jigsaw piece that just *fit*. He spoke to her more than to others, said the sweetest, dirtiest things she'd ever heard. Made her laugh and snort, made her fight.

His words had never resounded so deeply within her before. *Not a fling … A fantasy … Something more.*

The labels terrified her. How would they survive this, whether friends or casual lovers or the potential of Something More, when there was a baby involved? They'd been so solidly defined for so long, how would they pave a path into a new reality as … what? A couple? with a child involved in the equation?

"Bruce. Talk. Never stop talking."

She examined every feature of Billy's face, those amazing eyes, the dark hair that rested on his forehead, curling down into a wiry beard that she adored more than anything. She could spend hours following the individual zigs and zags of each hair as it trailed down to his tattooed chest.

She ran her hand over his wide chest, dropping her forehead to the familiar ink. Instinctively, his chin fell atop her head, his hand curling around her waist.

She became aware that she should say something, but her new nemesis – hormones – were getting the better of her once again. All because of towels.

He'd created a path in towels on the floor so she wouldn't slip. The simple thoughtfulness of the act made her want to cry, which, in turn, made her mad. She wasn't a crier! Who shed tears over linen?! Frustration melted into guilt.

How could she feel this way, so up and down and sideways? One minute she was literally dripping wet, about to orgasm from a shower and from Billy's fingers, and now ...

"I've spent so long being SO horny, and now I'm just ... not." Tears pricked her eyes once more, regret spearing through her, but she forced the thoughts from her mouth. "Mr Grumpy ... Billy ... it's not you. Either of you. Not at all! I wanted you so badly, and I was so close only a minute ago, but the switched flicked. I don't know what happened! One minute I'm all revved up and ready to go, and the next, my libido is as extinct as a damned dodo!"

"Honey, I told you, this isn't about me. Whatever you need, or don't," he added, "I've got you."

"You seemed like you had plans, though."

"My plans ... God." He exhaled roughly, and she saw him mustering his courage to speak. "My plans will take longer than just tonight. Tonight, I wanted to taste you. But my tongue and Mr Grumpy ..." His mouth kicked up into a gentle smile. "We'll survive."

She melted against him, and his familiar body.

"You used a contraction," she teased. "Must be serious." His deep, rich laugh rumbled through him, like he was a purring kitten, pleased with her. "So can we talk?"

He growled at the rhetorical question, like she knew he would. The warmth in his smile, the tilt of his mouth, the tiny rise of his brows all said to keep talking. With a grin wide as the Sydney Harbour Bridge, she continued.

"Your mum helped me so much this afternoon. She advised on new underwear, and why the elastic band position is important for comfort and healing, especially if baby is delivered via Caesarean. I see that expression, Billy Carmichael, and I know you're wondering if that's likely. Honestly, I don't know. As you probably guessed, I haven't been great at checking in with the good doctor Hargraves. But your mum, Billy, she found pants with just enough stretch AND pockets. She explained how maternity bras worked, and how to feed a baby."

The list continued. There were so many things she didn't know, simply hadn't considered, or never thought to ask.

Things Elanor would never discuss with her, because they weren't 'proper' for young ladies to know. Bre had never been proper. Too curious, she'd needed to know everything, and never quite understood why she was punished for seeking answers.

A yawn racked through her as she thought about the strange turns her life had taken this December. The way the Carmichael clan insisted on taking care of her, but still allowed her a dash of independence. How Holly and Sharee knew that Bre's version of 'rest' was to keep moving, simply changing the pace of her days without asking her to do the impossible and stop altogether.

God! She'd even gone shopping! It didn't get more out unusual than that. Shopping had never interested Bre like it did other girls. The thought of hours spent trawling every store in town was as enticing as slamming her head in Edsel's engine bay. She'd never stopped to consider her clothes – other than whether or not they passed the sniff tests. The fact that Holly and Sharee spent that time with her, asking, listening, advising, making it bearable with frequent snack and water breaks, had her emotions on a roller coaster she simply couldn't control.

"Come here, honey." Perching on the edge of the mattress, Billy patted his knee and Breanna sank into his lap. His grip tightening around her, he gathered her into himself. *Home.*

"I'm already exhausted with being a mum," Bre admitted, worrying her bottom lip, hugging him tighter. "I'm exhausted full stop. I know Reece is right; it's just so hard to let go, you know? It's so hot this summer. Is it always like the surface of the sun? Or is it just me? And honestly, what is Piers' problem?" She ranted and cried, sobbed, and stammered, unable to stop her mouth.

Billy quietly held her, allowed her to speak, even though most of what she said was nonsensical.

"And if one more person asks me how I am, I will absolutely lose my shit, grab a chair and prepare for a World-Wrestling-Smackdown-style spectacle that I know Piers will just *love* to see ..." She sighed. "It feels so good to just get all this off my chest."

Billy nodded slowly, dragging a towel closer with an extended leg, gripping it with his toes.

"You're shivering," he mumbled, lifting the fabric around them both, cocooning.

"You're something special, you know that?"

He huffed, lips quirking among the wiry hairs.

"Honestly," she said, cupping his face, thumbs stroking his bearded cheeks. "I don't know what I'd do without you, Billy. I don't know how I ever imagined I could ..." *live without you?* She bit the words down, because that was exactly the plan she'd made for her future. Be no burden. Ask nothing, of nobody. Survive as a single parent.

"I am here, Bre. Always."

"I know." The words whispered out.

If she were quite honest, she'd sometimes imagined what a life together as a 'proper couple' might look like. How she'd come home – to *their* home – dirty from working in the garage and covered in grease, smelling of metal and engine oil and faintly of petrol. She'd relived the fantasy, in detail, imagining how Billy would drag her into the shower and lovingly wash away all remnants of the day, his fingers tracing each bead of water down her smooth, freckled skin, like he had tonight. *This isn't a fling* ... He'd been right, of course. It was a fantasy. But it was also something more.

"What is it?" she asked absently, drowsily, snuggling into his damp warmth. "This thing between us?"

Another yawn consumed her. None of the dates her mother had arranged had been like this, or hinted at the comfort she implicitly felt with Billy.

He lay her down, curling beside her on the bed.

"We are best friends," he whispered, words rumbling low and decadent across her skin as he kissed her temple. "I am yours, forever, Breanna. You are ..."

Unconsciousness tugged at her edges, and she wasn't sure, but she thought she heard the word "mine" growled into her skin.

With all the energy she had left, Breanna smiled, she dragged his arm over her. Comforted by his solid body, she ignored the sticky summer heat his body brought with it, drifting quickly into sleep.

13

Kill Me With Want

Billy

CLOSING HIS EYES, BILLY focused on the tiny movements beneath Breanna's skin, and the way his whole hand curled so protectively around them both. He hadn't lied – Breanna was strong and brave. He'd let her fight her own battles in the past because she'd been able to handle whatever his brothers threw her way, and there was nothing she couldn't handle outside of herself. That was the problem, though. Now, she battled with her own body. The changes in her physical and emotional capabilities were forcing her to literally tear at the seams.

That deep, Neanderthal urge to protect and covet her grew stronger each day. Beside her in his bed, curled around her, where he belonged, he couldn't help but stare.

She'd been asleep for hours, peaceful and sprawling. He, on the other hand, struggled to leash the energy that still buzzed through his system at her acknowledgement that their friendship had morphed into something more – something beyond a fling, beyond fantasy. *Forever.*

All night, pillows abandoned, he'd cocooned his big body around hers, Bre's back plastered to his front, the fresh scent of her hair in his nose, and the fluttering baby in her belly communicating in its own language beneath his palm.

There was a good chance that he was the father of the child, but he wouldn't force the truth. The baby could emerge as a blue-tentacled alien of seriously questionable paternity and Billy wouldn't love or accept it any less. Now she'd started speaking to him again, the truth would come. He didn't need to rush it, or push Breanna away again.

She was communicating. Open. Unrestrained. Perfect.

Since childhood, Breanna had always been straight up and down – a 'beanpole' many insisted. Now though, she had curves. Swelling breasts, hips that flared, and a tight, rounded belly that fascinated Billy. His eyes drifted to it frequently, the tight little ball that made Bre feel so much bigger than she truly appeared. He caressed her, wondering how it was all at once so solid and so soft. Bre, once hard lines, was all rounded fullness, and he wanted to fill her up more than ever before.

Gentle kisses woke her from sleep.

"Hi." The word was muffled by pillow and red hair. *Gorgeous.*

"Good morning." He smiled down at her, hair a mess across

his pillow, gloriously nude beneath the towel and blanket he'd dragged over them both late last night. "Time to rise."

"Where are we going?"

Fabric between his teeth, he tightened the first buckle of his plaid, speaking around the tartan fabric. "Edsel."

She turned swiftly, her eyes wide. "Is everything okay with my baby? If Piers scratched Edsel I swear I'll–" Her balled fists said exactly what she'd do, and while Revv Ryder probably needed a dose of Breanna's brand of medicine, Billy couldn't let the TV host take the blame for something he hadn't done.

"Edsel's fine, Bruce." The look on her face said she wasn't so sure. He managed the second buckle, quickly pulling on socks and boots. He didn't bother with a shirt, the cool air a welcome caress against sleep-warmed skin. "Come."

Wrapping herself in his crisp white sheet, she rapidly shoved her feet into her Docs and reached for her Shit Show Supervisor cap before flying down the stairs, foot tapping as she waited for him to descend. His feet simply wouldn't work as fast as hers did; they couldn't, with her looking like *that* – ridiculous and transcendently beautiful, all bare neck and shoulders, a thin sheet, boots, and that worn hat slapped on her head.

She snatched a slice of bread and threw it into her mouth, her one arched brow daring him to comment. Strolling past, Billy opened the door, holding it until she'd emerged into the early morning.

"This way." Down more stairs, round the side, and into the trees.

"This feels a bit … murdery." She laughed, breezing her way through the misty morning air. "Or maybe we've seen too many horror films for me to see mist as anything but evil, foreshadowing an untimely death." The farm was bathed in hazy eucalypt greens, and she drew the sheet tighter, demanding, "Billy? Where's Edsel?"

With a nod of his head, he indicated a bright red gleam through the trees. "He's waiting."

"For what?"

Billy only smiled down.

"For you!" Sharee's voice sung, clear as a bell through the trees.

"Come now, we've got your breakfast ready." Holly stepped from the pines, taking Bre's hand. "You too, my little fournado."

Dutifully, they followed Holly through the remaining trees, to where Nick, Edsel and Sharee waited. Nestled in a small clearing, surrounded by pines decorated in twinkling fairy lights, her vintage Ford Utility waited patiently. More decorations wound around the restored wooden side panels of the utility, outlining the vehicle in tiny, soft white lights and tinsel. Blankets and pillows filled the tray of the back.

"What's going on?" Bre's hand flew to her hip.

"A maternity shoot, of course!" Sharee grinned widely.

"I don't even know what that is," Bre said, turning to face Billy. "You did this?"

"We all did." Holly beamed, siding her arm around her husband's waist. "You'll want some nice photos to remember this important time in your life. Trust me. Each of my four pregnancies was different and I'm so glad I captured those moments. Plus," she drew Bre in close, whispering, "it'd make a lovely gift for your mother. It's a special time, you know, becoming a nanna."

Tears welled in Bre's eyes, and Billy stepped forward, drawn to pull her to his chest, hold her there. But she shrugged him and Holly off, inhaling deeply.

"Let's get this over with. I'm not used to having my cooch out in the breeze like this."

Nick coughed, stepping closer to Billy in manly solidarity.

Snorting a laugh, Sharee clapped twice. "Great!" She assisted Bre into the back of her beloved 1943 Ford Utility, and arranged the white pillows for her comfort, despite Bre's objections. "The sun's risen just enough for some amazing natural lighting, and the fog is making it all misty and gorgeous. We'll just zhuzh you a little ..." Sharee whipped the cap from Bre's head, tugging the hair tie from the bun and rearranging her hair in sultry red waves. Pinching her cheeks, Sharee forced a blush to spread among Bre's freckles and repositioned the folds of the sheet.

"I feel as though I have stumbled upon nymphs in the wood," Billy mumbled to his mother. "Secret women's business."

"I also feel like I'm intruding," Nick said.

"Billy, you're my biggest son, but you're never an intruding presence." She patted her husband's cheek. "Neither are you, my dear."

They watched in silence as the sun rose, glinting off the cherry red paint of Edsel, tinging Bre's bare shoulders in gold and the top of her head with a brilliant ruby crown. His throat closed around the compliments he wished to say. *Exquisite. Flawless.*

His mother joined Sharee and Breanna, leaving Billy and his father alone.

"You know son," Nick said, eyes on the women, "Having a family is a lot like building a house." At Billy's raised brow, he continued. "There are so many parts, all relying on another, holding each other up. Sometimes, things fall apart. Things crack and fences need mending. But in the end," Nick sighed, patting his son on the back. "If the foundation is solid, son, then that's all you really need."

With a squeeze of Billy's shoulder, Nick smiled, walking back toward the house. He barely registered his father's absence, transfixed by the sight of Breanna.

"She really is one of a kind, isn't she?"

Billy could only nod at his mother's words.

Sharee wisely made quick work of the photo shoot, sensing Breanna's unease. Fair enough, he thought. He hadn't given her any warning, and she was mostly naked in a semi-public place right now, with a camera in her face. Still, she glowed, a goddess among the pines. He couldn't help but stare.

"So many tattoos, Billy. I can't keep up. Is this new?" Holly broke his trance by pressing a warm finger to the space above his heart. "A bee? No, two! It's such intricate work."

He nodded, unable to speak, transfixed by the rising sunlight that bathed Breanna in a veil of sheer exquisiteness. His whole body ached to touch her, just to ensure she was real and not a mirage his overactive imagination had conjured.

Billy felt the warmth in the encouraging squeeze his mother gave his arm, but he couldn't tear his eyes from the woman in the ute.

"How about you two together?" Sharee beamed, lowering the camera from her eye and waving him over with one perfectly manicured hand. "Billy and Bre – the two Bs!"

Holly squeezed his bicep, voice watery. "Oh, Billy." Pride shone in her tone. "My son, and my daughter of choice. It would be so lovely to see you two together." He heard the implication for what it was – the simple mirroring of his own desires. "Please, Billy? A few shots for the photo albums?"

He didn't need convincing. His feet were already striding to Edsel, where his best friend perched precariously on the lovingly restored tray. Reaching up, he offered his hand.

Bre snorted, commenting about how she wasn't a damsel, and she could climb down from her own vehicle, but took his offering anyway, tightening the sheet around her. Her hands, small and rough from work, closed around his. As she pitched forward, her hair tumbled down over her shoulders and he forced himself to blink, to attempt to look anywhere else but at her. He couldn't. Gently, Billy guided her palm to one of his shoulders, her other hand finding its place on the opposite side. She leaned against him, eyes never leaving his, as his arm cupped her arse, lifting her from the tray.

Slowly, he lowered her to the ground. The air, already too

warm, seemed to grow hotter, denser, in the remaining morning fog. Everything faded away, the world narrowing to the points where their warm bodies touched. Pressing his forehead to hers, his words came low and rough, "Honey, you are a fantasy. *My* fantasy." Her eyes fluttered closed, lips parting, cheeks flushed.

"Billy, I ..." For once, words seemed to fail her. For once, words weren't needed. Perhaps they were beyond the need for that kind of communication. Her body against his, the way she held him, fingers digging deeper, the comfort they immediately slipped into, that electric charge that built slowly from a strong and ever-present foundation; it was all a response that didn't require spoken language. Not anymore.

Holding her tighter, he could have sworn he felt the ghost of his right arm slid into her hair, pressing her closer. A thumb that was no longer there, save in his mind's eye, stroked her neck gently in the growing dawn. Bre shivered against him, breath hot against his bare chest.

"These photos will be so beautiful," Sharee said somewhere in the distance.

Billy vaguely registered his mother and their guest melting away as Bre tucked her head under his chin, inhaling deeply, holding him closer with a contented sigh, arms wrapping tight across his midsection.

A long while later, Bre blinked. "Oh, they're gone." She chuckled lightly, pulling back just enough to reveal the glint in her eyes. "I have to say, that photo shoot reminded me of a slightly more tasteful version of that time you took those pictures of me nak–" she paused. "You okay?"

Throat thick, heart full, he could only nod.

"What other plans did you have for me, now, Billy?" Her words came out sultry, followed by a sharply sarcastic, "because I doubt I'm allowed to complete many of my own pre-planned tasks today, am I right?"

Nodding, he said, "Doctor's orders."

"I'm guessing Edsel will stay here until the showboat arrives with Trudy and Jaxon?" Her eyes searched beyond, following the scorched line of earth back towards the house. "They mentioned filming interviews in natural light, with the trees in the background." Closing her eyes, she melted deeper into his bare chest, so close to the ink over his heart. "I will need clothes, though. I refuse to be naked with Piers around. He'll make some disgusting comment and force me to punch him in the dick, then where would I be? Not featured on *Crank Shaft*, that's for certain. And Constable Kenneally wouldn't be impressed."

With every flippant comment, happy confirmation bloomed within him. Perhaps Piers really wasn't the father of her baby. The thought grew ever more unlikely, and by now he'd eliminated the possibility of Elanor's set-ups as potentials.

Billy forced his throat to work. "Bruce ..."

Am I the father? He didn't look at her, knowing she'd read it on his face.

"I ..." He cleared his throat, forcing his features into neutrality. If she was ready ... *when* she was ready ... she'd let him know. "I anticipated that you may desire a quiet morning, before the inevitable hullabaloo Piers will bring to the day." The words scratched out and he wondered again at how this woman, her closeness, made his heart swell into a chokehold.

"Reece-mandated rest and appearing on my favourite television show alongside its disappointingly cocky host don't really correspond." Bre sighed, searching his face. "And who says hullabaloo?" She chuckled, tightening her arms around his waist. "Thank you, Billy. Really. This is perfect. The only thing that would make this better is snacks. I'm starving! This baby –" she rolled her hands over her stomach lovingly, "eats like a horse."

There were so many things he could say: comments, jokes, questions. She'd opened the door for the conversation, but he couldn't bring himself to ask for the clarification he needed. With a raised brow and a nod of his head, he drew her attention to the cab of the car. Ripping open the red door, Bre laughed, extracting a picnic basket stashed on the seat.

"You know me too well!"

Picking up the basket, she moved again to the back of the vehicle. "Help me back up? It was super comfortable in there, with all those pillows and throw rugs. Sharee really knows what she's doing with this design photography stuff." Placing the basket onto the flat bed of the ute, she added, "This is all so thoughtful." Emotion gripped her voice, startling him. "Sorry," she sniffed.

Rare as hen's teeth, he deposited the apology in the vault in his memory. Somewhere along the way, he'd started collecting the words, as they spilled from her lips, hoarding them like treasure. Now, as she battled with tears she clearly didn't want, he could only smile at the apology, letting it rumble from his chest as he repeated it back to her. "Sorry?"

"Hormones, you know? They're crazy things. I've been sleeping so well but I'm still too tired to try and hold my shit together anymore. So this is what you get. Me. Unfiltered."

"Unfiltered you is perfect," Billy told her.

"You're ..." Whatever she'd been going to say was lost as he kissed her. Hot, slow, immediately deep. "Wow."

He inclined his head. *Thank you.* He assisted her into the back of the utility, settling beside her among the pillows a moment later.

"Can you kiss me like that every time you call me perfect?" Bre teased, ignoring his raised eyebrow. She switched from sweet to silly in an instant. "Okay, Yogi, what's in that pic-en-ick basket?" she said, giving him her best Boo-Boo Bear impression. "Soft cheeses? Deli meats? Sushi? All the fun food I can't have while eating for two?"

"Correct."

"Urgh. Good. This big lumberjack over here and me, your incubator," she told her stomach, "we hate sushi. We think licking an armpit is probably tastier."

We. Every time she said it, his damned heart skipped a beat.

"Wait, how do you know I'm not supposed to eat those things while pregnant? Oh! You read the book, didn't you? No, wait, don't even answer that. It's rhetorical, obviously. Piers must be rubbing off on me."

Here she was, the woman who didn't let him get a word in edgeways. Smoothing a hand down his beard, he tried to hide his growing smile.

"So what *did* you pack?"

"Your favourites."

"Really?"

"Rhetorical," he warned, laying three foil-wrapped options beside her crossed legs.

"Fine! Don't tell me! My senses are in overload at the moment, so I can probably guess with a quick whiff."

Indulging her, he offered each of three parcels for her inspection.

"A fresh gherkin bagel from Friday's Café! Yes! And ..." she inhaled the second option deeply, "Granny May's lamb and rosemary pie! Billy, you're seriously the best!" Twisting a loose hair behind her ear, she eyed the third option.

Go ahead, he encouraged with a nod, hoping her ability to see right through him wasn't fully operational right now. The scent of her shampoo clung in his nostrils, the warmth of having her so close, so damned naked and alone, was sending a deep sense of longing through his body.

"Is it ..." She sniffed, brows drawn down. "Okay, I have no idea."

Plopping the bundle into her hands, he gently tugged the foil until two triangles of sandwich revealed themselves.

"Your favourite," he mumbled. "Banana and strawberry on

multigrain. Sliced the strawberries thin and placed them evenly over the smashed banana. And there are gummy worms and a KitKat in the basket for later."

"Billy!" Her eyes glistened. "What time did you wake up this morning? This is ... You didn't have to ..."

"I'd do anything for you, Bre. You know that, and I mean it." Cupping her cheek, he tried to soften the rough edges in his voice. To hold back the rumble of need that coursed through him, and the primal desire to show her that need, to possess her. Rolling into his touch, Bre kissed his palm, her lips soft, warm, and wet, tingling against his skin. Her breath was shaky, small puffs against his palm.

"Stop it."

She grinned. "Stop what?"

"Reading me."

"You have your books, Billy. I have you."

"You do."

Sliding his hand behind her neck, Billy drew her closer, tilting his head to one side. Their lips found each other perfectly, years of practice moulding every part of them into the other. Her tongue sought his as he shifted her into his lap. Wrapping her legs around him, Bre settled, pressed close. His forearm pressed down her spine, gently urging her closer.

Breathing heavily, he kissed down her neck, tugging at the sheet with his teeth until it fell slowly from her body.

"Do you remember," she asked as his mouth moved over her body, "when I first entered that competition, and we spoke about me and Edsel trying to get onto *Crank Shaft*?"

He did. Vividly. About seven months ago, they'd been lying on Billy's worn brown lounge in his above-the-tavern apartment that, despite his best efforts, still smelled like the pub downstairs. Her head in his lap, she'd held a tattered copy of *Motoring Monthly* like a tiny paper shelter, rattling off her list of plans as they unwound from another long night tending the busy bar.

She struck each item off on her fingers, eventually moving to include his five, flicking each fingertip. Thinking back, that really should have been an early indication of how consumed she'd become in her planning.

"He'll come to town, we'll film the show, and Revv Ryder will fall madly in love with me because I'm the hottest piece of arse in this whole town." She'd motioned to her dirty overalls with fingernails circled in black grease that never seemed to wash away, then her messy bun. Billy had made it even more nest-like with his fingers buried deep, scratching her skull.

He remembered the way she'd moaned for a massage, how hard his cock had become beneath the weight of her head, and how he'd tried to remain her very best friend – not a jealous occasional lover – as she salivated over the idea of Revv fricking Ryder.

"Fuck, he's hot," she'd said, all those months ago. "And not just because he's a celebrity and probably spends thousands of dollars a month on facial products to smooth out every wrinkle and shrink every pore into non-existence. He doesn't even have freckles!" She'd pulled the magazine millimetres from her nose, huffing. "I must have his share."

"Close your eyes," he'd told her then, as he did now. Both times she'd complied, completely trusting, and his heart swelled to bursting.

Pressing and circling, Billy's fingertips massaged away her worries. Temples, forehead, beneath her tired eyes, he connected each dot on her face, drawing constellations across her cheeks. That night, and now, this morning, he quietly named them.

"Cassiopeia. Andromeda. Taurus."

Billy had often heard himself described as a 'man of few words', but it had always been a bit easier with Bre. For Billy, speech was often the result of thought and reflection. He had never lost his words to anger, like his brothers, and he was not the impulsive speaker Breanna tended to be.

Perhaps their communication came easier than most because they'd grown up together, or because for the longest time, she'd been 'one of the boys', his Bruce ... until suddenly she wasn't. She'd become Breanna, then Honey, a term of endearment that meant so much more than Bre realised, the bee tattoos over his chest beating with his very heart. Now, there was no word for what she meant to him. Nothing seemed grand enough to express the way Billy felt – had always felt – around Breanna Henderson.

In the past, and the present, he found words, naming the stars scattered across her smooth, freckled skin.

"Sagittarius. Ophiuchus."

"Such beautiful words."

"For a beautiful woman." The sentiment echoed from memory. Was there a reason she brought up that night they'd spent together? The words exchanged in the darkness as she'd moved his fingertips across her skin, begging him to explore the freckles and constellations that stretched across her whole body? Bathed in sunlight now, he traced Capricorn and Orion's belt, his palm softly sliding over the peak of her exposed nipple.

As that night and this morning merged into one, he watched Bre's chest rise and fall, each increasingly shallow breath mirroring his own. Her hand pressed to the bees, the space above his heart, he mirrored the motion. Eyes locked, they breathed, time stopping, folding in on itself, speeding up as her hand drifted lower, sliding beneath the hem of his hastily belted kilt.

Billy's heart near jumped out of his throat, while other parts of his anatomy – much lower down – jumped hopefully towards her hand. Brow quirking, she offered a small smile.

Everything that existed and mattered to him had been right there on that lounge, and now, here she was again, the woman of his dreams, so firmly in his lap once more.

Swallowing roughly, he continued, "Cygnus," like he had that night, fingertips tracing the constellations on her shoulders and chest.

"Fuck, you're perfect, Bre." His mouth explored her skin while her hands dug into his hair. Between kisses, he admitted, "I love it when you do that."

I love you. The words hung, he knew it, but would he ruin this moment if he let that truth out into the world. He chose another tack, another admission.

"Woman, the things I want to do to you."

When she'd first proposed an annual Christmas fling, Billy hadn't quite believed his ears. The girl he'd known forever had become a woman he adored, and there she was offering the one thing he'd given up hope of, lest he hurt himself with his stupid desires.

He'd never known a moment where he didn't love her, and he'd comply with whatever she proposed. Whatever she was offering with those big eyes and her soft touch, whatever she wanted, it wasn't in his power to say no.

Then, several months ago, when she'd whispered her desires, her hair had been just a dark claret slash across the arm of his lounge. Now, she stole the words from his mouth, swiping them away with her tongue, swallowing them, her hair a blazing curtain that shifted around them, blocking out the rest of the world as he lay back, allowing her to lift the tartan of his family clan, and dispose of Mr Grumpy over Edsel's tray edge.

"Bre." It was too gruff, his voice. Too jagged. He hoped she didn't hear the desperation in its depths, and the growling beast of his longing that had outgrown their festive friends-with-benefits arrangement.

"Is this your contingency plan?" he managed to ask as she slid down his body. "To kill me with want?"

"What do you want, Billy?" She paused, lips dangerously

close to the hard length he desperately wished she'd suck into that warm, wet mouth. "Tell me."

He did. Held nothing back. Gripped her hair and tugged, unable to stop, as she granted his wish and drew his cock into her mouth. She hummed with approval, pausing for a moment to encourage. "Keep talking."

"Woman," he growled, eyes rolling back in his head as his hand searched. "Bring that arse up here." He dragged her hips closer to his mouth. "Sit."

With a gleam in her eye, she positioned herself above him, an approving rumble rolling through his chest as she complied. He sent a quick thank you to heaven, relishing the feast she offered, before burying his face between her legs. Nipping and licking, he basked in the way her body responded to his mouth, seeking more.

He'd tasted her before, but never so publicly. In fact, neither of them enjoyed public displays of affection. The thrill of being seen – truly seen – by Bre, and possibly anyone else on the farm, was an aphrodisiac. Giving and taking, they rose higher and higher, in perfect rhythm.

A breeze slid like silk across his hips and he realised Bre had removed his kilt altogether, the Carmichael tartan fabric flung open.

Completely nude, they writhed together beneath the wide blue sky.

Very few girlfriends had marked his otherwise sterling public reputation as a stoic bachelor, and none had seemed completely comfortable with his nudity.

He'd assumed it was something to do with his stump of a right arm, a part of him more easily forgotten when he was clothed, but starkly different to other men when exposed. It was the only place he'd never considered covering in tattoos. Unlike the rest of him, the upper half of his amputated arm was white-skinned and bare.

Regular exercise and physiotherapy kept his muscles impressive, his shoulders broad and defined, but the arm itself ... he wished he had it now, despite the fact that Bre wasn't afraid to touch herself when she needed to, or when he commanded.

Breanna had always been different. She was completely, blissfully comfortable with his nakedness; wasn't afraid to explore his body. She didn't shy away from any part of him, whether there, or noticeably absent, and had a knack for accepting his bookish, quiescent public nature alongside the louder, more commanding way he couldn't help but conduct himself when naked and alone with her.

Her body shuddered and rolled, the curve of her stomach pressing into his chest.

"Alright, honey?"

"Better than," she told him, eyes over her shoulder. "But ..." She spun, adjusting their position, a wicked grin growing as she prowled, feline, over him.

"Billy." She demanded his eyes on her as she straddled him. Positioning his hand on her hip, she held her breath and locked eyes as she slid down his slick cock. Inch by inch, he slid home.

She always did that, filled her lungs as he filled her pussy, holding the air and him within her, tight, for a long while. Seated around him, she was warm and wet and so blissfully perfect.

"Fuck, Bre. Push pause, honey. Hold still."

"I need to make up for lost time," she told him, her breasts and belly a brilliant sight atop him, bouncing, curves so delicious he wanted to nip at her skin, swallow her into himself. Hinging at the waist, he attempted to rise and do just that, but she shoved him back to the tray of the Ute, rocking, chin tilted to the sky. *Perfect. A fantasy. Mine.*

"Slow it down, Bre. Or I'll ... honey, I'm going to ..."

"Come?" She laughed, the sound clear as a bell through the clearing, her muscles clenching deliciously as he drove up and into her. "Come, Billy." The tension inside him built with every word from her lips. He liked this new Bre, the one who kept talking, speaking her needs as he drove up into her. "Fill me up. Ruin me. What's the worst that could happen? I'll get pregnant?" She contracted her inner muscles, making his entire body jerk.

"Fuck, honey." Gripping her hair, he dragged her head down, meeting her mouth with deep kisses, pounding home, wondering just how much she could take.

"You won't hurt me," she said, panting, grasping her own breasts as his hand dipped lower down, stroking, just the way she liked it. "You won't hurt the baby."

He slowed, braving the curve of her abdomen. She held her

breath again as the weight of his palm rested against her belly. It was hard, so much harder than he'd thought, the skin pulled too tight over a solid bowling ball.

"Does it hurt?"

"No."

He didn't believe her. Once, when they'd first been trusted with the chainsaws on the farm, she'd almost cut her finger off. Even then, with mangled skin and blood, white as a sheet, she'd refused to admit to any pain.

"I'm fine," she said, smoothing the tension in his brow. "Better than fine." She held his gaze until he nodded, acknowledging, moving inside her once more.

His thrusts became more sporadic, eyesight glossing over until there was only her – his red-headed little spitfire who'd fought her whole life to be heard. The girl called too 'boyish' and headstrong, who took no shit and lived by her own rules. Her lips pressed tight, fingers digging into his hair as she let go, losing herself as he sought her out, over and over again.

For Billy, there had only ever been Bre. She had been constant as the stars and shone just as brightly. The whole Friends-With-Festive-Benefits Plan had been her invention and his undoing. He'd never been more grateful in his life than the day she proposed that idea, complete with a list of rules, pitching it as though to a boardroom of CEOs. Breanna Henderson was the most well-prepared and planned person he'd ever met, with the exception of that night on the lounge, when he'd been so overcome, so unable to control himself that he'd become a man possessed, unable to stop, unwilling to leave her until she was boneless, and until the supply of condoms they kept in his bedside drawer hadn't been enough. The phrase 'fuck it' had changed everything, their recklessness overshadowed by exquisite pleasure.

Her nails scraped at his skin, and with one more push, they came undone, messy, sweating, unrestrained, all tongues and teeth and heavy breaths mingling in the early morning. Red hair fell over his face as Bre snuggled down atop him, curling around his body, mumbling apologies about her weight that he could only shake his head at, lost for words. When she continued to shiver, he asked, "Cold?"

"Just incredibly aware that I'm arse-up to the sky, mooning the birds right now, while your cock is still inside me. Seems a bit ... exhibitionist, maybe? Like we're throwing amazing sex in nature's face or something."

With a deep chuckle, he brought the tartan up over the point where they were still connected, asking her to help with the task on the other side.

As their hearts resumed a normal pace, breathing slowing, he remained in her, his body humming beneath hers. The baby in her stomach kicked against his belly.

"That's amazing." He slid his hand between them, feeling for the flutters, completely smitten with this woman and her child.

"You feel that?"

"I do."

Her slow, luxurious kiss melted into something deeper for a

long time.

"Do you hate me, Billy?"

"Impossible," he replied in earnest. "How could I possibly despise you?"

"Let me list it out," she said, readying her fingers to tally alleged reasons.

Gripping her fingers, he brought each one to his lips. "No more lists. No plans. Doctor's orders."

"Fucking Reece."

"I hope not." He growled. *Mine.*

She gave him a pointed look. "You know what I mean."

He waited for her to elaborate, thumb swiping back and forth. Releasing her hands, she reached for the buckles of his kilt, fastening it over his hips.

"I never understood why you insisted on buckles and buttons," she mumbled, securing the fabric. "I know you struggle to do them one-handed."

"You know why," he said quietly, pushing her hair back.

"You don't want anyone to think you're different, or lesser. You don't want people's perception of you to change ... I understand that." With one hand on her stomach and the other gently resting on the scarred nub at his elbow, she said, "You're not less, Billy. You are so much more than anyone knows. So much more than I've given you credit for."

He felt the words lodge in his throat. *I see you, too. You're perfect. I love you.*

"I see you, Billy. I see the things you're not saying."

Does it scare you?

Her long-held gaze said boldly, *I'm not afraid,* as her hands worked their way down, through the hair on his chest, to the twin bees.

"I'm not going anywhere, honey."

14

Mother Dearest

Bre

BLISS, SHE DECIDED, WAS best defined by the delicious ache between her legs and the heavy weight of Billy Carmichael's arm slung over her abdomen. Her mind kept rewinding, to Billy's drugging kisses, the scratch of his beard across her highly sensitive skin, and the deeply reverent way he looked at her, like she was a damned queen and he was prepared to go to war and back, just for her. She'd never felt so loved.

Love. They had yet to share with each other, that one, silly little four-letter word. She eyed Billy, his eyes closed and features slack from sleep. Did she love him? Was that the 'more'? Or was this train of thought just the result of a years of familiarity, numerous epic orgasms and the exceptional fluctuation of hormones rushing through her system?

The powerful urge to find a bathroom flooded her, and with some reluctance she pushed aside the latest list that was building in her brain – questions about love and lust and the future that she wasn't ready to fully realise right now. With even more regret, she realised that the closest bathroom was just beyond the dark line in the earth, at her mother's house. Eyeing the burned boundary, she almost considered stepping over it, the gherkin bagel gripped firmly between her teeth, when,

"BREANNA HENDERSON!"

"Shit! Mum! Hi." She clutched the sheet tighter, hoping Billy had the sense to stay hidden and covered by the pillows and plaid in Edsel's rear tray.

Hands on hips, Elanor's lips moved too fast, voice so low, as she stormed towards the boundary line, frilly apron frayed at the edges and slightly singed, probably from her flaming fence adventures. Bre watched her mother's mouth spewing curses like a witch, or – more likely – praying to the gods of wayward young women who refused to become good little housewives with a penchant for neighbourly disruption, like their mothers before them.

A few paces away, Elanor stopped abruptly, calling over to the Carmichaels' property.

"WHAT ARE YOU DOING?"

Bre's shoulders rose and fell helplessly as she wondered when rhetorical questions had become so in vogue.

"LOOKING FOR A UFO?" she shouted, unnecessarily,

back.

They were too close for shouting, but Bre assumed her mother was making some point or another with her volume, and going along with Elanor's charades often meant Bre could escape these awkward situations a lot quicker.

"SAW ONE LAND LAST NIGHT."

"SO, YOU'RE BACK?"

"WHAT WAS THAT? I DIDN'T HEAR YOU!"

"IS THAT RHETORICAL?" Elanor punctuated each word, eyes narrowed.

From inside Edsel, she heard Billy's roaring, signature laugh, the sound like a bomb exploding around them.

Elanor froze, eyes narrowing further, as if she could laser-beam the car into a melted hunk of metal.

"WILLIAM CARMICHAEL." Elanor's voice was icy. "STILL KEEPING MY DAUGHTER COMPANY?"

"He sure is," Bre said quietly, unable to stop her mouth, drawing that piercing, disapproving gaze once more.

Elanor chose to ignore the quip she'd obviously just heard. "WHY HAVEN'T YOU VISITED US?"

"HOW ABOUT YOU STOP YELLING, MOTHER, AND COME SPEAK TO MY FACE LIKE A CIVILISED PERSON!?"

Elanor's pointed glare dropped to the pine needles and the ashy line that separated them. Right. There were some lines her mother just wouldn't cross – at least, not in the light of day, or without a pocket full of matches.

"DINNER! CHRISTMAS EVE!" Elanor crossed her arms. "TELL YOUR BROTHER!"

In a flash, she spun on her heel and stormed back the way she had come – back to the cold little house Breanna had tried to substitute with the big, warm, and welcoming Carmichael home.

"BUT CHRISTMAS EVE IS THE CARMICHAELS' PARTY!"

Protests were useless. Her mother knew of the annual Christmas Eve party and was invited every year, along with all the residents of Moonshine. Elanor had probably chosen that date specifically to disrupt any plans Bre, Seth and the Carmichael clan had made together.

Plans, Bre reminded herself, that she wasn't allowed to oversee any more. Clutching the sheet tighter, she gritted her teeth as the house rattled, the window glass protesting as Elanor slammed the door.

Unable to contain her inner five-year-old, Bre poked her tongue out, mumbling, "Seth is gunna *love* being summoned, your highness." He might even show up completely covered in horse manure, just to be told he wasn't welcome to the table. It wouldn't be the first time he'd gone to such extremes to avoid their abrasive mother and the father who was so unobtrusive he might as well have been absent.

"She's as pleasant as ever," a familiar Scottish brogue commented as a weathered hand clapped on her shoulder. Jolting from thought, she spun, nearly knocking the hunched form of Billy's grandfather, Richard.

"That rolling accent made it sound like a compliment – almost. What are you up to old man?"

Dressed in a fresh linen shirt and his Carmichael tartan kilt, he sent a salute to Edsel. Billy's heavily inked arm flew up to wave in response. "Glad ye seem to have sorted things out with the wee one yonder," Richard chuckled. He then mumbled something about finding pickles, sending a rare flush of self-consciousness through Bre. "Ye'll have a grand ol' day, now. Canna get any worse."

"What are ye doing, Grandpa?" Billy asked from Edsel, eyeing the man with suspicion.

"Me?" Richard scanned the vicinity, as though there were some other aged fellow Billy might be calling to. "Oh, *nothing*." His tone was that of a child caught red-handed, up to mischief. "Just takin' ma'self for a wee coddiwomple through the trees."

"Who says coddiwomple?" Bre shook her head.

Richard gave a laugh; a deep, rich sound that reminded her of Billy's, only more refined. It was a tone she'd always loved. "Actually, I have somethin' fer ye, lass, tis right here in my sporran."

She moved closer, to save him the trouble. "Not another rabbit's foot, is it?"

He let out a very familiar rumbling sound as he searched the traditional Highland bag he always wore around his hips. "Nay, somethin' much better! Aha!"

In triumph, he lifted his curled hand from the sporran,

holding what looked to be a tiny flower. No, not a flower, she realised, a small stone carved and scored to look like a clover.

"Fer luck, lass. Fer the babe and –" his eyes flicked to Edsel, "the pickle, and all it entails." He chuckled, and ran a finger over the delicate carved lines of the design. She smiled at Richard and he waved off her thanks, continuing his trundle through the trees.

"Is he getting stranger?" she asked Billy as he appeared, dropping a small, hot kiss on the base of her neck, "or is it just me?"

"Nay, lass," Billy teased, "he's always been eccentric. Seems to love you, though." He hurried to add, "We all do," before pointing with his bearded chin to the Henderson house. "Was Elanor–"

"Her usual ray of freaking sunshine? She sure was. But you know what, William Carmichael?" He grumbled at her use of his full name. "We could make it better again." She waggled her brows suggestively, but Billy was shaking his head, wiping away the smile that tugged at his beard with a swipe of his hand.

"Piers, Trudy and Jaxon will be here very soon." He dropped his mouth to her ear, capturing the lobe before adding, "and ye smell like me, lassie."

"Is that a bad thing?"

His expression boldly stated, *Not to me.*

"You need a proper breakfast." At his mention of food, her stomach turned, the familiar queasiness lapping at her like waves. "Additionally, it will allow you the opportunity to give your last orders to our brothers." She liked the sound of that, and was about to comment to that effect when he spoke up once more. "Then, Breanna Henderson, you're overdue for a nice long day of sitting on your arse with your feet up."

"If my parents taught me anything, William Carmichael, it's that idle hands are the devil's playground. Growing up with five boys proved that." She bumped his shoulder, smiling up at those exquisite blue eyes. "I have to keep moving, but I promise I'll take it easy -er … Trudy said she was going to mic me up today, do the interview portion about how I restored Edsel, how long it took, my story, all that crap. And Piers wants to film more today, so I can't sit through the entire shoot. He said we'd go through the engine, do some weird close-up slow-mo shots of our hands running over the wooden side panels, take the tyres off then put them back on again."

She read the unspoken question on his face, sighing.

"Piers wants it to look like the final touches are happening while he's here. Can't let a woman do all the hard work and take credit for it. He wants to do some weird car-lovers version of Cinderella being re-glass-slippered with Prince Piers in shot. And no, *I'll* be doing it. One, because I don't trust him with my baby. And two, I *can* do it. But I'll take it easy, I promise."

Catching her chin between his fingers, Billy stooped, meeting her eye-to-eye.

"I promise, Billy."

He nodded.

"What will you be doing today?"

"The usual," he said. "Trimming. Weeding. Something. Everything. You know Dad runs a tight ship, especially at this time of year. Though I'd much rather see you bent over the boxes of decorations in the loft." He smacked her playfully, dodging as she went to swipe back at him. A wide grin spread across his face, the beauty of it and the expanses of ink causing her to stumble.

"Billy, you really are ..." She knew men didn't like to be called beautiful, but that's precisely what he was. Her eyes roamed his body, searching for the words among the stories inked into his skin.

Some of the stories she knew, like the mountains on his forearms resembling Gorukkin Gorge, where Nick used to take them all camping each October long weekend as children. The hammock and palm trees were reminiscent of the place they'd hidden as teens, drunk and giggling, that holiday of their first, most frantic, passionate kisses.

He watched her, brushing red tendrils back as they blew in the breeze. Bringing his wrist to his mouth, he bit at the hair tie he'd stored there, before offering it to her. Gripping the sheet close to her chest, he preserved her modesty – or what was left of it – while her arms rose to tie the flaming mane into its usual configuration.

"And the farm opens to visitors today," she reminded him.

I'm aware, his face told her.

"So, you'll be in your kilt every day from now on."

"Correct."

"Excellent."

His eyebrows rose.

With a wink, she added, "So when Piers decides it's too hot at 1pm and calls it quits, and you break for lunch … come find me in the barn. You can flip that skirt of yours in the loft of the barn, and I can jingle your bells." She chuckled, her knees threatening to give out with the very thought of it. "But right now, since I smell like you, I should probably sneak up the ladder and shower."

"*Crank Shaft* awaits," Billy murmured against her lips. "And so shall I."

15

Small Gifts

Billy

"I'm NOT GOING SIT and pretend to have a civilised, grown-up dinner with my uncivilised and very non-grown-up parents," Seth declared, when Billy relayed the morning's exchange. "No way. Not this Christmas. Plus, I'm not missing your family's party. It's the highlight of my year, and I've just about convinced Sharee De Luca to be my date." Seth waggled his eyebrows higher with each of those last three words, clearly impressed with himself.

"Funny," Billy said, handing the tree net to the customer they were assisting, "the twins said the exact same thing five minutes ago."

Muttering under his breath, Seth checked the tree one last

time for the pickle ornament, coming up empty. Billy tried to hide a smile, failing miserably, before wiping his forehead with the back of his hand.

The morning mist had burned off and the breeze had died, resulting in a particularly blistering summer day. With every trickle of sweat, he thought of Breanna, hoping she was relinquishing her stubbornness, and that Piers, Jaxon and Trudy were being true to their word – forcing her to slow down.

"I don't know this De Luca lady," said the customer, a red-faced man Billy had seen occasionally at his pub. "But I thought you were dating that girl in town, Seth. Lillian? Laura?"

"No girls in town," Seth assured him. "Not for a long while, anyway. Though I did meet that new bartender Liam and Connor keep going on about. Meredith is it?"

Billy nodded.

"She's a firecracker! Where'd you find her?" Turning to the customer, Seth continued, "She's basically from that movie *Coyote Ugly*. You wait and see. The Pope won't be recognisable as the friendly neighbourhood pub by the time that woman's through with it."

"Luckily I am the owner," Billy grumbled, helping Seth net the tree and load it onto the customer's roof racks. "And I dislike change." Until he said it out loud, Billy hadn't considered just how astute Bre had been in her observation of this fact. Was this why she'd avoided him all these months? Why she'd wanted to resume their festive plans as per normal? Because of his own stubbornness and dislike of change? Clearing his throat, he shook his head wearily, admitting that the idea had merit. "Plus, nothing gets past my rather meticulous, over-planning manager."

"Nothing gets past Bruce," Seth agreed. "How can my mother just expect us to drop everything and come home for one painful dinner? And, honestly, mate, I have no idea how your parents deal with this Montague/Capulet situation my mother's upheld all these years." He sighed, continuing on an honest, frustrated rant that reminded Billy too much of Breanna.

"My mum is blatant vandalism and disrespect. The desiccated fences, and minor terrorist acts – like that time they graffitied the letterbox and the barn walls? I didn't even know my mother knew that kind of foul language! It was kind of impressive, actually. But if I were Nick and Holly, I would have ensured old Constable Kenneally slapped cuffs on her long ago." Seth sighed again. "I wish I knew how it started. We all have theories of course, but ... By the way, speaking of theories, I have one about why my sister snuck into your place in nothing but a sheet this morning ..."

Billy blinked slowly, waiting for the customer to close their car door and start the ignition before responding. "You literally sat bare arsed in my mother's kitchen only a few days ago. Seems this naked bug is a Henderson affliction."

"Must be," Seth laughed, waving as the too-small car drove a too-big tree towards the gate of the farm, where today's greeter, Nick Carmichael himself, would check everything over.

"Your dad's hidden the pickle really well this year," Seth grumbled.

"Your mother stole the ladder," Billy replied, wiping his hand down his beard, trying to erase the smirk he felt growing there.

"Yeah, well, what can I say? She's ... different." Seth threw the customer's discarded tree necklace into the back of the ATV. "Has Bruce, you know, said anything about who the father is yet? I mean ..." Colour rose in his cheeks, freckles darkening. "What I mean is, I hope it's you. Is that too weird to say? I know you guys think you've been so sly all these years, but, mate, we're adults now. You're not fooling anyone. There's literally no need for that ladder anymore. So while I don't condone my mother's kleptomania, or her complete lack of maturity, I do think what she's done isn't actually so wrong ..."

Billy clapped his hand onto Seth's shoulder, the smile blooming wide across his face.

"Thank you, Seth. That means a lot."

"You're my brother." Seth shrugged. "I hope ... I hope she tells you. One way or another, you know? Eventually."

"Me too, mate, but honestly? Knowing wouldn't change a thing." Billy leaned in to check Seth's watch. "Gotta go."

"See ya." With a wave, Seth peered down at his wrist before rubbing his hands together. "Sweet! Lunch time."

Days passed, the farm settling into the rhythms of all work and little play as Christmas drew nearer.

Trucks loaded with fresh seafood came and went from Warner's Bay, delivering stock for his mother's famous prawn cocktails. Boxes of decorations shifted from one place to another, the farm transforming each hour into a more dazzling, glittery, explosion of festivity.

Everything seemed to progress smoothly, until Iris, the local florist and owner of Bloomin' Brilliant, arrived. After speaking with his mother about arrangements for the Christmas Eve party, Iris spoke at length with Breanna about Jillian Maitland – Bre's best female friend and Iris' employee.

"Struggling," Iris explained, shaking her head. "The passing of her mother has hit hard, and she's retreated from a lot of social interaction as she tries to get a grip on her grief. I worry for her. Has she connected with you, Bre?"

He saw the weight of Bre's guilt in her hung shoulders. Making the effort to reach out, she messaged Jillian and tried calling a few times. She stared so longingly at her phone, waiting for her other best friend to reply, that Billy began to feel jealous of the device.

Each evening, he asked her to leave the phone with its shiny new glass screen, and they'd wander aimlessly through the pines, true nemophilists, haunting the trees. After long, heated days spent in the midst of noise and crowds, their evenings became an eagerly awaited cool, quiet solace.

Each night, they gazed up at the stars and Billy matched the constellations to her freckles, kissing the patterns into her skin like a brand. He'd leave imprints all over her with his lips and tongue, before claiming her with his cock when she begged him to do so. They chatted – everything from philosophical discussion to local gossip gleaned from Meredith as she tended the bar in their absence.

Often they shared thoughts about Sharee and Piers, how their respective projects were progressing, and how, after all, Breanna hadn't needed to be so worried about micromanaging it all. Billy waited for Breanna to broach the subject of her baby's father, but there was nothing beyond general discussions of her pregnancy. Reece came and went, concerned about her ability to cope with the summer heatwave.

"It doesn't matter. It will not change anything," Billy repeated to the doctor, head hung.

"It won't change anything," Reece acknowledged lightly, "but still, you should probably know."

As Christmas Eve drew nearer, Bre settled into a pattern that merged productivity with leisure. Filming with Piers consumed her mornings, while the thermometers read just below a million degrees. Then, the crew would spend their afternoons editing in the van, or on their laptops in the cool air-conditioning of the house, and Piers would lounge by the Carmichaels' pool, scrolling his phone constantly, looking utterly bored and often a little intoxicated.

Bre would assist Billy's mother, grandmother and Sharee each afternoon, creating the candy cane bonbonnieres, making wreaths of eucalyptus, banksia and flowering gum, and ordering Graham, Liam, Connor and Seth to move this box or that ridiculously sized ornament two centimetres to the left so it was perfect for Sharee's shots of the big event. Still contributing, and able to assert herself, Bre seemed content, the swell of her stomach growing each day.

"You Carmichaels really know how to throw a party!" Sharee chirped. The woman was joy personified. Unlike Revv, she was a sheer delight to be around. "I can't wait for the big event!" Sharee continued, pleasure and pride in her voice as she eyed the big barn that would house the annual gathering.

"It will make for one hell of a blitz!" Holly laughed, showing the influx of page visits and social media followers to Billy's reserved grandmother, who was up to her elbows in dough for yet another batch of his mother's festive phallus cookies. "Sharee, you have been an absolute delight! Thank you for all that you've done. The insight. The kindness. Breanna's dr–"

Both Sharee and Breanna shushed her, Holly's mouth slamming shut. Billy's eyebrows drew up, but all the women refused to look at him, or acknowledge his curiosity. All except Bre. Snagging him with those glinting hazel eyes, she only shrugged, oddly wordless, before going back to glueing Santa hats to tiny koala and kangaroo ornaments.

"I can wait," he told them, eyes still locked on Bre. "I am sure it will be worth it."

"Holy Jesus in a manger, I did it!" Bre stormed inside, arm held high like Lady Liberty.

"You did ... what?" Graham asked, dropping the *Moonshine Gazette* to the table.

"Pick your nose?"

"Pick a wedgie!"

"Pick a–"

The children's guesses grew increasingly revolting.

"Hush, you heathens!" Bre grinned widely at the assembly. "I found the pickle!"

"No way!" Max exclaimed.

Lachlan smacked his forehead. "Aw, c'mon!"

"That's *so* unfair!" Leo added.

Only Billy wasn't surprised that Breanna had managed to locate the ornament. They had taken their evening walks when the lights from the windows shone at just the right angle to catch the glint of green in the trees closest to the house. She'd been sneaky, pretending she hadn't seen the pickle two nights in a row, before mysteriously disappearing this morning for an 'additional coddiwomple', returning with it in her hand, wearing a grin bigger than the house.

"Good for you, Aunty Bre," piped up the quiet voice of ten-year-old Callum.

"Thank you, sweetie." She laughed, and raised her voice. "You know what that means?"

"Favours," grumbled the adults, sounding like a group of misbehaving schoolkids who'd been kept in by their teacher at playtime.

"My area of expertise." Piers winked, and was completely ignored by everyone in the room. Even the children had stopped giving him the celebrity treatment he so badly craved.

"Actually, I was really excited to open a present." Bre grinned at the children who'd already risen from the table, bouncing on the balls of their feet. "C'mon, kids, you can help me choose which gift I'm going to open early!"

The screaming that ensued was loud enough for the townsfolk of Moonshine, a few kilometres away, to hear.

"Settle down, wee ones! Yer great grannie is asleep!" Richard scolded the youngsters with a grin, unsuccessfully attempting to trip them with his cane as they scrambled to the base of the beautiful tree that now dominated their living room.

"Which one will you pick?" wondered little Leo, wide eyed. "There are so many!"

"Most are for us, numbskull," Max scoffed, full of eight-year-old sass.

"This one says 'Bruce'. That's you, right, Aunty Bre?"

"Sure is, Lachlan. Good reading!"

The three-year-old beamed.

"I think you should open this one," Callum offered, sliding a suspiciously large, suspiciously wiggly gift her way.

"If you've put a snake in there, Callum Carmichael ..." Bre warned. The children drew back, squealing, Callum swearing he didn't.

"Connor? Liam? Is this one of your pranks?" She eyed the

shifting box.

"Never seen it before, Bruce," the twins both claimed.

Billy saw her consider them, the twins' genuinely curious expressions eventually convincing her of their innocence. Nick and Holly drew near, eyeing the red-bow-topped package that rustled with each shaking motion.

"Neither have I," Seth commented, approaching cautiously.

No one expected Billy to respond, which was perfect. He was a terrible liar. "Open it," he encouraged, adding, "carefully."

Never one to back down from a challenge, his formidable best friend squared her shoulders. Plopping cross-legged before the big red bow, she tugged gently, evidently expecting something to explode out.

"Oh my god!"

"What is it?!" the children chorused, peering closer, despite the adults' wary attempts to keep them well back.

"It's a puppy! I always wanted a puppy!" Diving into the now open box, Breanna extricated a fluffball of black, white and brown, pure joy lighting her face from within.

"He's your pickle present," Billy said quietly, pleased with himself.

"A Kelpie? No ... Australian Shepherd." Nick nodded, approvingly. "Probably the only dog who could keep pace with you, Breanna. Good farm dogs. Great companions."

"When Reece and I stole your planner," Billy told her, running his hand over the pup's head, "we found your Life Plan."

As the furball licked her vigorously, tears welled. "I remember … my Steps to Living a Happy Life. The first thing I wrote was 'Adopt a dog'." She laughed lightly, snuggling the pup before looking up, up, meeting Billy's eyes. "Thank you, Billy. For everything."

"You are most welcome, honey."

He'd never used the endearment in front of his family before, but nobody reacted.

"Aye, what a clever lad ye are." His grandfather chuckled as he made his way past, walking cane tapping his ankle lightly. "Yon lassie will be able te sit for hours now, doin' nought but fussing and bossing that pup, instead of yer brothers." He chuckled again. "Clever man indeed."

With a small nod, Billy acknowledged the praise. What he didn't confess was that he had many, many other plans for Breanna so she could tick off what remained of her first and most important list – *Steps to living a Happy Life.*

1- Adopt a dog.

2- Travel the world.

3- Never. Have. Kids.

4- Always come home for Christmas.

Like all her plans this Christmas, the list had changed somewhat, but Billy would ensure that these items were struck off, one way or another. All he needed was a little time.

16

The 'Wild Child'

Bre

"DOES MY BUM LOOK big in these arseless Elf chaps?" Bre queried, peeking over her shoulder as she presented her posterior for his inspection. "I want to look good for Mum's big dinner tonight."

Wiping his hand down his face, he struggled – failing – to hide his wide smile. With a flash of white teeth, he loosed a booming laugh that rippled through her blood and made the sleeping babe in her belly startle, turning towards the sound.

"I know, right. My darling mother will adore them. Unfortunately, her reaction to any of my life choices is an expression of disappointment I've seen so often, I could probably mould it into a clay mask. Do you think Sharee, with all her talents, could make that into a viral Instagram product?" She sighed as Billy rose from the bed, where he was reading to her from *What to Expect When You're Expecting*. Wrapping his arm around her, he drew her close, comforting and kissing her temple. Reaching up, she gripped his stump, dragging him closer, pulling him around her like a big, protective cape.

"Thanks, but no thanks. I can see you thinking about offering – again – to go with me. It's fine. Seth will be there, and Dad." She mustn't forget her father, the barely-there ghost of Christmases past and present. "As we speak, Mum's probably rushing him into the shower and, what did you call it – *scurryfungle?* Tidying the house in a mad rush just before guests arrive?" She chuckled. "You and your strange collection of words."

Keep talking, she told herself, feeling the panic rise. *Just keep talking, let it out, and breathe ...*

A yawn filled the room. Maybe her growing exhaustion would curse her with a thousand-year sleep, and she'd miss the year's least-anticipated event altogether.

"Should you need me, Bre ..." The depth of his tone, the softness she heard, made her heart twist in her chest.

"Your Spidey Senses will tingle, I'm sure. Plus –" She bent down, hoisting the pup from the floor, where it had been happily chewing on the edges of her discarded planner. Weird how the sight of tiny shreds of masticated paper made her happy. In fact, she was rather glad of that mess, and the relief it had brought. "Mr Pickles here will need you to stay and take him for a wee coddiwomple –" she air quoted the term, "– so he can *wee* anywhere that isn't in my boots!"

Stepping into the warm, wet puddle this morning was not an experience she'd like to repeat. Ruffling his ears teasingly, she plopped the Australian Shepherd into the waiting crook of Billy's arm. Heading for the door, Bre paused as he called her name.

Turning, she couldn't help but smile at the sight before her. The pup was nibbling at the ends of Billy's beard, his white button-down shirt open, exposing the tattoos she'd been slowly cataloguing over the past few weeks. Her eyes travelled down the flat plane of his stomach to his kilt, the smooth calves that emerged below, and the bare feet, surrounded by shredded plans. Her stomach rolled, heart beating faster, louder in her ears. *Breathe.*

"Good luck." Even with his one arm full of puppy, he managed to flick something her way. She caught the little blur of grey, laughing when she realised what it was.

"Richard's rabbit's foot! Gee, thanks, Billy."

"I mean it," he said, placing the puppy on the ground so he could run that hand down his beard. "Good luck. You will need it if you go dressed as you are."

"Right. The chaps."

Changing quickly, she tried to ignore the heat in his eyes, the way his dark pupils seemed to eclipse the brilliant blue of his irises. With a not-so-silent prayer of thanks to Holly, she slid into the world's most comfortable stretch pants and a halter that seemed to balance her out, the exposure of her white shoulders drawing attention from the roundness of everything south of her chin. At least, that's what Sharee had claimed. Piers, oddly enough, had agreed in a rare moment of genuine and well-intentioned flattery, and as she looked in the mirror, Breanna had to agree.

"I actually look good," she commented, tying her hair up and nodding to her reflection.

The heat in Billy's gaze told her, *Always.*

"Now, be good boys." She playfully patted both Mr Pickles and Billy on the head. "Mumma's gotta go speak to the witch in the woods. Slay dragons. Build a rocket to the moon, shaped like a 1943 Ford Utility who is going to be on national TV in a few days! You know, all the usual damsel in distress stuff."

"Later." Billy nodded, his expression full of adoration that had her chest tightening.

Later ... She really needed to tell him. Get it over with. She wasn't a damsel, and he refused to be a white knight. She could tell him about the father of her baby, and Billy wouldn't feel obligated to change anything about their relationship. He wouldn't feel trapped by the child, not when they'd mutually agreed that their friendship had outgrown its rules and boundaries and had become something More.

"Later." She nodded, exiting before her eyes decided to leak all over again.

So much had changed. So much was still in the process of changing. But Billy and Bre, they were solid. Which was fortunate, because as she crossed the scorched boundary line between the Carmichael and Henderson properties, she'd need that strength to survive this dinner.

"We're glad you could come. Both of you." Elanor's clipped tone didn't sound glad. Not at all. Breanna and her brother exchanged a glance.

The oppressive heat of the day barely stirred in the oppressive little dining room as the ceiling fan struggled around in wobbly rotations. Elanor had attempted a festive scene, a twiggy 20-year-old plastic tree propped in the corner, shedding fine, dark-green tinsel shards on the floor that looked like it hadn't been vacuumed in years. Cheap bon-bons sat at the head of each place setting, above mismatched cutlery, and ancient, chipped plates.

"Thanks for having us, Mum." Seth tried a smile; it looked as though three-year-old Leo Carmichael had drawn a line on his face. It was the exact look Elanor had given Seth when he arrived, still in his workwear – heavy duty shorts and a shirt made of Carmichael tartan. Bre was glad that he'd at least forgone the traditional kilt. Having her brother's junk hanging free at yet another dining table was something she'd rather not have thought about.

"We're glad you agreed to bring the dinner forward by

a few days," Seth continued, "so we could still attend the Carmichaels'–"

Elanor's sharp glance had his lips pressing tight.

At the head of the table, their father dutifully chewed his peas, eyes glued to the plate. Despite the summer heat, Elanor had insisted on cooking a roast meal – a turkey so small and dry it scraped like sandpaper on Bre's tongue. The potatoes were charred to crispy black mounds that grated like charcoal between her teeth. Fresh peas, overcooked to mush, were spotted around the plate under a slathering of thick gravy that tasted to Bre like a burnt concoction of beef stock and vinegar – too salty and tangy for the lacklustre meal.

"Yes. Well. We will take any time you offer us." Her smile was brief and tight-lipped. "And it was time we all sat down to talk."

"You mean *we* as in you and me, right, Mum?" said Bre.

"If you decide to finally talk like a *civilised* young lady, I'll listen," Elanor said.

Seth's face said *Here we go*. "Mum ..."

Her eyes remained firmly on Breanna. "Don't you look lovely tonight, Breanna," she said, her voice flat.

"She does, actually, right Dad?" Seth found no allies. "And she's doing really well–"

"I wouldn't know."

"C'mon, Mum."

Breathe, just breathe.

"Your sister clearly doesn't know how to pick up the phone and call her mother. She does, *however*, know how to flirt her days away with that Revv-Head Ryder, heavily pregnant and completely unmarried, and on national television no less!"

"That's not a crime," Bre managed between clenched teeth. "At least, not since the eighteenth century."

"There you go with that reckless, uncouth attitude. You didn't even deny it! I saw the trailers, young lady! The way you throw yourself at that man–"

"Mum, you're being unfair," Seth interjected. "I'm equally single and older than Bre, and Revv's been a bit of a jerk, but he's mostly kept to himself these past few weeks, since the boys all–"

Bre's eyebrows rose. "Since the boys all *what*?"

Colour bloomed in Seth's cheeks, blurring the spray of freckles that had multiplied recently. "Since we ... threatened to yabby-pump him if he kept his attitude up."

"Yabby pump?" Elanor's nose screwed up.

"Hold him down. Punch up and down, like what your hand does when you're pumping for yabbies," Bre explained with a casual wave of her hand. "I can fight my own fights, Seth. Billy can, too."

"Breanna!"

"What? I wasn't the one who threatened to do it!"

"Seth is different," Elanor snapped. "He wouldn't actually do it. But it sounds like you know too much about this violence, young lady. You are the wild one."

"THE WILD ONE?" Bre was on her feet, palms planted on the table. Her father kept chewing, eyes downcast. "For knowing how to throw a punch? Or for becoming a mechanic instead of a wife? I know you've always wished I was more like you."

"Being a wife, or a *mother*, for that matter, isn't a terrible career choice, Breanna." Her sharp glance cut down to Bre's bulging stomach.

She felt sick. Weak. Dizzy.

Breathe.

"Do you know who the father is?" Elanor addressed the question to Seth, whose mouth opened to reply, then froze. Her pitch grew higher. "Do *you*?" Elanor asked her daughter.

"Yes. I do. Because despite the several *horrible* dates you insisted on organising for me, mother, in this weird quest to find me a suitable husband, only one man showed up at The Pope who was decent enough to ever consider. Only one man in that whole tavern gave a shit about me and what I actually wanted!"

"And who was that?" Elanor demanded curtly, her mouth and eyes pinched.

"NONE OF YOUR DAMNED BUSINESS!" Breanna swayed with the sudden explosion of her voice. "Mum, no offence, but you and me? We're done. Okay? I love you, but I don't understand you, and the way you make me feel ..." She shuddered, and then Seth was standing beside her, his hand around her back, supporting her. "I'm about to have a baby. It should be the happiest time of my life. But you make it so stressful that I feel physically ill. I thought it was the food but ..." She shook her head as her mother's jaw dropped, eyes darting to the husband who was still pushing mushy peas around his plate, his own eyes downcast. "And it isn't worth it to be here. I'm not tiptoeing around it anymore. It's not worth another panic attack–"

"Another?"

"See you have no idea, Mum. No idea who I am and what's going on with me. It's okay. We're just different. I don't hate you, but this … this isn't working." Turning to Seth, she said, "I need to leave."

Straightening to her full height, she cast weary eyes on her father, who was still refusing to engage in the conversation, and her mother, who demanded the whole world centre around her.

"There's no use pretending we have anything in common, other than a few genes." Her hand roamed her stomach, and the growing baby housed there. "I'm going to be a damned good mother. With a present husband." Her eyes watered and she forced herself not to look at her father. "In a home full of laughter and teasing and love." Her tongue stumbled on the word; her brain filled with visions of Billy and the baby. "And I might not have it now, or even two years from now, but I'll have it all, eventually, because I deserve it."

"Breanna." Elanor followed them to the door. "Seth! Wait!" She dropped back as they exited the house, like she was too scared to step beyond the doorway, watching them stalk off.

"Bre, I'm so sorry." Seth whispered at Bre's back, voice thick.

"It's fine." She sniffled, slowing. "Nothing unexpected. I need …"

He nodded, understanding. *Space. Quiet.*

"Take an ATV. Go for a ride. I'll let Billy know. Hey ..." Safely on the Carmichael side of the burned boundary, Seth took his sister's shoulders. "Mum was way out of line. I can't believe she spoke to you like that."

Bre sighed. "She wants what she thinks is best. I just wish she saw me, for me."

"We see you, Bruce."

"I know."

"Can I ask ..."

Breathe. She nodded weakly, ready, finally, to just let the cat out of the bag.

"Is Billy the father?"

The look she gave him answered everything.

"Oh, Bruce. Go on, go for a ride. See you at later? We're all going to watch *Die Hard* ..."

With a shrug, she threw a leg over an ATV, turned the key, and rode off.

17

All I Want for Christmas is You

Billy

THE ANNUAL CARMICHAEL CHRISTMAS party was by far the busiest twenty-four hours on the farm. As Piers joked for the umpteenth time about 'all hands on deck', Billy's family and the other farm workers swirling in and out of the house, utterly ignored him.

Billy struggled to resist the cave-man urge to konk the celebrity over the head with a blunt stick, then dress him up as an elf, and sit him in the back of Edsel as a prop. He wasn't a violent man by nature, but a few weeks of forced proximity to the narcissist had potentially changed him at a fundamental level.

At least filming for *Crank Shaft* was officially done, and within the next few days, Piers, Trudy, and Jaxon would vacate the farm altogether – a loss that would only be lamented by Sharee De Luca.

Sharee's patience and positivity enabled her to cope with his ill-timed and ill-mannered quips. She'd taken him under her wing and even joined him by the pool most evenings. The Carmichaels, on the other hand, were exhausted by long days in the sun, hard labour, and the exertions of not assaulting the *Crank Shaft* host for his generally loutish attitude. Big dinners, cold showers, and early bedtimes helped them through.

The day flew in a festive haze of tinsel and trees. The finishing decorative touches had been put on the big barn, and with the kitchen working overtime, Holly was well prepared to send everyone into a food coma.

His mother had always believed that food brought people together, and tonight, it would bring the town of Moonshine to the Carmichaels' tree farm for their Christmas Eve party. Everything was ready. Tables and chairs had been set, excessive lights strung over the alfresco area, and the musicians had arrived early, setting up beside the huge tree that towered over them all, brushing the very rafters of the barn. Edsel waited beside the big barn, ready for family photos with 'Father Nicholas' who was playing Santa, the huge bags of presents beside Bre's Ford ready for gifting to every guest.

Hours ago, Billy had vacated his bedroom, carrying out the chores on Bre's evening list, as requested, while she allowed his mother to fuss over her. For years, Holly had attempted to play dress-ups, but this year, Bre must've been too tired to refuse. Chuckling, Billy had closed the door on his mother and Breanna, who'd been in a stand-off about makeup.

"Just a little" was apparently "way too much" and his mother was well-prepared for the fight. Grateful to excuse himself, Billy had spent the afternoon completing the To Do list.

The first item read.

- Check in with Sharee

As Bre probably anticipated, this had proved unnecessary. The stylist was glowing, calm, and prepared for the final shebang she'd planned with his mother.

"Tonight, our socials will sparkle!" they kept saying, an inside joke they refused to elaborate on. Their house, tree, and barn decorations weren't "sparkling" in any extraordinary manner, but he left them to their smug little giggles.

Next, Breanna's list told him:

- Assist Trudy and Jaxon with the preparations for the final *Crank Shaft* film session.

After weeks of too-close proximity to Piers, Trudy and Jaxon had gone rogue. At least, this was according to his bartender, Meredith, who had spent an inordinate amount of time of late appraising him of the local tavern gossip. Jaxon and Trudy, Meredith had confided in a whisper that could have been heard in Antarctica, were "done". According to his drama-loving employee, the last straw had been that "too-hot-to-trot Revv-head hogging the spotlight from the farm owners and event coordinators" – aka Billy's parents.

Over dinners Billy and Bre had attended for ever-shortening amounts of time, Piers had managed to cement a plan that showcased his winning, public-facing personality. Somehow the TV star had convinced Nick and Holly to allow him to assist with distributing gifts to party guests, demanding Jaxon film while Trudy caught every fake compliment that dripped from his mouth.

"PR stunt if ever I've seen one!" Meredith had hissed into the phone, outraged on behalf of Nick and Holly, who she'd never even met. The opinion was followed by the slap of a glass on the bar.

"All's well there?"

"Oh, boy, totally! And as soon as the last patron leaves The Pope tonight, I'm going to drive out there, scope out this amazing farm everyone keeps banging on about." Her voice turned sulky in a way he doubted Breanna's ever would. "Plus, I kind of miss the twins. But I didn't call to talk about your brothers and the fact that your biggest security guards have been sorely missed here at The Pope. I called to warn about Piers ..."

Billy prayed that seeing a magnanimous Santa Claus wearing a leather jacket and sunglasses indoors wouldn't ruin Christmas for Moonshine's children. But while Piers planned to show-boat and steal the spotlight from Billy's parents, Trudy and Jaxon had other plans. Staging a coup, Piers' team would focus their energy on Edsel, the true star of the show, and

Breanna, in all her pregnant glory. This plan, Billy approved.

The third item on Breanna's list had been the easiest.

- Be my date for the party.

He loved that she hadn't made it a question. He had no choice in the matter anyway. Whatever she wanted, he'd find a way to give it to her. Acting as her date at parties had been a large part of their Friends With Benefits Plans over the years.

As he waited at the bottom of the stairs, he idly wondered which of the strong-willed women upstairs had won the battle of the makeup. When the door at the top of the landing squeaked open and Holly rushed out, tears in her eyes, he worried for the answer.

"Mum?"

Gripping his forearm, she pulled him close, kissing his cheek. Cool wetness lingered as she pulled back, beaming at him, before her eyes flicked up. He followed her gaze, wondering what could shake his mother so thoroughly that her grip on his tattooed forearm trembled.

The world slowed as two hazel eyes found his, and step by step, tentative and unsure and so unlike her usual self, Breanna emerged.

Only, this wasn't Breanna. This vision before him didn't stomp down the stairs in her familiar Doc Martens. She wasn't smothered in the loose fabric of baggy overalls and t-shirts, or a dirty Shit Show Supervisor baseball cap, and her flaming hair wasn't twisted up and off her face in a messy bun. She wasn't glistening from farm work or greasy from fixing cars.

This woman was …

"Exquisite."

"Isn't she just?" Holly beamed. Somewhere behind him, Sharee's camera clicked. At least, he thought that was what the sound was. It could well have been the sound of the fabric of reality tearing apart as this vision – his fantasy – stepped into reality.

In simple flat shoes, she trod down, down, closer, the swish of fabric parting with each step to reveal shapely lean legs. With thin straps over strong shoulders, the material was a deep forest green trimmed in Carmichael tartan. It hugged her belly and breasts, a deep V showing more of her neck, chest, and cleavage than her clothing ever had before. She was resplendent.

Waves of lightly curled red hair tumbled down her shoulders, framing her face in ways he didn't realise it could.

His right arm, or the ghost of it, at least, reached out, needing to touch her, while the rest of him stood rooted to the spot as she descended from his room. *His. Mine.*

She hesitated as something like self-consciousness flitted across her face – a face, Billy noticed, enhanced with a light dusting of something sparkly, darker lashes, and red lipstick. So, his mother had won after all.

"We all good?" *We.* His throat closed completely, overwhelmed by the splendid vision before him. Nodding, he reminded himself to breathe, inhaling and exhaling shakily as his mother, still beside him, grinned and practically held him upright.

"Oh, dear, *please* no more rhetorical questions," Holly groaned, pinching the bridge of her nose.

"We are ..." Bre seemed to lose her words as she took him in. His spine straightened under her assessing gaze, her growing smile and that sparkle in her eye indicating her approval.

In a fine linen shirt, his Carmichael plaid, traditional sporran, and hose, including the little Sgian-dubh knife tucked into the top, he was every bit the tall, broad, dark-haired Highlander his ancestors had been.

He tried to swallow the lump in his throat – the one she put there simply by existing. Failed. Tried again.

"We are ..." Billy repeated the affirmation in a low grumble that sounded too harsh. A thrill ran through him as his best friend's eyes lit up.

"We are." Bre was nodding, confirming, though what, precisely, she confirmed, he still wasn't sure. Was it a 'We are ... a we'? 'We are ... a fling to forever'? *We are ...*

Finally, Bre reached the bottom step.

"You two are perfect." Holly beamed, pride glowing from every pore as her eyes flicked between them. Taking Billy's hand, then Breanna's, his mother fit them together as if it was the most natural thing in the world.

"Merry Christmas Eve, you two. May the best present you receive be those straight from the heart." His mother said the words, but they barely registered as she drifted into the blurry background.

"I'm guessing you like?" Bre looked down, nose crinkling.

"Still can't touch my toes, though. Or see them, for that matter."

"Nobody will be looking at your feet, honey." The words were a growl, and a threat to anyone who even thought about coming near her tonight. She was his. Now and forever.

"Come here," he demanded, pulling her into his chest. Instinct drew her arms around him, tucked her face into his neck. His chin rested on the top of her head, and together, they breathed. In. Out. In.

"Bruce ..."

"You can't call me that anymore."

He froze.

"I'm not that little girl who demanded equality with you and our brothers. I'm not that tomboy who could do it all and keep up, be just as tough, just as fearless, just as dumb." She smiled up at him. "I'm all woman now, Billy. I have the breasts and the baby bump to prove it."

His hand slid to her rounded stomach, his thumb caressing; nodding, wordlessly encouraging her to continue, entranced by the red of her mouth, the loose waves of her hair.

God, what I wouldn't give to touch her, all over, all at once. Instead, he'd have to go slow. Too slow. With only one hand.

Squeezing his hand, she led him out of the house, towards the big barn, the fairy lights and stars overhead lighting the way.

"You can't call me Bruce anymore," she repeated.

"Who ..." The lump caught the word, and he coughed lightly, freeing the rest of his query while trying to remember how to work his feet, stumbling more than usual. "Who are you, then?"

She paused, throwing him a bashful look. And was that ... regret? He wasn't as adept at reading faces as she was, but since December first, when she climbed in his window – what seemed like a lifetime ago now – he'd taught himself to be more observant, to see the nuanced way her face spoke volumes when she couldn't find the words.

"I'm yours, Billy," Bre told him gently, guiding him through the trees. Heart swollen to bursting, all he could do was swallow, breathe, and follow her blindly.

Others joined them. He registered the familiar shadows of family, their friendly faces blurred beyond his direct line of vision – vision that started and ended with Breanna Henderson.

"I've always been yours. Your family knew it. You knew it! You said we were something more. I knew that too, but I was too stupid to name it." She lowered her voice, pressing closer as the children joined the throng that moved towards the big barn for the party. "As anything beyond Friends With Festive Benefits, anyway," she finished, smirking up at him. "I was too dumb to realise that I had my head in the sand this whole time. Too chicken-shit to name it."

"Name what, Bre?" What was his fantasy saying?

Bre's smile widened. "I'm getting there. Be patient." She flicked her hair, irritated by the length tickling her shoulders. He watched the motion, transfixed.

"After slowing down this Christmas, actually talking to

everyone, not just bossing them around, it seems they all knew before I did."

"Knew what?" It sounded rhetorical, and a shudder passed through his body as he asked it. But he needed to be sure that what he was hearing was, in fact, what Breanna was trying to tell him.

"Billy, I know I've treated you unfairly. I've been ..." she sighed. "If I'm perfectly honest, I've been too scared to pop the bubble. Saying the words makes everything real, instead of this made-up world we've created, when we hoard time together. That's not normal, Billy." The crowd seemed to swell around them as they continued into the barn. "Friends with Benefits is just a fling masquerading as two mates whose friendship will *inevitably* implode when one person catches feelings and demands more. We never did that, Billy, don't you see?"

He didn't see, and she read it in his face. Pausing in the wide doorway, she smoothed her thumbs over his eyebrows, he let her loosen the deep V that had formed on his brow.

"We never imploded, Billy. Because we both caught feelings. We both knew the fantasy was something more ... something more *permanent*, but we were both too scared to upset the status quo. Both of us knew it was something else, and we both wanted more, but we were chicken shit and didn't chase what we really wanted. Don't look at me like that, you know it's true!" She laughed. "We were comfortable with whatever time we had or that we took, to explore each other and this thing between us. But it was temporary, even though it's been years." She laughed again, lightly, the sound hitting him straight in the chest.

She placed his palm on her stomach. Swift little kicks moved beneath his fingertips as they moved into the barn, family and friends swirling around. Vaguely, he was aware of his family drawing closer around them. Familiar shapes and faces blurred as his world again narrowed – to the racing of his heart, and the baby's movement beneath his fingertips.

"Wanna know what's more permanent, Billy?" She beamed up at him. "This baby. He gets so excited to hear your voice. Little shit kicks like a world champ soccer player whenever you're near. He is *so* excited to meet you."

"He?" The word somehow tore itself from his body.

"Of course," Bre beamed up. "I'm just guessing the gender, but it seems to me like all Carmichaels are boys."

His.

The world tilted on its axis. The baby was his. "Mine?"

From the encircling crowd, a brother stepped forward. "I do believe that was a rhetorical question," Connor warned, leaning an elbow up to his brother's shoulder.

"Two, actually," Liam added, breaking ranks and taking up a mirror pose on Billy's other side. "He? Mine?" He mocked their youngest brother, ruffling his hair playfully to break Billy's wide-eyed trance.

Bre shrugged, nonchalant. "Chances are good. Like, *really* good." She smoothed a wayward lock of hair from her face, and he beamed down at her, heart bursting. "Reece says that several shitty dates prearranged by my batty mother involving zero sex will statistically end in zero babies. But multiple hot evenings with you, Billy? Not being as careful as we should have, after all this time? Being too comfortable with each other and just trusting we were being careful enough ... That'd do the trick." She read something in his face, and added quietly, "There wasn't anyone else but you, Billy. There hasn't been for a long, long time. I might have insinuated there was, to other people, because I'm private like that, I suppose. My sex life," she stroked his arm, "my *love* life, is nobody's business but mine. I'm sorry if you've ever had the wrong impression."

Her love life? Was she saying ... A dog yapped, clawing its way up and under his kilt. Jerking back, he found Mr Pickles trying to gnaw the fringed edge of his sporran.

"I know about *him*, too." Bre chuckled. "A very cute distraction from my usual planned activities." She raised one eyebrow, smile widening. "Playing on my growing maternal instincts by giving me a fur baby to look after, William Carmichael you rascal!"

She swatted his arm playfully – the right one, or what remained of it. She'd never been afraid to touch him, and such a simple act, her teasing, her casual touch, the admission – finally – of the baby's paternity – it all made him feel more whole than ever before. His missing hand reached for her. His mind felt it, felt *her* beneath the gentle caress of her cheek.

She leaned her head to one side, her eyes closing, as if she felt it, too. Contentment spread across her features.

"My fling, my fantasy. You, me, our baby ... Billy, we're

forever."

Something inside him clicked – a missing piece finding its way home. His heart swelled, throat closing around the flood of words he wanted to say, eloquent responses and possessive demands, praises for this woman who said what she meant, and she'd said she was his, forevermore.

"'Tis all ready fer ye, lass!" Richard's voice stage-whispered from somewhere behind Billy, whose jaw struggled off the floor.

"Ready?" Billy managed, his usually gravelly voice more a mouse squeak.

"I called in all my Christmas Pickle favours," Bre grinned, taking his hand once more and leading him towards the open centre of the wide barn. Jaxon and Trudy followed them, their own personal paparazzi. Billy's gaze swung round, but Piers was nowhere to be seen.

"Revv is outside," Bre beamed, reading his mind yet again and unable to contain her excitement. "That was Pickle Favour Number One – to get him out of my sight. I thought being on *Crank Shaft* would be this magical television experience where I could share Edsel with the world, when really, my whole world is already right here, and Edsel is such a big part of our lives already." She laughed. "So, Piers is gone. Making out with Sharee DeLuca of all people! I think she feels sorry for him or something. It's kinda sweet, and *completely* fucking gross. We'll have to disown her after this."

There she went again, speaking without abandon, dropping the smallest words that made his knees buckle, just so he could grovel at her feet. *We. Our.* He wanted to taste them on her tongue and add his own: *Mine.*

Reaching the centre of the room, his family, his nearest and dearest, surrounded them.

"Lianne!" Graham broke from the crowd to rush for his wife. Tiredness crept from her pores as she clung to her husband, smiling pure sunlight.

"I made it!" she told them all, eyeing Bre and her hand clasped with Billy's. "What's going on?"

"We'll explain later," Graham said, kissing her temple. "In the meantime, you get to look after Mr Pickles."

"Mr who? Oh! Puppy!" Her tiredness lifted marginally as the dog was unceremoniously shoved into her arms. "Aren't you a cutie!" The pup instantly started chewing on the ends of her long hair while her four boys rushed to welcome their mother.

"My second Pickle favour involves Trudy and Jaxon."

At her voice, Billy turned then looked down, down, to her face, now at his waist. On one knee before him she glanced up, the smile on her red lips steady and wide.

"Bre, honey ..."

Jaxon and Trudy moved closer, camera on and mic dangling above.

"William Carmichael," Bre said. "I have a confession to make. A few confessions, actually. But the biggest one is that I think I love you. No," she corrected, "I know I do. I know it so truly that I asked the *Crank Shaft* crew to immortalise this moment, but not for TV ... just for us. I know it's kind of intense, because this is kind of public ..." A chuckle rippled through the family. "But I won't hide how I really, truly, *deeply* feel anymore. Not from you, at least. I can't promise you marriage, because I still don't even know if I want that, honestly. My mother has completely ruined the notion of it. But babies? A life together? As best friends and as lovers and more ..."

She paused to allow the wolf-whistling of the entire Carmichael clan to die down, colour high on her cheeks, blurring each constellation into one beautiful pink.

"Whatever I have, William Carmichael, I offer it to you. Our past plans, and our future ones ... the common denominator is that we're together. You, me, our baby ..."

Nearby, Holly let out a tiny, excited squeal, snuggling into Nick's side. Connor, Liam and Seth stood side by side, trading *See, I told you so*'s and *Pay up*s. Richard and his wife shared a hankie, dabbing at watering eyes. Graham, Lianne, and their four boys leant against each other, like a grove of individual trees growing stronger as one.

Billy wanted that, he realised. He wanted that with Bre. That comfort and security, that sense of strength in family.

"Bre–"

"Let me finish," Bre demanded. "I might be on one knee, rather painfully I might add ..." Rushing forward, Billy helped her up, Bre teetering side-to-side as she once again found her feet, looking up into his eyes. Tucking that glorious hair behind her ear, he did as she asked, waiting for her words to spill and spill until they came no more. "I love you, Billy. You hear me?"

He wanted to repeat the words. To scream them from the heavens. To drag her against him and brand the phrase onto her lips with his. But he didn't have to. In that way of hers, she always knew what he was thinking.

Dragging his hand to her stomach, she cupped her palm over his, pressing them both into her belly. "*We* love you, William Carmichael."

We. Us.

Without further ado, Billy moved his hand to the back of her neck, guiding her lips to his. Cheers exploded in the barn and with a squeal of a microphone, Nick announced, "Welcome all!" The barn doors rolled open and the township of Moonshine flowed in and around them.

"The other Pickle favours?" he murmured, leaning close, trying to preserve this moment that was just for them – and hoping she hadn't sold her soul to their brothers in exchange for whatever else she had planned for him this evening.

She merely pointed up.

Following her finger, Billy tilted his head, and a long, rumbling laugh erupted from the very depths of his soul. All around them, the party goers raised amused faces to the roof, giggling.

Countless bundles of mistletoe, all sporting googly eyes, glared down at them from the pitched barn ceiling. In green, red, gold, and tartan ribbons, they dangled menacingly above, making Christmas kisses inescapable.

"Aw, yuck!" one of Graham's kids declared as his parents

quickly embraced, numerous other couples following suit.

Already closing the distance between them, Billy put every unsaid word into his deep, luxuriating kiss.

You were never a fling.

I love you.

I've always loved you.

You're mine.

The baby's mine.

We're going to be a family.

"You know," Breanna murmured against his lips, pressing up on her tiptoes to wrap her arms around his neck as he gently moved her to and fro, "mistletoe started this."

It was exactly what she'd said on the first of December, when she'd climbed in his window, for the sake of tradition.

"Actually," Billy countered, clearing his throat with difficulty, "Adam James did."

"I have never been more grateful for childish dares in my life," Bre told him, curling into the space underneath his chin and tugging at his beard. "You'll need a new tattoo now," she told him seriously. "To remember this story, and tell it to our grandkids when we're all old and crotchety."

"Not all of us Carmichaels end up shoggley," Richard intervened, appearing suddenly beside them, digging in his sporran.

"What have ye got now, Grandfather?" Billy asked, slipping in a little of the accent he knew Bre loved hearing so much, watching his words send a shiver over her bare skin with satisfaction.

"Just a wee chookin' bon."

"A ... chicken bone?" Bre clarified as Richard deposited a gnawed V-shaped wishbone into her upturned palm. "Gee ... thanks ..."

"Fer luck, lassie. That's three now, te cement it. The rabbit's foot, the clover, an this wee wishbone!" Richard nodded. "Three's a lucky number, see? But four? Four's better!" He cackled, pointing to Graham, Connor, Liam, then finally, to Billy. "Go on then. Grab one side each an' make a wish."

He watched her small, strong fingers grip the tiny section of grey-white bone, his much larger fingers following suit.

"I wish every Christmas could be like this one," Bre said. "Except for the anxiety and Piers, maybe. But everything else has been amazing. Top-notch organisation, I say."

"Shut up, Bre." Billy laughed, dragging her closer and swallowing her jokes.

"But ... yon wee chookin' bon?"

"Later, Richard," Breanna told him, taking Billy's hand. "We've got some stargazing to do."

"Oh, aye?"

Stars glittered in the inky sky as they snuggled in together, between the trees, eyes roaming the constellations. Curled into his chest, they felt *right*.

"I don't know if I can forgive her," Bre said quietly.

"Your mother?"

He felt Breanna nod.

"Her, but Dad, too. They're not stellar role models for parenting. And what if that shit's genetic? Nature and nurture and all that. I worry ..."

"You are nothing like them."

"But what if, one day, I am? What if having kids is the thing that bonds the nature and nurture elements of my personality, and I turn into my mother after this baby is born?" Bre's sigh shook through him. "I want to have a good relationship with my parents, like you do. I want to have that relationship with my – our – child." She smiled, and it lit up the night. "We're just so different. I don't see a way forward with Mum and me."

"Start with honesty," Billy suggested, meaning it. "Communication is key."

She snorted. "Can I communicate in grunts, like you do most of the time?"

"That is acceptable only when I'm on top of you," he whispered, pulling her close. "When I'm inside you, buried deep and warm ... Then, honey, you can grunt all you want. I won't mind."

"You're naughty."

"I am nice."

"You, sir, are both. My favourite Christmas List personified."

Dazzling in the deepening evening sky, the stars shone down, each twinkle making his fingers itch to touch her and trace those constellations across her skin. Instead, he reached into the pocket of his shirt, extracting a slip of paper.

"Speaking of lists ... Breanna Henderson's Life Plan. New Years Eve, Age 13. Steps to living a Happy Life," he read, smiling down at Breanna. *"One – adopt a dog."* He nodded towards the bounding Australian Shephard.

"Mr Pickles! Who, by the way, William Carmichael, is *so* sweet but I think he'll have to stay here on the farm."

"Reece will foster him."

"Oh, thank Santa in a red fucking sleigh! That is a load off my mind, honestly. I love the little shoe destroyer, but a new baby and a new puppy will be too much, and I thought you two were trying to LIMIT my panic! But Reece having Mr Pickles, that's good. I think he's lonely ..."

"*Two,*" Billy continued. "*Travel the world.*"

His hand traversed her curves slowly, before he laced his fingers with hers, the paper crinkling between them. "Whenever you're ready, lass." He added the accent for fun, "I'd like to take ye to Scotland. We can start there. Next year, in five years, in fifty ... Whenever you want. Though, I might like to go while my grandparents are still alive. I've not been to their home since I was a wee boy."

"Yes, Billy! I'd love that!" Tears sprung to her eyes, but she blinked them back fiercely, squeezing his hand tightly before releasing it to wipe at her eyes.

"*Four. Always come home for Christmas,*" he continued.

"Every year, Breanna, we will be here. You. Me. The stars. Our family and Mr Pickles ... Every element adds up to perfection and it would not be Christmas without you."

Still blinking, she choked out, "You forgot the third item on the list."

Shaking his head, he indicated, *No, I haven't,* holding the note before her face.

"I amended it."

He watched her hazel eyes squint, then widen, as she read the words out loud. "*Three - Never. Have. Kids ...*"

"Unless they are with me," he finished, heart racing as his hand curved over her belly. "You and me, Bruce. A horde of kids. Three dogs."

"Horde? Three dogs?" she scoffed. "No one likes Gaston vibes, Billy!"

"Stop back chatting and listen." He kissed her gently before continuing, loving the way her hands found their way into his hair and smoothed his beard, such a gentle caress for a strong woman. "Breanna, honey, I have said it before, but I am going to repeat this over and over until I die ... All I want for Christmas is you. This year. Every year. That's my plan, and my promise to you."

The baby kicked his palm, responding to his touch and his voice. His heart jumped into his throat, swollen so big he battled for a long time to swallow it down.

"I know you never planned any of this, and this Christmas Contingency will not be the last of the amendments we will make in our lives. Time-share a dog *with me*. Travel the world *with me*. Have children–"

"With you?"

"Exclusively," he rumbled, leaning his forehead against hers, breathing her in.

"All I want for Christmas is you, too," she whispered. "Make sure you tell me that when things get a bit hectic, okay? When I'm tired from mothering, or my mother is being a pain in the arse, or we've been too busy with our own stuff for too long, or I just need reminding that we're in this together ... tell me, okay?"

"All I want for Christmas–"

"Is–"

The final word wasn't needed to seal the promise. Not when his lips were otherwise engaged. With slow, deep kisses and gentle caresses, Billy promised himself to Bre, and to the baby merrily thumping beneath her skin – forever.

Epilogue

Four days before Valentine's Day

Billy

"He's here. It's happening." Breanna's voice rattled down the phone line.

"Bruce, honey, please be more specific."

The last time she'd said those exact words, Revv Ryder had driven into their life, nearly ruined Christmas, then left for Bali – to everyone's eternal surprise – with a smitten Sharee DeLuca!

While the family had been glad to see the Revv's taillights shrinking in the distance, they had been sad to see Sharee leave.

Sharee's efforts, combined with his mother's, had skyrocketed the Carmichael Christmas Tree Farm, and all its endeavours, into the international spotlight. If 'breaking the internet' had been Holly's and Sharee's goal, they achieved it, with plans for rapid expansion of the tree farm business, and a sub-branch dedicated specifically to what blogs, newspapers and podcasts had dubbed 'Mrs Claus' Naughty Bakery.' Plans for the industrial-sized bakery had already been submitted to Moonshine Municipal Council for approval.

Crank Shaft's ratings had also been through the roof, but with Revv 'unavailable' in Bali, Trudy and Jaxon had been the ones to celebrate the news with Breanna, over a quiet, intimate dinner at The Pope. For hours they'd laughed at tweets, emails and social media comments that had actively encouraged Breanna to throw down her hat and wallop Piers Ryder.

Billy, or any one of his 'hot kilted brothers', according to the wild west of the internet, had encouraged everything from courses in disability awareness to burying him in a deep hole in the woods.

The family's lack of restraint had received continuous, overwhelming praise, and Trudy and Jaxon were quite pleased with themselves for capturing the 'real' Revv Ryder for his adoring fans. This had been the final nail in the *Crank Shaft* coffin, the producers actively seeking a new host for the next season.

"You want me to be more specific." Bre groaned, her words bringing his mind back to the present. "Fair enough. So, you know how I literally just left The Pope after finally catching up with Jillian ..."

He grunted in acknowledgement, inhaling the thick scent

of beer that filled the air. Throwing the towel down onto the bar, he recalled how happy Bre had been to see her friend, and how well Jillian Maitland had looked this afternoon. With her floral dresses and gentle disposition, Jillian was the vision of femininity that Elanor had always wished for Breanna.

Elanor had no idea, of course, that Jillian was occasionally a nudist and that she was planning to attend the annual Greasy Pig Chase out at the old Brumby Homestead – a dirty and decidedly unladylike endeavour.

The more Billy thought on it, the more similarities he found between his Bruce and Jillian. There was a time Billy had considered them to be complete opposites, but both women were, in one way or another, grieving the loss of their mothers, and each woman was her own biggest obstacle.

For the last few hours, the women's laughter had filled his tavern – and his heart – with joy. Breanna looked so light, so at ease, and it fuelled him in strange ways to see her so peaceful.

Thankfully, after a busy Christmas period, Jillian had reconnected with Breanna, resulting in the last few hours of reminiscing, and generally catching up on the last few months of each other's lives. Billy had been too busy behind the bar to ascertain what, if anything, Breanna told Jillian about the events of Christmas, and their new relationship status as More Than Just Friends.

They hadn't announced it, exactly, but neither assumed it was necessary. Moonshine was a small town, and gossip travelled fast. Let people believe and think whatever they wanted – all that mattered lie between Billy and Bre anyway. It was no one else's business but theirs.

"So ... yeah ..." Breanna continued, "my waters just broke."

Billy's spine snapped straight, his feet already carrying him around the long wooden bar, across the carpeted floor that, despite being new, still smelled of too many beers spilled, and out the door. The phone rustled as she moved.

"I still can't see my toes, but they feel ... well, let's just say I'm pretty sure I dropped my lady juices all over them. And – ooh!!!"

A pained noise echoed down the phone, halting his retort to her less-than-ladylike descriptions.

"Bre? You okay?" Heart pounding, he ran for the car park where Jillian Maitland had just escorted her – his – their – best friend.

"No!" Bre whimpered as he reached her. "I'm not okay, Billy." Reading his face, she added, "We had plans for later this week – Valentine's Day. Our first Global Day of Romance as a proper couple and my body goes and ruins everything ... again! I really should just give up on making any sort of official plans with youuuuu ..." Her voice strained as her body shuddered. "Billy!" The word was a whimper. "He's not waiting! This is happening. Call Reece. Get the bags. Get–"

"I've got you, honey. Hold on."

He considered the distance between The Pope and the hospital, helping Bre shuffle back towards the tavern.

As soon as they made it through the door, he growled at the nearest patron, "Call Dr Reece Hargraves, *now*," clearing a path with glares and Bre's heavy breathing, towards the stairs that led to his apartment upstairs. The pub floor was not the place to birth a baby.

"Well, this little baby adventure started upstairs," she said, somehow reading his mind even now. "Might as well finish up there, too."

If worry wasn't pumping through his veins instead of blood, he might've laughed. Loosed one of his wall-shaking booms that still seemed to catch Breanna off guard and make her face light up like she'd just won the lottery.

"Ooooohhhh!!" What had to be a contraction racked through her body as Bre doubled over, hand on her stomach. "Fuuuuuck …"

"You need to keep walking, Breanna."

"Could *you* fucking walk inside when Seth kicked you in the balls that time? No. It's physically impossible to keep your feet moving when all hell is breaking loose in your nether regions!" she snapped, her mood changing two seconds later. "Billy, I am so sorry. You didn't deserve that." He hoarded the apology, dropping a kiss to her temple.

"That is a fair point," he conceded.

"Meredith, we'll need towels and ice. Upstairs."

"Girl, you're having your baby?" the bartender squealed in unrestrained joy.

"MEREDITH!" Billy boomed. "NOW!"

Meredith stopped her cooing and launched into action. "You got it, boss!"

Bre curled into his side, his arm slung low, supporting her as best as he could. The stairs took forever to scale.

"If Richard thinks he can not-so-subtly request more of your huge babies to come out of this body, he's got another think coming! All that shit about four's better and wishing for ... ooohhhh!!!!!"

"You were the one who wished every Christmas could be the same." He earned a fiery stare, shrugging it off. "Pregnant every summer? Sounds nice, right?"

"Shove your rhetorical questions up your clacker!" she told him curtly, throwing her Shit Show Supervisor hat off the bed. It had been the only thing she'd worn for him last night. His cock twitched at the memory, just briefly, before concern replaced all other feelings in his body.

"Ah, home." She sunk down onto the bed, telling him, "I am not moving, unless Reece brings a crane. I hope you're not attached to these sheets, because we're throwing them out once this baby is out of me."

We. The word still sent a thrill through him.

"Need anything?"

Her hand reached out, inviting his strong grip. "Talk me through it all again. The list. Are we ready for a baby?"

"We have everything we need," he reassured her. "The bassinette sits in the corner. The legs have more teeth marks than wood thanks to Mr Pickles. We bought the change table, that creepy googley-eyes teddy bear–"

"*Cute* googley-eyed teddy bear," she corrected, squeezing his hand tighter as another spasm rolled through her. Billy checked her watch, keeping time, so he could tell Reece how far apart the contractions were.

"And we have a huge pile of nappies ..."

He'd been practising how to change the bear one-handed, using his teeth to undo the Velcro side panels. Some men would have let the mother change every nappy, even if they had two hands. But there was no way Billy would let that happen, especially when he was capable of the task. Hell, he looked forward to the raspberries he could blow on that baby's belly, and the giggling that would ensue. Plus, he knew Bre would never ask for help, but he sure as shit wouldn't let that stop him from offering it.

"We are ready."

"Billyyyyyyyy!"

"I am here, Breanna."

"Don't leave me." The words were a whispered plea, a prayer. "I love you so much. I do want to marry you, one day. I'm an idiot for saying otherwiiiiiiiiiiiiiiiiiise!!!"

"Bre, honey, this is all happening too fast."

Bre huffed. "The wedding talk?"

"This birth. The books indicate–"

"Here's your ice and towels!" Meredith's head appeared in the doorway. "Holy shit, girl, I can totally see that baby's head!"

"GET OUT!" Breanna screamed, hurling the bear towards the door.

"Okay, okay, no need to be so grouchy, girl!" Meredith slunk back to the stairs, pausing halfway to yell up, "The hot doc just pulled up outside! And he's *running* ..." The word purred from her mouth, but Billy focused his attention back to Breanna.

His Breanna, who gripped his hand so tightly.

Reece appeared at his side, saying something Billy couldn't hear, thanks to the pounding in his ears. "Billy? Billy!" Both Reece's hands gripped the sides of his face, forcefully focusing his attention.

"You here, Daddy? You with me? We need you, okay? She's not making it to the hospital. Typical Henderson, this kid is its own master and isn't playing by anyone else's rules. This baby is coming now."

With a short nod, Billy's head was freed.

"Right." Reece dug into his bag for medical gloves. "Let's do this."

An hour later, the babe tucked into her bare chest for skin-to-skin time, and Reece downstairs organising celebratory drinks, Billy gingerly climbed into the bed beside Breanna.

"Just look at this perfect little baby," Breanna cooed.

"He is perfect." Billy kissed her temple. "Just like his mother."

"Let's hope he got your eyes."

"And your hair."

"Oh, God, this poor kid. He'll fit in with all the other redheads in Scotland, though, so it'll be okay."

"We're going, then?" They'd never revisited the idea of travelling together, but she seemed awfully certain now.

"How many more years will you have with your

grandparents, really, before they won't be able to travel anymore? I'd like little Will to meet them."

"Will?"

"Aye." She beamed up at him. "It's a bit of a wasted name, since you never use it. Figured he might as well have it."

Brushing stringy tendrils of hair off her face, Billy showered her in kisses, one for every freckle on her face. After a long while, she giggled, saying, "Stop. I must be bowfin right now."

A wide smile parted his beard. "You could never be gross to me, Bre. And I will never stop loving you," he told her seriously. "I cannot. You ..."

She waited for him to loosen the words that had lodged in his throat. Billy took in his woman, his baby, and the home he'd made for them here, above his bar.

"I love you, Breanna Henderson. I always have, and I always will. You, me, *us*. Here. Honey, if this isn't a fantasy, then I don't know what is."

"I agree completely." She yawned, closing her eyes, and snuggling close. "Hold us."

Sliding his arm gently around them, he could have purred like a cat, he was so content. Breanna breathed deeply, one hand reaching up to idly play with his hair.

"I can't wait until next Christmas," she said dreamily. "Little Will is going to love the farm in December. The lights, the cameras–"

"The action?" Billy waggled his eyebrows, struggling to contain his own laughter as she snorted into her hand, trying not to wake the baby.

"We'll see about that."

"We might need a ladder."

"And condoms."

Billy chuckled, the deep sound spreading ripples of warmth through his chest. "I will make a list."

"Okay," she said contentedly. "You do that. I'm done trying to plan things."

"Bre?"

"Mmmm?"

"All I want for Christmas is you. And little Will."

"And the Christmas Pickle?"

A chuckle rolled through his chest, shaking them all. "And that. I already have a few favours I will ask you for ..."

"Good." She patted his cheek blindly, sighing blissfully. "Me too."

Please consider leaving a review of
A Merry Little Christmas Contingency.

Whether on Amazon, Goodreads, an email to the author,
a recommendation to a friend, or all of the above.

Like water to a flower, reviews help authors grow!

Thank you.

Acknowledgements

In true Breanna style, I'm going to list my many thanks in a super organised manner. So, for this book, I would love to acknowledge:

o **The Caffeine Club** – This book wouldn't have happened without the caffeine injections so generously provided by Clare, Kirsten, Margarita and Tenniele. Your donations via https://www.buymeacoffee.com/bcdean lubricated and caffeinated my brain and got me through the tough times. Your support is so very appreciated.

o **My Beta Babes** – Cassie, Annemarie, Melissa, Tara and Louise. I don't deserve you, your fast turnarounds and your encouragement. Thank you for being so on board with Billy and Bre and their creative festivities. Also, Melissa, congrats on your beautiful bub! Having an official Pregnancy Advisor really helped me out with this book and I cannot wait to squish those chubby lil bubba cheeks.

o **Dural Christmas Tree Farm** – Leo Demasi, thank you for answering my many, *many* questions about Australian Christmas Tree Farms! Your insights into the industry were so helpful and I loved learning about the amazing work you do.

o **Editor Extraordinaire** – Sue Copsey – once again, you've polished and perfected my words. You make the editing process enjoyable and I continue to learn so much from your comments and insights. I hope we can cross oceans to sit and have a coffee (or a wine!) together one day.

o **Snow, Fucking Snow** – You know, that white fluffy stuff the movies insist on year after year? What even is that?! I've certainly never seen it in December. I want to acknowledge it, here, in this random note, because this is NOT the experience of everyone at Christmas. Thanks, snowy movie scenes, for making me write this sweaty, sexy summer story. Australian Christmases deserve some spotlight, too. Rant over.

o **My own 'Baby Daddy'** – (excuse me while I gush) James, you sir, oh inspiration to all of my characters (insert eye roll here) not only fathered my children, but you put up with me when I was hormonal and angry crying about that half-eaten Cherry Ripe you so callously threw out after a week on the bench. You listened when I needed lunch, but my ankles were too swollen, and the shooting pains up my calves (a burning fire I still feel to this day) were simply too painful to stand in the kitchen. You ran me a cold bath, made a makeshift table, crafted a ridiculously delicious sandwich, then sat with me as I sobbed and sniffled around each bite. I appreciate all you do, and all you put up with. You're a bit of alright. I think I'll keep you.

o **You, lovely reader** – Thank YOU so much for picking up this book, for social media follows, for comments and messages, for coffees and encouragement. I never thought my quirky little kissing books would bring me so many amazing new friends, from all over the globe. Thank you for being here, and reading all the way through the Acknowledgements! I thank you, lovely reader, from the deepest, most achy parts of my full and grateful heart.

I hope to see you back in Moonshine again soon. Now, go have a ripper Christmas!

Hope it's a hot one! *wink wink*

Want a sneak peak

at the next

Moonshine Romance?

Read on

Fake Dating Dr Darcy

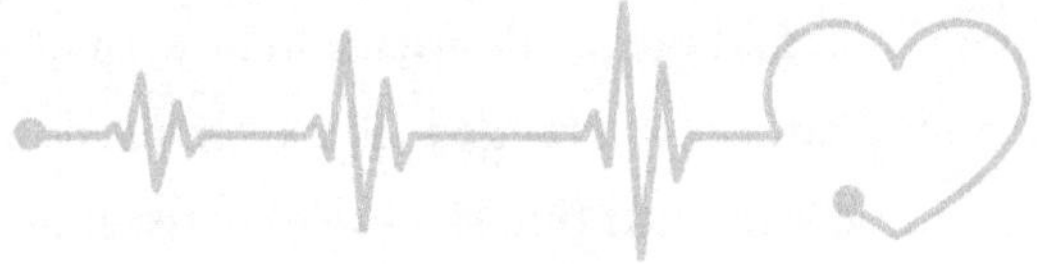

Meet Reece and Laura
in the next Moonshine Romance novel –
Fake Dating Dr Darcy

Reece

It was a truth universally acknowledged that a young doctor should never ... *ever* ... turn his back on an elderly patient with a penchant for semi-public nudity. And yet, there Dr Reece Hargraves was, turning in his office chair to find an expanse of wrinkled skin he'd promised himself to never see again. He'd planned to implement precautions – like simply keeping eyes on the cheeky old bugger – but plans and practice were two different beasts.

Of course Harold Compton had no pants on. They weren't even scrunched around his varicose-veined ankles. Nope, those grey track pants had been thrown from the examination table in the short time it had taken Reece to retrieve the information he needed from the computer.

Some men just liked getting their dick out. Reece wouldn't bat an eyelid to give Harold the penile attention he desired.

Keeping his face carefully arranged in a stoic mask he'd adopted long ago, he scratched one sideburn, massaging the ache his clenched jaw placed there hours ago.

"Alright Mr Compton, everything looks in order."

Harold's face fell. "Doctor Hargraves, I'm worried about my … you know …" the old man pointed to his pecker, hanging lifelessly and pointing to the floor.

"Urinary issues? Infection? Erectile dysfunction?" With every question Harold grew more outraged. Reece waited.

Eventually, Mr Compton's shoulders slumped. Nodding, he mumbled, "That last one."

"Perfectly normal, I'm afraid."

"Could you just take a quick look …?"

Reece scratched the sideburn again before snapping on gloves. He administered a swift, professional exam, questioning a few of his life choices.

He loved being a doctor – one of two in the small rural town of Moonshine, Australia. He enjoyed co-owning the practice, the extra hours at the hospital, and being on-call when people needed him the most. But all that responsibility came at a personal toll and he was tired of people asking when he'd settle down, when his last date was, and his favourite – "Are you some kind of monk now?" Even more than that, he was tired of going home to a big, empty house whose tiled hallway echoed too loudly as he entered and exited.

Sure, he had partial custody of a dog whose boundless energy took him on many long walks, and the river running behind the house provided opportunities for fishing, swimming, and the occasional Sunday float on his giant donut inflatable. But Pickles the Australian Shephard was with his other humans right now and while he loved the water, fish were very poor company.

As giggles and chatter slid through the gap under the door, Reece reminded himself to be careful what he wished for. There was attention you wanted, and then there was the attention he would find – and didn't want – in the world beyond what he could currently see; His office, and Harold's crotch.

He wasn't sure if there had been an official memo sent out, but the mothers of Moonshine seemed to hold regular meetings in the clinic's waiting room. They fluttered around like he was the last male left on the planet, thrusting their often alarmingly young daughters into his orbit.

They hoped for marriage, of course. To those who cared about social standing, being wed to the town physician was a fine match in a small town. Moonshine was small AND old-fashioned in some regards, but society *had* progressed since the 1800's, when young women threw themselves at single, eligible gentlemen of a certain standing (and bank account) in the community. At least, he liked to think so.

Standing, he retrieved Mr Compton's discarded pants, shoving them toward him with a rueful smile. Harold had a healthy disrespect for privacy, but Reece was a gentleman.

"Maybe," Harold coughed, snapping his waistband around his gut. "Maybe just a new prescription for those little pills ... the blue ones ..."

"Of course, Mr Compton." Reece kept his face carefully neutral and binned the gloves, reaching for hand sanitizer. No harm in being extra careful. Unlike his best mate, Sam, Reece had a healthy respect for cleanliness.

The teetering of Moonshine's mothers floated into his office once more, the printing prescription swallowing the sound. Thankfully, this day was almost over.

"See you next week, Mr Compton." Reece shook the man's hand, consulting his calendar for the last patient of the day.

As Harold shuffled out, Reece called, "Ahn, Laura!" into the waiting room.

He didn't greet her at the door, as he would for other patients, escorting them into the black leather chair that faced his desk. Instead, he focussed on work, filing final notes on Harold Compton and opening Laura Ahn's extensive file, all the while ignoring the feminine commotion in the waiting room.

A moment later, the door clicked closed. Turning, he looked up, pleasantly surprised.

Reece allowed himself a moment let his eyes roam over the platitude of conservative layers, the small pearl buttons that trailed up her high-necked shirt, and the hair that was so tightly pulled back, it must've hurt. She wore no makeup, simple stud earrings, and a serious expression he mostly saw in the mirror each morning. Only her eyes gave her any warmth – a lovely deep brown that sparkled out at the world, shimmering as though she, too, kept a truth hidden from the world.

"My mother doesn't know I'm here," she began.

A secret indeed, he thought, trying to hide a smile behind steepled fingers.

Laura

"My mother doesn't know I'm here," she confided, adding, "Did you know a handful of women are sighing at your closed door?" For some reason, she felt the need to mention this, to warn him about the hoard of tutting mothers, their still-single daughters, and the unusually large amount of baked goods, jams, and iced tea awaiting him beyond this office. "And there's a man who just barged in, demanding to see you-"

The doctor cut her off with a surprisingly warm, "Ni hao,

Ahn, Laura."

"Ni hao, doctor Hargraves. Though, there's no need to be so formal. She's not here." Laura said, crossing her arms – something she would never do in front of her mother, who believed it was the height of rudeness.

"Alrighty then." Reece leaned back in his chair, pressing his fingertips together like a prayer before his face. Did he think that hid the small smile that momentarily graced his handsome face? "Where is your mother today? I thought this was her appointment, not yours."

"It's always fun having the same name as the one who birthed you." Sarcasm. Another 'height of rudeness', according to Laura Senior. "Mix ups all the time. But to answer your question …" Laura sighed. "My mum is carrying on about Mr Bingley's Ball again."

"Ah."

He started typing notes, all business, careful to look at the screen instead of at her. Her mother had him well trained, or, perhaps, the good doctor had done cultural awareness training and knew these tiny efforts made a big difference – using the surname first, looking at his screen and not the patient to show he was more invested in his work than idle chit-chat with a woman. All these things impressed people like her mother.

Laura Junior couldn't care less, though she appreciated the effort on her mother's behalf. Doctor Hargraves was a good man, though his face was so serious she wanted to reach out and smoosh his cheeks together, just to see if that hard mask would shatter into a smile. Laura spent many appointments here, while accompanying her mother, wondering what Reece Hargraves' smile might look like.

"She swears I am Elizabeth Bennet and my sister is Jane." Laura continued. "I tried asking where Kitty and Lydia were once, but she became hysterical to the point that I seriously considered calling you."

"Why didn't you?"

It was a fair question. Most Moonshine residents called for the doctors for the smallest ailments and house calls were frequent. The hospital did have an ambulance, but that was reserved for emergencies – mostly incidents occurring on the expansive farms surrounding the rural town, or vehicular accidents on the highway straddling the town.

"I didn't call because I made the metaphorical bed and I was going to lay in it. I did the wrong thing."

"You played into her delusions," he guessed, correctly.

"It's so much easier!" In some ways, at least. "I know I'm not supposed to."

"Is her medication helping?"

"Sometimes. When she's lucid she's ..." Laura's eyes misted. "She's my mum again. But the other times ..."

"I see." He continued typing.

"What can I do?"

The phone on his desk buzzed, trilling over his attempted response. Picking the handset up, the doctor placed it straight back down.

"What I suggest-"

The phone rang again, the shrill sound making her jump.

"Excuse me," he said, two seconds before a terse, "Yes?" Then, forcefully, "No." He stood up from behind the desk, scratching at one long, dark sideburn.

Laura rather liked his hair. The old-fashioned style framed his handsome face well and it was no wonder her mother saw him as Mister Darcy. The resemblance was quite astounding, though Elizabeth Bennet's Darcy would never gape open-mouthed the way Doctor Hargraves did right now. His never-changing stoic face was suddenly the portrait of sheer panic.

With a deep swallow, he said, "Thank you," into the receiver before slamming it down. Beyond the door, she heard the receptionist's voice rise, a second person arguing loudly back.

"What's wrong?" Laura stood too, worry flooding her system. "Is it mother?"

"Worse."

"What could possibly be worse?"

Reece stalked around the small office, just a few steps at every turn, before his gaze flicked to her.

"Doctor Hargraves? What is it?"

He looked her up and down, his expression anguished. "I'm sorry, Laura Ahn."

"Sorry?" Her heart rate kicked up as the commotion beyond the door intensified. "For what?"

What was going on? An emergency? Was it her mum? In one long stride he stood before her, much closer than was comfortable for a doctor to stand with a patient.

"I know this is highly unprofessional, but ..." His smooth hands rested on each side of her face. "Please forgive me."

Her lips parted, about to respond, to beg for an answer, when all at once, in rush – it came.

Doctor Hargraves swooped his face down, pressing warm lips to hers. His mouth moved while she stood frozen. Eyes wide. He was *kissing* her? What the ...

His tongue brushed her bottom lip, so gently it barely registered, but somehow, her knees turned to jelly. Her eyes fluttered closed. Reece Hargraves knew what he was doing, that was for sure. His lips molded to hers, his thumbs sweeping her cheeks as he lifted her face to his. It was just a few seconds, really, but Laura swore she could've forgotten her own name, with a kiss like that. Her body urged her to move. To reciprocate, or run away.

A tiny moan escaped, much to her horror, as she threw her arms around his neck and moved her lips against his, right as the office door burst open.

Welcome to Moonshine

Read other interconnected standalone stories in the Moonshine Romance series:

- Meet Me in Moonshine

- The Write Way for Love

- The Insufferable Adam James

- A Merry Little Christmas Contingency

- Fake Dating Dr Darcy

Love a little freebie?

- Small town romantic adventure
- Mysterious notes of love and longing
- Skinny dipping
- Greasy pig chase

Available in paperback,
and as a **free ebook**.
Grab your copy today!

Writing about intimacy can be awkward, but someone's gotta do it ...

Samuel Harthrup — AKA romance novelist Sammie Hart — has lost his mojo. His sexy MasterChef-inspired smash-hit *Heat in the Kitchen* left readers voracious for a sequel, but Sam's muse ran off with a hulking, tattooed biker, and his new manuscript is more fizzle than sizzle. Sam needs help – a special ingredient to inspire the spicy scenes his editor (and career) demands. When the circus rolls into the small town of Moonshine, Sam stumbles upon Anita Fortuna, a psychic who firmly believes that wishing upon a star will make your dreams come true. Together, they resolve to whip his manuscript into shape, and succumbing to personal temptations is not an option – no matter how enticing the offer might be.

On a deadline, and with Sam's career at stake, can Sam and Anita find the write way for romance, define their own stories, and discover whether words are enough? Or is the whole deal a recipe for disaster?

The Write Way for Love is a dual POV Aussie rom com with an adorkable beta hero and a curvy FMC. If you like cheesy food puns and found family, this interconnected standalone will be to your taste.

ISBN: 978-0-6456910-2-3 (PRINT)

ISBN: 978-0-6456910-3-0 (EBOOK)

**One immature dare.
Two childhood enemies.
Three kisses to bring him
to his knees ...**

Clarissa Wilson *hates* Adam James – his dentist-white smile, his ridiculous body built of muscles-upon-muscles, and that movie-star swagger that carries him into every room. So, back in their hometown of Moonshine – sixteen years later – with a revenge body and a new name, it's a guilty thrill when Adam wants her ... and has no idea she's the chubby girl he teased throughout school. As 'Lissy,' she's determined to live life by her own rules and hide her old scars – meaning she needs a plan to deal with Adam, their past, and the present. Luckily, his cheeky dare offers Lissy the perfect opportunity for payback: she has three kisses, and three chances to seduce the man who ruined her life ... then leave him in the dust. But Adam is playing with her heartstrings and rewriting their history, revealing things aren't what they seem. Now, Lissy must decide who she really is and what her heart desires, because three kisses can't undo a lifetime of hate ... right?

WINNER- BEST INDIE BOOK AWARD 2024 – ROMANCE

The Insufferable Adam James is an enemies-to-lovers rom com with a droolworthy MMC and a sassy FMC. If you like banter and secret cinnamon rolls, this interconnected standalone is for you.

ISBN: 978-0-6456910-4-7 (PRINT)
ISBN: 978-0-6456910-5-4 (EBOOK)

About the Author

BROOKLYN DEAN is a perpetual daydreamer from rural Australia. She lives with her super supportive husband and children, and a sock stealing Labradoodle named Noodle.

When she's not writing, Brooklyn is often training to become the world hugging champion, drinking coffee, throwing her head back in laughter, or stealing time to nap in the sun.

Connect with Brooklyn on social media:

Wattle Tree Press is a small, independent publisher, located on the picturesque Central Coast of Australia. WTP believes that everyone has a story (or two) within them and aims to bring Aussie storytelling to the wider world.

Their growing catalogue can be found at:

www.wattletreepress.com